DINOSAUR CONQUEST

"The Gairk are gone," Mundo told them. "The camp-fires are totally cold, and it looks like they cleaned out most of their belongings. There's no smell of them, and it doesn't look like anyone's been here in a week or more."

Despite what Mundo had said, the Gairk village still smelled of Gairk to Aaron. A scent of death and filth clung to the dirty, misshapen buildings. Garbage littered the ground; further up the hill, tailings from their copper smelting operation fouled the earth.

"They're gone all right," Peter said. Like the rest, his Roman sword was out and ready. "What's that smell?" he asked.

He was answered by the rending of trees and a roar.

Behind the group, a monster's head suddenly leered at them, open-mouthed, through the screening fronds.

"Allosaurus!" Aaron cried. "Run!"

R A Y   B R A D B U R Y

PRESENTS

DINOSAUR CONQUEST

Ray Bradbury's Dinosaur Series #1
DINOSAUR WORLD
by Stephen Leigh, illustrated by Wayne D. Barlowe

Ray Bradbury's Dinosaur Series #2
DINOSAUR PLANET
by Stephen Leigh, illustrated by John Paul Genzo

Ray Bradbury's Dinosaur Series #3
DINOSAUR SAMURAI
by Stephen Leigh and John J. Miller,
illustrated by Brian Franczak

Ray Bradbury's Dinosaur Series #4
DINOSAUR WARRIORS
by Stephen Leigh, illustrated by Nicholas Jainschigg

Ray Bradbury's Dinosaur Series #5
DINOSAUR EMPIRE
by Stephen Leigh and John J. Miller,
illustrated by Nicholas Jainschigg and Cortney Skinner

Ray Bradbury's Dinosaur Series #6
DINOSAUR CONQUEST
by Stephen Leigh, illustrated by Cortney Skinner

TIME SAFARI, INC.
SAFARIS TO ANY YEAR IN THE PAST.
You name the animal. We take you there.

RAY BRADBURY

PRESENTS

DINOSAUR CONQUEST

A NOVEL BY

STEPHEN LEIGH

Illustrated by
Cortney Skinner

A Byron Preiss Book

J. T. Colby & Company, Inc.
Purveyors of Time Travel Instruments and Accessories™

J. T. Colby & Company, Inc.
Purveyors of Time Travel Instruments and Accessories™

Dinosaur Conquest

"Time Safari, Inc." is a trademark of
Byron Preiss Visual Publications.

Library of Congress Cataloging-in-Publication Data
Leigh, Stephen.
Ray Bradbury Presents Dinosaur Conquest.
        (Ray Bradbury Presents) "A Byron Preiss Visual
Publications book."
p. cm.
        [1. Science Fiction—Time Travel. 2. Fiction—Science
Fiction—Adventure. 3.] I. Skinner, Cortney II. Title. III.
Series: Ray Bradbury Presents.

J. T. Colby & Company, Inc.
Purveyors of Time Travel Instruments and Accessories™

Manhanset House
Dering Harbor, New York 11965-0342
bricktower@aol.com
bricktowerpress.com

ISBN: 978-1-59687-749-8
January 2019

This one's for Mary, John, and Andrew
from their ogre Steve

Table of Contents

Prologue—
A Synopsis of
the Previous Adventures

Aaron Cofield and Jennifer Mason are sitting on the hill behind Aaron's house in Green Town, Illinois, enjoying the summer afternoon. Their talk is interrupted by a commotion in the woods below. They investigate and find a clutch of very odd eggs. The two call their friend Peter Finnigan, but the trio is suddenly hit from behind by a running, badly injured man.

The reason for the man's flight becomes obvious as an angry allosaurus crashes through the trees. The stranger kills the beast with his rifle; as the dinosaur crumples, so does the stranger.

The youths take the man back to Aaron's house. The stranger—Travis—regains consciousness long enough to tell the three teenagers his story. Travis is a time safari guide from two hundred years or so in the future. While escorting a group of hunters through the Mesozoic era in order to kill a Tyrannosaurus rex, there was an accident: a man named Eckels went blundering off the special path laid down by Travis. On their return home, the time travelers found history changed—for the worse. When

Travis attacked Eckels in a rage, Eckels fled for his life in the time machine. Unfortunately, the machine met itself in the Mesozoic, and the resulting paradox caused the explosion of Eckels's machine *and* the destruction of the floating path.

Travis, in pursuit of Eckels, came upon the wreckage. Infuriated and despairing, Travis was about to return to his own time when the allosaurus attacked. Running through the jungle, Travis came across a piece of path still floating a few inches above the ground. Instinctively, he leapt upon it—

—and landed in the Green Town woods with the allosaurus close behind.

Travis lapses into unconsciousness after relating his strange tale. Later, when Jennifer goes to check on Travis, she finds the man gone—slipped out of the open window.

As they sit in the kitchen, Aaron spies a triceratops nibbling on the grass at the edge of the incline. In a second, the three are up and out of their chairs; the triceratops snorts in surprise and fear and makes for the cover of the trees with the teenagers in close pursuit. Grandpa Carl hollers at them to be careful, but he can't stop them.

Once in the woods, the three are separated: Aaron, out ahead, falls on a section of the broken path—and finds himself with Travis and the body of the dead T-rex in the Mesozoic.

At the same time, Jennifer and Peter find a section of the path themselves—another piece entirely. Jennifer insists that they step on the path. Despite Peter's reluctance, they do so . . .

. . . and enter a world they have never seen before; lush with primitive plants and strange reptilian life. Jennifer is excited—certain that this is the Mesozoic that Travis was talking about. They explore and find footprints leading into a cave. Entering, they are ambushed by Eckels. The man is raving about talking to dinosaurs, going on and on about things that make no sense to the two. He ties up the two and leaves the cave, saying that he's going to offer the two teenagers to the dinosaurs. While Eckels is away, Jennifer and Peter manage to escape.

They are trying to return to the section of path when they are captured once more—this time by a group of sentient man-sized dinosaurs armed with spears.

The dinosaurs place Jennifer and Peter within a barricaded compound. The dinosaur in charge of them, Jennifer learns, is a young female named Struth.

Over the next several days, Jennifer attempts to learn the dinosaur language, though it is difficult for her human throat to reproduce the various honks, trills, and bleats with which the words are sprinkled. Jennifer and Peter learn that the Mutata (as the dinosaur tribe is called) are one of two sentient species of dinosaur, that they have been troubled recently by invasions from what they called "Floating Stones" and by someone they name the "Far-Killer." The Gairk, a tribe of warlike, sentient dinosaurs similar to allosaurus, are also upset by the changes within their valley, and the Gairk are also searching for this Far-Killer.

It also becomes obvious that Struth is not exactly in the best graces of the dinosaur called the OColi—the Eldest—who is the head of this Mutata tribe.

Struth captures the Far-Killer and brings him back to the encampment. The Far-Killer is Eckels. Eckels claims not to remember abducting Jennifer and Peter. In fact, he gives a very different telling of Travis's tale. According to

Eckels, *Travis* is ultimately responsible for the destruction of the path and the timestream. The explosion of the time machine knocked Eckels here, where he wandered confused and a little mad for a time—that is why he can't remember their first meeting. He asks for their forgiveness. Peter shrugs; Jennifer is not quite so inclined to believe him.

The three plot to escape, though Jennifer holds back. She doesn't want to do anything which might hurt Struth, with whom she is beginning to share a friendship.

There are other forces at work, however. In particular, Frraghi (or "Fergie," as the humans call him), the OColi's second-in-command, is pressuring Struth to dispose of the humans. The Mutata are set in their ways, following a half instinctive set of rules called the OColihi, or "Ancient Path." Struth's mentor, Raajek, once attempted to upset the outmoded Ancient Path. Raajek wanted to lead the Mutata on the OChihi, or "New Path." Her attempt failed, and Raajek left the Mutata, exiling herself.

The OColi gives Struth one boon—if Jennifer can show that she is "intelligent" (and thus knows the Ancient Path), he will allow them to live.

Eckels killed one of the Mutata during his capture. The OColi insists that Jennifer be brought in to perform a part of the ceremony they call "Giving," though Struth is instructed not to teach her any of the rites. Jennifer will succeed or fail entirely on her own.

Confronted with a ceremony she doesn't understand, Jennifer manages at last to stumble through well enough to impress the OColi. Peter, on the other hand, has not been so fortunate. Eckels and Jennifer can live, the OColi rules, but Peter is to be killed and his body shown to the

Gairk as proof that the Mutata have done something about the floating stones.

Struth is unable to conceive of disobeying the OColi. She has only one option—to allow Jennifer and the others to escape, even though that will mean her own death. Struth makes that decision, but before she can put the plan in action, they are interrupted. The Gairk have sent an emissary who insists on seeing the humans. They are presented to him, but before the Gairk can act, a strange lightning storm begins. Devoid of rain, coming upon them with no warning, the lightning flashes display shifting patches of other realities, both known and unknown. One of these small worlds happens to appear where the Gairk is standing, and half of him simply disappears, killing him instantly. Fearful, Fergie orders the humans killed.

Struth, in desperation, seeks out Raajek, who, though blind, has sensed the omens. Raajek agrees to return to the Mutata to help Struth. In a confrontation with the OColi, Raajek uses a clever deception to save the humans.

In the Mesozoic, Aaron deals with a badly hurt and rather unstable Travis. In a rage, Travis orders Aaron into his time machine and they return to Aaron's "present," finding only a desolate, cold waste utterly devoid of anything human at all. Travis goes mad, shouting that Eckels has destroyed known history entirely; Aaron is also shocked, wanting to disbelieve all of this since it also means the end of Green Town and his own time. When Travis is nearly killed by the plant life of this odd future, Aaron convinces him to take the time machine to *Aaron's*

HomeTime. Aaron is certain that he will find Jennifer, Peter, his family, and Green Town intact.

But he doesn't.

This world is far too much like the world they just left. Aaron is shattered. His entire past is gone, all of it. Eckels has destroyed the timestream entirely, changed the past so much that nothing is the same. Aaron's family has never lived, nor Jennifer, nor any human at all . . .

As the two are about to return to the Mesozoic, a whirlwind attacks them, changing shape as it comes. Worse, there is no sign of the time machine—it has disappeared.

In defiance, Aaron strikes at the whirlwind, which dissolves into a fantasy-cover wizard. The creature—whom they address as Mundo, though it actually has no name—is an extension of the world-mind, a consciousness that spans all living creatures in the world. Mundo doesn't understand much of what Aaron and Travis are worrying about, doesn't understand their "alone-ness" at all, and certainly doesn't share their concerns. However, Aaron convinces the being to return with them to the Mesozoic—since if they *don't* do that and Eckels is still alive back there, then Eckels will change history yet again and destroy Mundo in the process. Aaron convinces Mundo there's no danger, since not only can they return him via the time machine, but the section of path that leads from the Mesozoic to Green Town now must connect to *Mundo's* present, not Aaron's.

The strange trio returns to the past, but the trip is very disturbing to Mundo, who goes into a shrieking fit as this part of him is suddenly disconnected from his greater whole. Aaron calms him, and they go off to find the pathway. Before they can do that, however, a time storm much like the one witnessed by Jennifer and the others assails them. When it passes at last, Aaron—more desperate than ever now—sets off with Mundo.

They find the section of broken path and step on it.

It's with incredible surprise that Aaron finds himself in the Green Town forest once more. Mundo, angered, bolts and runs, cursing Aaron for having tricked him. Aaron starts to go back to get Travis, then stops. He's home now. If he goes back through, he might find himself trapped once more.

Instead, Aaron moves through the familiar, comfortable forest toward his house. He spies Grandpa Carl on the porch. Waving, shouting, Aaron goes to greet him.

* * *

Aaron finds that Green Town isn't exactly the familiar place he remembers. The house is run down, Grandpa Carl is strange and irritable, and the newspaper has odd headlines about time storms. Worst of all, Aaron finds that twelve *years* have passed in this world, and that his parents are dead.

Carl is visited by an officious-looking man from a place called the "Compound"—evidently a quasimilitary establishment near Green Town. It's obvious to Aaron that his grandfather is in trouble with the authorities and is being blamed for the time storms and odd visitations. Aaron decides to go into Green Town himself.

Green Town is as strange as Carl and his house. A statue of a dinosaur dominates the square, and Aaron meets a schoolmate of his, now thirty years old. When the man becomes suspicious of Aaron and threatens to call Sheriff Tate, Aaron flees. On the way back to his house, Sheriff Tate's car, with two sinister passengers, one male and one female, passes him as he hides in the weeds at the side of the road. Back at the house, he finds that the three are waiting for him to return. Aaron watches from the woods for hours—and then, in the middle of the night, he sees Mundo approaching the house. Tate and the woman see him as well, and the woman shoots at Mundo, then pursues him into the woods. Aaron flees too, since they're heading right for him, and eventually finds himself near the piece of roadway to the Mesozoic.

Aaron decides he needs help and returns to the Mesozoic to find Travis—while back at the house, Carl is arrested. If Aaron needed any more encouragement, a time storm hits as Aaron and Travis are talking—odd fragments of alternate realities go flickering past them.

Even though they spend only a few minutes in the Mesozoic, months have passed when they return to Green Town with the time machine. Carl is gone, and the house looks deserted. Aaron is furious, and he decides that they must *do* something.

Travis performs a small experiment with the time machine—he finds that he can't go any further UpTime than the present. This tells him that Green Town is *not* Travis's past at all, but another alternate reality entirely. Things start to fall into place: evidently the pieces of roadways cross not just time, but various shadow-worlds where history has taken other turns.

Aaron convinces Travis to send the time machine back to just after Tate and his two cronies took off after Mundo. They do so, and materialize just in time to see Carl being put into a car. The two are fired upon, and Aaron is shot. He falls unconscious.

Carl sees Aaron fall back into the time machine, but the car drives away then. The woman in charge of the mission, Captain Michaels, takes him to the Compound. There, he is shown the piece of the roadway the authorities have found—the roadway that Jennifer and Peter stepped on, though Carl isn't aware of that. Carl, taking advantage of a momentary lapse, jumps onto the path and is transported . . . somewhere.

In the place Jennifer and Peter call "Dinosaur World," the attacks continue from the Floating Stones. More persistent than even the samurai are the huge pterosaurs (called "saorod" by the Mutata), who attack recklessly and fearlessly from the sky after crossing over from one of the pieces of roadway. The OColi and Frraghi are getting more impatient each day, and Struth and Raajek do what they can to keep the OColi from ordering the death of the humans. Peter and Eckels seem to have their own plan, and Jennifer finds herself alone in wanting to trust Struth and Raajek.

The conflict is affecting the entire Mutata community—Jennifer witnesses a ritualistic duel to the death between one of Raajek's followers and another Mutata. It is clear to her that the fragile peace is falling apart.

It is worse than she thinks. The OColi himself is under pressure by his counterpart among the Gairk. The Gairk OColi has issued his own declaration: the humans must die by the day called OGhielas (the summer solstice), or the Gairk will declare war on the Mutata.

Struth and Raajek redouble their efforts and find the piece of path that Jennifer and Peter came through. They take Jennifer to see it for identification. On the way, they meet a Gairk, who tells them that he has just killed a "soft, pale thing" just like Jennifer a bit up the path.

Jennifer is horrified, afraid that Aaron is dead. The Gairk guides them back to the body. Jennifer does indeed recognize the person lying there:

Aaron's grandfather Carl.

Aaron returns to consciousness still at his farmhouse in Green Town, but several months in the future. Travis tells Aaron that he pulled him into the time machine, returned fire, and then brought them here after the car took off with Carl inside. Aaron and Travis spend a few weeks recuperating, then return to the fateful night a bit later. There they find a dying man, Tate's crony, who tells them that Carl was taken to the Compound. Troops arrive from the Compound then, and they capture the time machine and Travis. Aaron escapes into the woods, where he meets Mundo. The two decide to join forces: an uneasy alliance. Aaron and Mundo attempt to get into the Compound via the storm sewer system.

Jennifer buries Carl as Struth and Raajek look on in puzzlement—that is not the way the Mutata deal with their dead, after all. Then the three go on to the Floating Stone. Jennifer reluctantly decides that with all that has happened, she should take this opportunity and go for help. She breaks away from Struth and Raajek and jumps on top of the Floating Stone.

Nothing happens. The pathway between the worlds is closed.

OGhielas arrives, and with it the Gairk Envoy. Struth and Raajek attempt to demonstrate that Jenny has done what was asked of her—found a way to seal up the pathways between the worlds. She demonstrates that she closed up the one path to her own world. The Gairk seems unconvinced, and at that moment, Eckels and

Peter play their own hidden card. When the Mutata captured Eckels, they broke his rifle, but they didn't take the cartridges, not understanding the technology. Eckels and Peter have made a small bomb with the gunpowder, and they light the fuse and run, calling to Jennifer. Jennifer is forced to make her own decision. None of the dinosaurs understand the danger, and Jennifer sacrifices her own chance at escape to save the Mutata and Gairk. Thrown away, the bomb explodes harmlessly while Peter and Eckels disappear into the jungle.

A death sentence remains on Peter and Eckels, but Jennifer is spared.

Travis is interrogated by Captain Michaels as Aaron and Mundo steal closer to the Compound. A time storm hits as well, and a gigantic creature of lightning and cloud escapes from one of the passing realities. It rages through the Compound, tearing down walls and creating chaos—a confusion that allows Aaron and Mundo to reach Travis. The piece of floating path has been moved somewhere else by the force of the creature's passage, though. They have one choice: to take the time machine and use it to move back a few hours. Captain Michaels turns out to be more sympathetic than they'd realized. She tells them how they've learned that the gateways are powered by fragments of Eckels's temporal mechanism, imbedded in the pathways by the force of the explosion when his time machine met itself. Take away the fragment, and the gateway is sealed; put them back, and it reopens. Grateful, Aaron, Travis, and Mundo get into the time machine.

In the laboratory a few hours before, they move the time machine through the pathway and into a new world: Dinosaur World.

Peter and Eckels have holed up in Eckels's old cave, trying to escape the various Gairk and Mutata hunting parties now searching for them. Peter, out hunting food, is surprised by a Gairk and followed back to the cave. To escape, Peter and Eckels climb out a natural chimney in the rear of the cave. Peter, his claustrophobia kicking in as he manuevers through the tight, dark crawlway, quickly loses Eckels, who is already up and out of the chimney. Peter is nearly at the top, but almost falls. A hand grabs him—the hand is Mundo's.

Mundo pulls Peter out of the crevice, and he is greeted by Aaron and Travis. They heard Peter calling for Eckels and came to help. The reunion is shortlived—they hear the distinctive sound of the time machine in its local travel mode: Eckels has stolen Travis's vehicle.

Jennifer, with Struth, is out searching for Peter and Eckels herself when they see the Gairk Klaido rushing past. Realizing that the creature is in hot pursuit of someone and desperately afraid that she knows who, Jennifer and Struth follow as quickly as they can, but lose him. They find themselves very near where the Mutata are guarding the Floating Stone to the samurai world. Realizing that a time storm is about to break, they stay there, waiting for the storm to pass. The storm hits, and in the chaos of fleeting realities and strange visions, Jennifer sees the time machine heading for the Floating Stone with Eckels at the controls. The machine glides over the Floating Stone and disappears.

At the same time, she sees something that lightens her mood: Aaron. The two reunite quickly, and then everyone—Aaron, Jennifer, Peter, Travis, Mundo—follow Eckels through the portal to the world of the samurai.

From that point on, they are thrown into a succession of strange, alternate histories: a North America where the Japanese, not the Europeans, have discovered the continent; an ancient Aztec Mexico in a world where Montezuma won his war with Spain; and the world of the saorods.

In between, they came back to Dinosaur World, to find Raajek now installed as OColi, and the Gairk still after them.

They escape once more, first to an ancient Egypt where the pharoah collects pieces of other histories, and where the Gairk Klaido too has come, still bearing his death-grudge against the humans, and then to the Rome of Nero's time—but where Nero is an aspiring actor and singer, not emperor, and where Struth must save the humans from the pursuing Klaido.

And now, with little choice, they have come back to Dinosaur World once again . . .

1

Sstragh's Return

SStragh stepped unsteadily from the floating stone into moonlit darkness, her bones aching from the cold, her nostrils full of the sharp smell of ozone from the time storm, her neck raw and torn from her fight with the Gairk Klaido. Tiny glowing sparks clung to her scales— the legacy of her trip between the worlds—and she brushed them to the ground.

She blinked, still dizzy from the passage between the worlds and the loss of blood, and gave an involuntary hoot of joy at recognizing her own world.

At last! After all those horrible places beyond the floating stones, at last! I am home. With the thought, a resolution came to her, as if from the voice of the All-Ancestor herself.

I will not leave here again.

The pleasant aroma of her world swelled around her in welcome: the richness of damp, black earth, the sharp fullness of the leaves, the varied odors of the Mutata themselves. Through the thick, twisting branches of the cycads, she could see the familiar domes of her village gleaming under a star-drenched sky. The constellation of the Nesting Mother hung high above SStragh, the fingers of the Mother's hand stroking the flank of the moon. The sight of the star-shape caused SStragh to gasp in a melding of relief and amazement. If the Nesting Mother was up in the night sky, then much time had passed in this world—and SStragh desperately needed that to be the case. Her body, heavier every day with the ripening eggs, yearned for it.

The Nesting Mother . . .

Every second appearance of that constellation at the edge of the sky was the herald for the Birthing Walk. Long centuries of instinct within SStragh yearned to participate in this particular Walk—because it would be her first as one of the breeding females. For a moment SStragh wondered whether the reason no one was watching the floating stone was that the Mutata had already departed the valley for the Nesting Grounds near the sea. With the thought, a wild despair made her shiver.

I'm too late! They're already gone . . .

But no, the night breeze held the musk of life.

SStragh smelled Lhath's approach before she heard or saw the Mutata, and she greeted him as he blundered through the nearby trees, moving with the usual slowness of a Mutata awakened in the cold night. "Lhath!"

"SStragh!—it *is* you and not some horror from a Dreaming Storm? I heard the thunder . . ."

"Yes," SStragh said. "Why is no one guarding the floating stone? Why is it here instead of in the Gairk village?"

Lhath's head lowered and he sent a faint scent of admonition toward SStragh. "Nothing has come through any of the floating stones for hands upon hands of days, SStragh, not since you helped the humans escape. The female human appeared once just after you left and gave me this scar." Lhath touched the side of his head, where a short line of white marred the dappled aquamarine of his scales.

SStragh puzzled over that—did he mean Jhenini? That wasn't possible, since she had been with SStragh all along.

"What happened to your neck?" Lhath asked, and SStragh remembered the treachery of Klaido, of how he had struck her with the *broaii* in his right hand, the hand that was only used to kill animals—the Ancient Path, the rules that governed life for both Mutata and Gairk, said that you never struck intelligent beings with anything other than the left hand.

"A sad betrayal," SStragh answered Lhath cryptically. "And how have things been here?"

"Since you left," Lhath continued, "the Dreaming Storms have become far worse, but the floating stones, at least, have been silent. As for the Gairk—look at the sky, foolish one." He jabbed his spear toward the moon and the Nesting Mother. "They have already gone on their Walk, two hands of days ago."

Lhath's scent altered strangely, and SStragh noticed even in the darkness that the bands of blue and green of his scales were brighter than usual. For some reason, the realization sent a momentary quiver through her. Lhath noticed it too; he stared appraisingly at SStragh, and that strange male scent about him deepened. Then he seemed to shake himself, and he pointed his spear at the floating stone.

"Why did you come back, SStragh? The OColi may decide that you are to be Given because of what you've done."

"I don't care," SStragh answered, surprised at the ease in which the words came. "There was nothing for me on the other side of the floating stones, Lhath. I know that now. Nothing."

"And where are the humans?" Lhath asked. "OColi Raajek will want them too."

SStragh looked at the floating stone. In the joy of being home, she had almost forgotten her companions. The floating stone hung empty, its whitish surface bright in the moon's glow. Jhenini had said that they would all follow right behind her, but SStragh could tell without understanding their language that some of the others had not wanted to return to SStragh's world—had they decided to remain behind, then? Had they put another one of the glowing magical pieces in it? Had they gone back to their own world at last?

"I don't know," she said truthfully. "They were supposed to follow me."

"Then we will need to place a guard around the stone again," Lhath said. "I will call Frraghi."

"There's no need for that, Lhath," a deep, booming voice said.

Frraghi came through the underbrush. Like Lhath, his colors were brighter than SStragh remembered, and when Frraghi looked at SStragh, his usual scent was overpowered by an earthiness even stronger than Lhath's odor. The scent made SStragh want to change her own odor to a musk of receptiveness. She fought with her body against the urge, wondering at the sudden strength of the compulsion. She had never felt this way before. Strange, frightening feelings were crashing unbidden through her mind and she could barely keep her thoughts on the words of the two males before her, lost in their scent.

The time of the Nesting Walk is a time of strangeness. Raajek had told her that once. *The small madness of emotion will take hold of you, and you won't understand what you feel or why.*

SStragh looked at Frraghi and felt the small madness take her.

"The thunder woke me too," Frraghi told them. "The humans have invaded my dreams for the last hand of nights, and I knew. I knew you'd return, SStragh. I knew you'd show up again, just when the All-Ancestor seems to have turned Her back on us. What calamity have you brought with you this time?"

"I've brought nothing," SStragh answered, straining to ignore the smells. "Only myself, though I thought—" *I thought that Jhenini, Aaron, and the others were following just behind me. Where are they?* SStragh decided not to mention the humans. "How is Raajek?" she asked, trying to concentrate even though Frraghi's scent made her itch to move closer to him. She faced away from the wind— that helped a little.

"The OColi is alive," Frraghi answered harshly, but his stance was wrong; the way he stood, the way his tail was held—the language of his body said something different, something softer. "Is that all that worries you, SStragh? Then let me tell you the worst of it. The Gairk nearly declared *ciosie* on us after the humans escaped. They blamed the Mutata, and they've refused to give us protection for the Walk. They've already left. When we go on our Nesting Walk, we'll have no help from the Gairk. The Floraria will be waiting for us when we leave the valley now, SStragh, and the Gairk won't be there to keep them away. I wonder how many of us will die needlessly because of your foolishness."

"Frraghi . . ." SStragh didn't know what to say. The words were so harsh, yet his body was so open . . . What was Frraghi trying to tell her? If what he said was true, then all of them were in danger.

The Gairk might be stubbornly proud and far too quick to fight, but their fierce protection shielded the Mutata from the attacks of the Floraria, the Gairks' sharp-toothed and nearly brainless cousins, whose only driving force seemed to be the hunger in their bellies. Gairk and Mutata had always gone to the nesting grounds together: the Mutata feeding the Gairk from their stores of dried fruits and leaves gathered in the months before the Walk, while the Gairk protected the Mutata in return. Without the Gairk . . .

SStragh had seen the ferocious, mindless attacks of the Floraria. Once they struck, only death would stop them. "I'm sorry, Frraghi," she said. "But you don't understand why I left. Jhenini . . . she still believes that the humans—"

"The humans have lied to you all along, SStragh," Frraghi snorted, and the smell of his hatred for them was strong. "You're still too stupid to see it. The Dreaming Storms tear up our land. They come every day now, without fail, always taking away pieces of our valley and leaving behind strangeness. Show me the humans, and I'll do what we should have done from the first. Maybe then the All-Ancestor will end this chaos."

Frraghi glared at the floating stone behind SStragh. His spear trembled in his hand. SStragh knew that if Jhenini or any of them stepped through now, they would be instantly killed. But the floating stone remained adamantly, strangely empty.

"Get Khieli and some of the others," Frraghi barked at Lhath. "Guard this stone for the rest of the night, just in case. I will take SStragh to the OColi."

Frraghi looked at SStragh for a very long time, until she could no longer stand his gaze and turned her eyes away. His scent was stronger than ever, and it made SStragh almost afraid. "I wish you hadn't come back,"

Frraghi told her. "At least then we could have died in peace."

OColi Raajek turned her blind eyes from the brazier over which she stood, sniffing the curling smoke of aromatic spices burning on the coals. She lifted a small wooden bowl, took a pinch of brick-red powder, and sprinkled it on the blue flames. "This last one has just the right hint of citrus, don't you think, SStragh? A pleasant complement to the bitterness of the *capoli* wood." Raajek sniffed again and sighed.

"Yes, OColi," SStragh agreed, taking a deep breath herself. The odor made the scales on her back shiver, as if she were cold. "When did you take up the scent-art?"

"After you left with the humans that first time," Raajek answered. "It was something I'd always wanted to try, but I'd never felt the moment to be right—there was always so much to do: teaching you, discussing the merits of the Ancient Path . . . My own OTsio had been a Scent Master. After you and the humans were gone, it seemed the time for me to begin: my last student gone, the OChihi—my New Path—in shambles. I felt that there was nothing constructive left for me to do." Raajek leaned over the brazier again, inhaling deeply. "I'm still not very good at this. I wonder whether I'll have the time to really learn."

"Of course you will," SStragh said reflexively. "You have many seasons—"

Raajek waved a hand, and her white, blind eyes seemed to search for SStragh. "You misunderstand me, my dear student," she said. "I'm not talking about my own life. I wonder how long *all* Mutata have."

SStragh said nothing to that. She could smell Frraghi's presence at the door even through the thick veil of

Raajek's brazier. SStragh stood as patiently as she could, her head raised properly and her stance submissive, but she wished that Raajek would simply pronounce her sentence and let her prepare to die. She would ask OColi Raajek herself to Give her soul to the All-Ancestor, as a gift from an OTsio to her student. Raajek would not—could not—refuse that. That would be a small consolation for SStragh to take with her when she stood before the All-Ancestor and had to answer for the actions of her life.

"The art has sharpened my nose." Raajek, maddeningly to SStragh, circled the subject again. "I hardly miss my eyes anymore. I smell Frraghi, for instance, and I notice how your own scent has changed, SStragh . . ."

Raajek came over to SStragh, close enough that SStragh caught a whiff of the rotting skin around the sores on the ancient Mutata's skin. Raajek reached out and explored the wound on SStragh's neck. "You will need to put some *jhafi* weed on that; it will heal," she said, and then stroked SStragh's belly, pressing hard. SStragh endured the examination, wondering. Finally, Raajek stepped back with a sigh.

"I thought so," she said. "You are full with your eggs, SStragh. I'm almost sorry . . ."

Raajek fumbled for a gourd of water sitting on a ledge near the brazier. She poured the water over the coals; they hissed while fragrant steam curled upward toward the domed ceiling of the OColi's room.

"This changes things. SStragh," Raajek continued, "I had intended to order you to be Given. I *should* offer your life to the All-Ancestor, hoping She'll finally have mercy on us. But there are so few of us, so few . . ." Raajek shook her head. "I can't afford to sacrifice a female who bears eggs."

"OColi, I am not afraid to be Given."

Raajek smiled at her. "I know. But I am afraid. I am very afraid." Raajek went to the brazier and sniffed. She blew softly on the ashes, reviving the coals. "I had a vision," Raajek said. "A month ago, when the arm of the Nesting Mother first showed above the horizon."

"You saw something in a Dreaming Storm?" SStragh asked, but Raajek only pulled herself erect, her frill rising as she gave the sharp scent of rebuke.

"It wasn't a Dreaming Storm," she said, "but a dream that came from the All-Ancestor. In that dream, I saw the Mutata nesting grounds, and all the nests were empty, barren. What few eggs there were had been broken and lizards scampered among the shards, licking them clean." Raajek lifted her head, and her blind eyes seemed to glare at SStragh. "I fear this may be the last Nesting Walk of the Mutata. I fear that there won't be enough children born this time. I fear that none of us will ever come home again."

SStragh shook her head, denying what Raajek had said even though she could smell the truth of her words. "OColi, no. Aaron, the human, he has told me that he knows a way—"

"Humans?" Frraghi nearly roared the word. "What have they ever brought us but death? The humans don't offer solutions, only more problems. SStragh, listen to me: I will kill the humans if they come here again. I will take my spear and—"

Raajek waved a hand at Frraghi, who snorted but went silent with his leader's gesture. "SStragh, we are too few. Only a handful of us are left who are of breeding age. So I cannot Give you. Not now. Your body has saved you, SStragh. If we no longer need you, we need your eggs."

"And the humans?"

"If they come again, I will not listen to them. I will close my ears to their words."

The words were unemotional and cold, but they made SStragh feel comfortable. She knew that Jhenini, with her strange human wildness, would have been plunged into despair or perhaps anger, or some odd combination of many emotions—with humans it was hard to tell how they'd react. Humans (especially, she told herself, the males) were creatures ruled by chaotic thoughts. For SStragh, Raajek's simple declaration only made her sigh with relief. She *knew*, now. She knew whether she would live or die; best of all, she knew that she would be given her chance to lay her eggs, and somehow, at this moment, that meant the most to her.

"I will abide with your decision, OColi Raajek," she said, and the scent and stance of Raajek indicated a mild amusement.

"You have not heard all of my decision yet, SStragh. It is my right as OColi to decide who will give life to your eggs. I have also made that decision."

SStragh knew what Raajek was about to say before the words came, and in that instant, very humanly, she felt some of the wild panic that Jhenini must have felt.

Raajek leaned over the brazier and tossed a pinch of dry herbs onto the coals. The OColi took a deep inhalation of the fragrance as the leaves curled and blackened. "Frraghi will be your mate," Raajek said.

She did not look at either of them.

2

Alterations

Moonlight dappled the perfectly circular patch of cobalt blue sand that had sheared off the top of the hill as if by some supernatural knife—a piece of some other world brought here by the Dreaming Storms and left behind. From the hilltop, SStragh could look over the moon-silvered valley and see other, larger pockets of other-places, like lesions on the skin of her world. The Dreaming Storms had ravaged the valley far worse than any other place she had seen, it seemed. Who knew what strangeness they had brought? Who knew what abominations now walked here?

It is humans' fault It is Eckels's fault, and I can understand why it is that Raajek and the others want the humans destroyed . . .

SStragh had already smoothed down the sand around a glassy black rock. Now she reached out with her hand, leaning over the sand with her tail out for balance. Her clawed fingers drew triple parallel lines around the stone, and then a line curling gently away. SStragh stepped back, her head cocked, gazing down at her handiwork.

The night's coldness made her slow, made her feel like she was part of a dream.

The wind, in SStragh's face, touched the grains, *tumbling* them into the miniature canyons she had drawn, smoothing the grooves. She liked that. Somehow, it reminded her of how fragile and fleeting everything seemed to be now.

"How is your neck?" The voice startled her. With the breeze blowing the other way, she hadn't heard or smelled anyone approaching. SStragh turned to see Frraghi half glaring at her.

"Better," she said. "Raajek was right—*jhafi* weed took the pain from it."

"What are you doing?" Frraghi moved closer, and she saw his eyes narrow as he saw the sand and the marks she had made.

"The humans do this," SStragh told him. "It is an art, like scent-mixing. Do you remember the hard-shelled ones, the ones Jhenini and Aaron called 'Jhapaneese'? They built gardens like this in their houses, though the sand wasn't this color—an area of white sand with a few large stones set in it. They would draw lines in the sand with a tool like a claw on a long stick." SStragh held her hand up, fingers extended. "I didn't understand the art, but I liked the sand-drawings. There was something . . . *pleasant* about gazing at them."

"The humans have infected you, SStragh," Frraghi said angrily. SStragh could smell his irritation. The moonlight showed the colors brightening on his beaded skin. "They have stolen the soul the All-Ancestor gave you and left behind an emptiness, like the sickness the Dreaming Storms leave on our world." Frraghi pointed at the sand.

SStragh widened her stance in mute denial. "You're wrong, Frraghi. The humans have taught me more than

I ever believed I would know," she said. "I have seen that there are many other worlds and many other ways. And I have learned this: there is more than just one Way. There are many more paths to follow beside the OColihi."

"That is why you came up here. You are going to run away again. You will not obey the OColi Raajek and bond with me." Frraghi snorted his disapproval. "You would let the Mutata die because of these experiences of yours."

SStragh looked down at the sand. She gave the scent of rebuke to Frraghi. "No. That is not what I mean. I will do as I said I would do. I will obey OColi Raajek."

"You accept me as your mate?"

SStragh looked at Frraghi, so haughty and proud before her, and yet at the same time, she could sense the fear underneath his arrogance. It was a strange realization: Frraghi was frightened, too, as scared of this commitment as SStragh herself was. That knowledge made SStragh smile sadly. Softly, she answered him: "Yes. I will."

As she said the words, she felt her own acceptance. The emotion burned inside her, yet the heat was pleasant. SStragh found that she was not at all unhappy with the choice.

This is right. I feel it—my own OColihi. My own path . . .

Frraghi's scent changed. It became deeper, like sandalwood laced with musk. His spinal frill lifted, and even in the moonlight, SStragh could see that the earthy colors on his body became deeper and brighter. SStragh could feel her own body changing in unbidden response, her scent altering to an inviting sweetness, and her skin tingled as the wind brushed by her. "Frraghi—" she started to say, but stopped, uncertain. The ghosts of ancestors seemed to move around her, binding SStragh to this path she had just chosen.

Like all Mutata, she took solace in ritual. In instinct. In the OColihi, the Old Path.

"You will be Mutata now," Frraghi growled. "You will forget the humans and their destruction. We will go on our Nesting Walk and we will bring back with us younglings. Yours and mine."

"Yes," SStragh answered. The agreement came easily. The heaviness in her belly filled her, swelling, and she could hear the sound of Mutata younglings, mewling in their high-pitched voices. In her mind, she could see them, gangly and awkward, running around her feet and racing away again, a tangle of clamoring arms and legs and tails. SStragh was almost frightened at the intensity of the emotions. Rushing, clamoring, they threatened to overwhelm her. She could barely hear or smell or see through the interior assault. SStragh's only experience of attraction was that of the humans—of Jhenini and Aaron. Jhenini said that she loved Aaron, that she hoped one day to be with him, but the human attraction seemed tame and slow compared to this sudden whirlwind that had swept her up.

Your OColihi is not our way, Jhenini had once told her. You have a whole other history; there's no possibility Mutata and human can ever see or experience or respond to things the same. We are too different for that.

It seemed Jhenini was right.

Frraghi was gripped in the same rushing excitement. His stance was formal. "We will walk together," he told SStragh, and she could feel his nearness, like a heat on her skin. The words were the ancient words, the words that all mates spoke together before the Nesting Walk. The web of ritual had caught them, and SStragh surrendered herself to it gladly. For the first time in many months, she felt safe. Frraghi's head came forward and rested alongside hers. She pressed against him, and marveled at the pleasure the touch gave her. "We will nest," she answered, the words of this OColihi, the Path of Mating, rising from centuries of instinct and habit. "My eggs will be yours."

"We will give our strength to our younglings," Frraghi answered, the final statement of the bonding ritual. SStragh felt a sudden, almost physical sense of completeness.

Frraghi evidently felt it too, for he stirred to move closer to SStragh. As he did so, his foot scraped over and into the sand patch, scattering the bluish grains and destroying the pattern that SStragh had placed there.

SStragh saw, but she said nothing. The marks in the sand had come from the small part of her that was like the humans, and the ritual and the urgency of her biology had destroyed that part of her. SStragh was Mutata again. She would be Frraghi's mate, since that was what the OColi had decreed, since that was what she seemed to want herself.

Beyond that, she no longer cared.

In the blue sand, there were only the footprints of Mutata.

"Frraghi?"

SStragh woke to see Frraghi standing near the entrance to the dome in which they'd spent the night, his head cocked to the side so that he stared up at the sky with one eye. "A Dreaming Storm is coming," he said. "Listen."

A moment later, a soft thundering came from the blue sky. Dark clouds formed overhead in an instant, a boiling gray-black fury spreading madly across the sky until it blotted out the just-risen sun. The first stroke of lightning flickered down like a glowing snake's tongue, hissing and sparking, leaving SStragh momentarily blind with the brilliance of its passage, and deafened at the thunderclap that accompanied it. SStragh shrieked in instinctive terror, huddling back against the wall. Frraghi grabbed one of the spears near the entrance and tossed it toward SStragh. He looked worried, and his scent was cinnamon concern.

"Here! We may need this. Stay here; I have to go to the OColi." He took a spear for himself and went out into the storm, narrowing his eyes against the swirling, angry wind.

"Wait!" SStragh shouted, and she followed after him. Frraghi had already ducked into the OColi's dome, next to his own. Mutata were scattering everywhere as more lightning flickered high up on the blue hills of the valley. SStragh could see something there: ramparts of white stone, studded with slender towers. There was movement along the walls, gleaming, running sparks that might have been creatures carrying torches, but they were so far away that SStragh couldn't tell what type of beings they were. Then the lightning flashed again and the walls vanished.

SStragh turned away and loped toward the OColi's dome.

Lightning threw a sharp, fleeting shadow of herself on the ground ahead. SStragh blatted in alarm, and tried to skid to a halt, for the earth in front of her had changed. A circle of wide-packed black had appeared instead, and racing across that blackness, roaring like a mad Gairk, was what the humans would have called a *ma-cheen*, an orange and blue teardrop screaming in metal fury, the blinding light-throwing eye on the front of it focused directly on SStragh as it bore down on her at breakneck speeds, sparks flying from ridged metal wheels that tore at the utterly flat hardness under it.

SStragh knew that she could not move out of the way in time. This metal thing would run her down. As she stood, wide-eyed and frozen, someone hit her from the right, knocking her aside even as the next lightning flash stole the *ma-cheen*—inside which SStragh could now see faces: human faces, which somehow did not surprise her—and took the thing back from where it had come. Strong hands gripped the stunned SStragh and dragged her into the nearest dwelling.

"Frraghi?" SStragh said, trying to catch her breath. She could smell him, and one other. "OColi Raajek?"

"Here," said Raajek, and a gruffer voice answered also: "I am here." A hand touched her: Frraghi. She could see his eyes gleaming as her eyes adjusted to the sudden dimness after the glare of the *ma-cheen*. "I asked you to stay. The Dreaming Storms are dangerous—you know that. If I had not been there . . ."

"I wanted to be with you," SStragh answered, almost surprised to find how true her words were. She spoke almost angrily, and her scent was sharp. "I have given you my bonding. We go together from now until our eggs have hatched, Frraghi—we will stay together whether that means on the Nesting Walk or into some strange world of Dreaming Storm. I have given you my bond, and I will not lose you now. If that bothers you, then tell me and we can ask Raajek to release you from your vows. But you'll walk alone if you do, and I will find someone else to give their seed to my eggs."

Frraghi snorted, and Raajek gave a bark of amusement.

"You see, Frraghi," Raajek said, "SStragh is the ideal mate for you—she has a strength of will to match your own. Tomorrow, we will begin the Nesting Walk."

Frraghi snorted again, but SStragh felt his tail curl around her own, warm and comforting. As Raajek uncovered the glowfires so that a warm greenish light filled the room, Frraghi handed SStragh a spear from the rack on the wall. "Watch with me, then," he said. "Together, we will protect the OColi."

For the remainder of the Dreaming Storm, she stayed close to him.

3

Following The Leader

Aaron Cofield stepped out onto the floating stone
through the blinding sparks and bitter cold of the gateway
and immediately took a roll into cover behind the nearest
cycad, alert for attack from any of the Mutata or Gairk.
He expected a spear to come hissing above his head, or
to hear the roar of a Gairk, but there was nothing but the
faint rustling of ferns in the breeze and the chittering of
small animals in the brush. He shook his head to clear it
of the last lingering effects of the disorientation. Then
Aaron clutched the bronze sword he'd picked up in their
mad rush out of the Emperor Julius's banquet and stood
up cautiously.

"Struth?" he half-whispered. "You around here? Darn it
anyway, Struth, speak up . . ."

A lizard on the branch of the nearest fern looked at him
curiously from one eye, but otherwise there was no
answer. Aaron let out a breath. He stepped cautiously into
the clearing. He could see the domes of the Mutata village
through the trees, but there was no sign of activity around
them. In fact, the entire area seemed suspiciously empty.

Aaron wondered what had happened. They'd agreed to wait a few minutes to let Struth check out the area before they all went through, but Struth hadn't come back. When five minutes had gone by, Aaron had decided to go through himself. *"We'll go through one after another."* he'd told them. *"I'll go first."*

But no one else had come through the portal, and the last remnants of clouds from the time storm caused by Aaron's passage had faded away. *Uh-oh. We have a big time differential between here and Rome*, he realized suddenly: the stream of time flowed much faster on this side of the portal than the other. A minute there might be hours here—and that meant that Struth might have been here for a few days already.

Time enough for a lot to happen. Time enough for Struth to be dead and buried—except, of course, that Mutata never buried their dead . . .

Aaron decided to look around. A time storm would warn him if anyone else came through from the Roman world. Taking a firm hold on the sword, he headed toward the village.

The paths between the domes were empty and silent. Aaron went to the first dome—one of the dwellings— and peered inside. The interior was normal enough for a Mutata: a set of pillows arranged against one of the sloping walls, a high table with a set of their hand-built pottery on it, glazed with abstract patterns of blue and brown. Toward the back of the first room, near the arch leading further back, was a small niche in the wall. Usually, those were full of fruit and grain: the Mutata equivalent of a kitchen cupboard. This one was empty.

"Obviously I have Mother Hubbard's house," Aaron muttered. He moved further into the residence, sword held out ahead of him. A noise from the next room suddenly made Aaron dart to the side of the archway, putting his back to the wall. He listened. There was a rhythmic scraping sound: *Scritch. Scritch. Scritch.*

Aaron took a breath. He turned and leaped into the room, his sword at the ready.

A huge praying mantis as long as a yardstick and as thin as a year-old sapling peered at him curiously from a window ledge. After a long stare, it went back to cleaning its claws: *scritch, scritch, scritch.* Aaron shook his head, feeling his pulse pounding in his head. "You just about got cut in half—you realize that? Next time you want to make noise, warn someone first." The mantis watched Aaron, its head swiveling on the anemic body. "Great," Aaron said. "Now I'm talking to insects. Next thing you know, I'll be having conversation with trees. Where the heck *is* everybody?"

The mantis didn't seem to have the answer to that. Aaron moved on.

An hour later, he'd convinced himself that all the Mutata were gone—just in the last few days, by the look of things. He was also beginning to worry about the rest of his companions, none of whom had come through the Floating Stone yet. The sun was beginning to angle down toward the west, tossing long shadows over the roofs of the Mutata dwellings, and Aaron had no intention of spending the night here alone. He was about to give up and go back through the doorway himself when he heard the low rumble of distant thunder.

Aaron glanced up to notice clouds boiling darkly at the zenith, sprouting impossibly from clear blue sky. The sun ducked behind the screen of thunderheads, and a lightning flash cast a glare brighter than the vanished sun over the Mutata village. The building from which he'd just come was gone, replaced by a circular patch of ice on which a polar bear sat staring at Aaron in befuddlement. The bear started lumbering toward Aaron, who began looking for the nearest tree, when another lightning flashed again, followed instantaneously by the deafening thunder.

Polar bear and ice vanished as if they had never existed.

Aaron hardly noticed. He found himself swaying at the edge of a jagged black emptiness, the mouth of a cave gaping open at his feet. The tips of his Roman sandals extended over the edge of the unseen depths, and a cold wind swept up into his face. Aaron scrambled back, pebbles cascading over the lip of the cavern and down into the gaping maw. At the same time, Aaron heard a sound: a thousand tiny drums beating wildly, the rustling of a million bedsheets on a universe of clotheslines.

A dark cloud erupted from the cave mouth: a swirling, ebony cyclone shrieking as it came boiling out into the air. "Bats!" Aaron cried. They rushed and shrilled past him as he ducked. The wind of their passage buffeted him, their high calls dinned in his ears and their wings beat at him like miniature fists. Aaron threw himself on the ground.

Lightning flashed again; thunder growled. Aaron lifted his head to find the cave mouth gone, though the cloud of bats still wheeled and swelled in the sky above him. The clouds were already melting overhead, the sun making its slow, cautious return.

"Veil," said a very bad Transylvanian accent from behind Aaron. "Vould you vant to drink my blood?"

Aaron looked around, startled, the hair on the back of his neck standing erect. Then he rose to his feet and grinned. "Jenny! That's got to be the worst Dracula imitation I've ever heard, and man, am I ever glad to hear it."

Aaron ran to Jennifer, hugging her tightly for long seconds. Neither one of them said anything—the embrace was enough. At last, reluctantly, he let her go and let out a long breath. "I've been here for hours—just like what happened to you in Egypt. I was beginning to worry."

"I followed right after you, like you said," Jennifer told him. "It wasn't any more than a few seconds, over there." Jennifer suddenly looked worried. "Oh no. Struth . . ."

"Yeah," Aaron told her. "She probably had days here before I came through. Time enough for everyone to take off, anyway. No one's here, Jenny—not Struth, not Fergie, not Raajek. The place is deserted." Aaron ran fingers through his hair. "Which may give us a real problem."

"We'll see," Jennifer told him. "No use worrying about it now. Let's wait for the others. They should be along any sec"—she stopped—"*hour* now," she finished. "Looks like we're going to have to spend some time alone. Darn."

She grinned.

By the next morning, they had all come through the Floating Stone: their friend Peter, Mundo, Travis, and Eckels. Aaron filled them in on the situation. "The bottom line is that the Mutata are all gone. Jenny and I found tracks leading toward the mouth of the valley. From the looks of it, every last Mutata went that way a few days ago."

"What about the time machine?" Eckels said. Whatever could be said of the man—none of it good, in Aaron's opinion—he was at least consistently self-centered. "The heck with the lizards—good riddance. All I care about is the machine and getting out of here."

"So far we haven't found it," Jennifer told him. "There's no sign of it anywhere in the village. I don't know what they did with it."

"Great." Peter had been moody since he'd come through the portal from the Roman world—hardly surprising, since Chantico, the young woman with whom he'd fallen in love, had decided to return to Kemet rather than stay with him. Peter nudged the shards of the temporal machine, piled in a heap near him. "At least we can go home. I say we stick the hunk of Green Town-linked stuff in the nearest piece of roadway and go home. I don't care how it's changed or what's going on, I'm tired of *this* place."

"What about *me?*" Mundo whined. "I can't get home, not without the machine." The white-furred ape frowned. "You can't leave me," he told Aaron defiantly. "Not after everything I've done for you."

"Yeah, you've been a terrific help," Peter said. "We're lucky we're not all *dead* from all your help."

"I've done far more than you, marching around in that tin-plated armor like some puffed-up fool," Mundo snarled, and the ape's fingers curled, the claws bright in the morning sun. Aaron thought Mundo was going to launch himself at Peter. He started forward to intercept the attack, but Travis moved between the two, limping badly on his wounded legs. Fluid was seeping through the bandages Jennifer had wrapped around them.

"Shut up, both of you," the guide said wearily. He looked more tired than ever, his skin pale. He seemed to sway slightly as he stood, but his face was stern. "This bickering's getting us nowhere. Aaron, what's this plan you've come up with?"

They were all looking at him, and the pressure of their gazes was enormous. His throat threatened to close up, his heart seemed to be trying to leap out of his rib cage. *As much as anyone, you're the leader. Your job is to try to keep them together—as impossible a task as that seems sometimes.* Aaron tried to sound a lot more certain than he felt. "If my hunch is right, we'll need the time machine. The

Mutata had it; they know where it is. For all we know, they could have taken it with them. We can't afford to let them disappear. I say we all spend a few hours looking for the machine. If we find it, great; there's an experiment I'd like to try. If not . . ."Aaron shrugged. "Then we'll go after the Mutata," he finished.

"You keep hinting about 'experiments' and 'ideas' and 'hunches,' " Eckels grumbled. "Why don't you tell us what they are?"

Because I don't trust everyone, and most especially you, Aaron nearly said, then decided that honesty was not always the best policy. *Already a politician . . .* he chided himself.

"I'm still sorting things out, Eckels. Considering that the batteries in the time machine were getting pretty low, we don't have a lot of room for mistakes. I want to get it all straight in my own head, then I'll go over it with everyone else."

"Yes, O Great Leader," Peter said sarcastically from alongside Eckels. "We'd hate to soil your pristine thoughts with our lousy input."

"Hey, Peter . . . Aaron began heatedly, surprised at the sudden attack. He stopped, realizing that they were all frightened and more than a little tired, and this was exactly the wrong tack to take with them. But it was already too late.

"What, Aaron?" Peter answered, moving forward. Aaron could see the anger in his eyes, and he realized that Peter wanted the confrontation to turn physical. He could see Peter gathering himself for a fight, and the hardest thing Aaron had ever done was to not respond in kind. He kept his hands at his sides. "You have a problem with someone thinking for himself, huh?" Peter taunted, and with the last word, Peter shoved Aaron hard.

Aaron let his hips turn with the push, and it was Peter that nearly went sprawling as the resistance he expected disappeared. Peter stumbled, catching his balance with one hand on the ground. He sprang up, turning sideways into a martial stance, his hands up and ready.

Aaron wasn't sure what he was going to do. Peter's face was as red as his hair, and muscles bulged at the corners of his jaw. He knew Peter: the next attack wouldn't be anything so innocuous as a push—it would be a full-bore attack, fists and feet.

One of them would end up hurt, no matter what happened. Worse, they would both have a hard time forgetting, even when the fight itself was over.

Jennifer saved him. She stepped between the two, giving them each a look of exasperation. "If the two of you haven't noticed, we're wasting time," she said, hands on hips. "Or is this display of stupid machismo more important than getting home?"

"Just get out of the way, Jennifer," Peter told her. He stayed in stance, his eyes locked on Aaron. "This doesn't have anything to do with you."

"Or what, Peter? Are you going to hit me, too?" Jennifer advanced on him, her arms waving. "I'm sure that'll solve everything. Oh sure, a bloody nose, a few loose teeth, maybe even a broken arm or a concussion, and I'm *positive* the heavens will open, the Dreaming Storms will stop, and everything will be back to the way it was." Peter retreated in the face of Jennifer's tirade, his hands dropping a little lower with each step. "How *dare* you say that this doesn't have anything to do with me? How asinine can you *be*? Do you think this will bring Chantico back? She made the decision she had to make, and if you really loved her, you'd understand that.

If you were thinking with your head instead of your . . . your . . . *Ohhh!*"

Jennifer flung her hands wildly. Peter, his eyes wide, took a last step backward and bumped into the trunk of a cycad. "Ouch!" he muttered.

"At least we know who's *really* in charge," Mundo commented drily.

Aaron looked at Peter, with his back against the tree trunk, with Jennifer still fuming in the midst of them. A chuckle, utterly unexpected, burst from him. Jennifer whirled around at the sound. For a moment she scowled, then slowly her expression softened, and she smiled, joining in Aaron's laughter. The others joined in the amusement, the tension slowly draining from them. Peter didn't join in the laughter, but his hands dropped to his side and he seemed to relax slightly.

"All right," Aaron said at last. "Jenny's right. We're wasting time. Let's spread out and see if we can find the time machine. Everyone meet back here around noon, and we'll decide what to do next." Aaron looked at Peter. "We'll *all* decide," he added.

Peter just grunted. As the others scattered in various directions, Aaron watched Peter. Aaron knew that it was just the stress of their situation, but he wondered just how long their friendship could last under the continued strain.

"Peter, I'm sorry. I really am," he said, but the words were only a whisper and Peter had already gone.

"I didn't find a thing," Mundo told them, "unless you're counting those biting flies down by the marsh." Mundo scratched at his furry chest with both hands and an overdone frown. "I found *plenty* of them."

The ape was the last of the troupe to report back in. No one had seen any evidence of the time machine. Aaron grimaced. "At least no one found any Gairk, either." He glanced at each of them in turn, trying to read from their faces what they were thinking. Jennifer was checking Travis's bandages; her tight frown told Aaron she now wore her doctor's hat. Eckels seemed almost angry, and Peter had on what Aaron thought of as his "martial artist" mask: his expression betrayed nothing about what was going on inside his head. Mundo was content to sit in the dirt and scratch himself.

I wonder if Mundo would tell me what they're thinking? Aaron wondered, and with the thought, the ape looked up at him.

"Not a chance," Mundo said. "You wouldn't like it, anyway."

Aaron got to his feet. "We need to go after the Mutata, then," he said. "They've either hidden the time machine or taken it with them. Either way, the only way to know is to go after them."

"Go *where?*" Peter asked. "They could be anywhere by now."

"*I* can track them," Mundo said.

"When did you become the Great White Hunter?" Peter retorted. "I thought that was Travis's role."

"I have nothing to prove to *you*" Mundo answered. "I said I can do it, and I can." Mundo turned to Aaron. "I want to go *home*" he said. The words were plaintive and soft. "Please. I'm tired of being alone."

"I'd like that too, Mundo," Aaron said to the ape. "We're all tired." Aaron nodded to each of them. "Look at what we've been through already: lost in time, stranded in a time line where the Japanese found America, captured by pterosaurs, trapped in the middle of Aztec rites, lost in ancient Egypt and captured in Rome. The thing is, we've gotten through it all alive. We know more now than we did when we started this. Tezozomoc told me that his visions said we would 'fix what was broken.' I think that means the shattered timestreams. Even if we do *nothing*, we still need what's in the time machine: the weapons, the medical supplies, the technology. What I'm asking is for a few more days of strength from each of you. We'll find the Mutata, find the time machine, and see what we can do. A few more days, and we'll know. What do you say?"

"I'm in," Jennifer said quickly. Travis echoed her, grimacing as he tried to stand. Mundo nodded. Aaron looked at Eckels, who shrugged noncommitally. "Peter?" Aaron asked. "What do you say?"

Peter scowled, arms folded on his chest. "I guess the votes are in. Doesn't matter what I think, does it?" He scuffed at the dirt and walked away toward the village. Aaron, his face flushed, started after him, but Jennifer caught his arm and shook her head. "Let him go," she told him. "He'll be okay."

Aaron stared after Peter. "He'd better be," he told Jennifer.

Evening found them at the Gairk village near the mouth of the valley. The trail of the Mutata moved along the river snaking through the valley—"Any idiot could follow *this* kind of trail," Peter had said disdainfully when he'd seen the deep impressions left in the mud and foliage by the Mutata's passage. They moved at a jog, hoping to gain ground on the Mutata, who—Mundo claimed—were progressing slowly. Around them, they could see signs of the time storms that had ravaged the valley. On the side of a nearby hill, a tumbledown, deserted castle sat leaning heavily, like a plaything dropped by a child. A wide circle of tall bladelike grass blocked their progress at one point. The empty husk of a ten-foot-tall beetle gleamed darkly half in and half out of the river, and, grasped in its dead legs, they could all see the skeleton of a Gairk. Several times, they had glimpsed through the trees buildings whose architecture was so strange that they knew nothing human had ever designed them, and once, Aaron could have sworn that he saw a kangaroo hop by.

This world of dinosaurs, it seemed, was being assaulted by other times and histories.

The group slowed as they approached the Gairk village, remembering the fury of Klaido and the fact that the last time they'd been there, they'd been prisoners condemned to death by the Gairk OColi. Mundo went ahead, coming back several minutes later. "The Gairk are gone, too," he told them. "The campfires are totally cold, and it looks like they cleaned out most of their belongings. There's no smell of them, and it doesn't look like anyone's been here in a week or more. The Mutata trail goes right past the village—they're still heading out of the valley."

"All right," Aaron said. "We'll follow, then. Everyone keep your eyes and ears open—I don't want to be surprised by a Gairk who got left behind."

Despite what Mundo had said, the Gairk village still smelled of Gairk to Aaron. A scent of death and filth clung to the dirty, misshappen buildings. Garbage littered the ground; further up the hill, tailings from their copper smelting operation fouled the earth. But proto-birds, like lizards with tufts of feathers clinging to their leathery bodies, prowled the area unchallenged, and smaller dinosaurs—Coelusaurus, Aaron thought; whip-thin, bipedal, striped scavengers about six feet long—looked up, startled, as they approached.

"They're gone, all right," Peter said. Like the rest, his Roman sword was out and ready, and he had a spear in his other hand. "I wonder why? The Gairk leave, then the Mutata . . ." Peter suddenly frowned. "What's that smell?" he asked.

Aaron sniffed, and Mundo's nose was wrinkled as well. Aaron thought he caught a whiff of something. He noticed that the Coelusaurus had all lifted up, their heads craning around. As if some unheard alarm had gone off, all of the fleet dinosaurs suddenly bounded away like a herd of deer. "What spooked them?" Eckels asked.

He was answered by the rending of trees and a roar.

Behind the group, a monster's head suddenly leered at them, open-mouthed, through the screening fronds.

"Allosaurus!" Aaron cried. "Run!"

4

Narrow Escapes

"No!" Travis barked even as Aaron gave the command. "Don't run. Stand still. Stand perfectly still!"

"Do as he says!" Aaron said quickly, realizing that, of all of them, Travis knew the huge carnivores best. The truth was, Aaron didn't think any of them could really outrun the tons of hungry muscle staring at them from fifty yards away, and their puny swords and spears would be like knitting needles against a charging lion. Still, remaining quiet and calm while the allosaurus snuffled and peered in their direction with its head cocked sideways was very nearly the hardest thing he'd ever done.

"They look for movement," Travis whispered. "The allos are like lizards—they don't like dead meat. They want their prey alive and moving. If you stay perfectly still, they can't really see you—you just blend into the background. But if you move . . ."

Travis didn't need to finish the rest of the statement. They all understood. "What about smell?" Peter asked, not daring to look at Travis, all his muscles locked. "That thing's sniffing this way."

"Their sense of smell's good, but I don't think he'll actually strike without noticing us first. Besides, I don't think it's looking for us. See—it keeps glancing behind,like it's watching for something following it."

"Anything willing to hunt *that* is something I don't want to meet," Jennifer said fervently. Aaron was tempted to agree with Jennifer, but then they all went silent as the allosaurus came fully out into the open. Watching it, Aaron felt a sense of mingled awe and terror. There was a certain evil beauty in the creature. The beast was a perfect machine of death, muscles rippling under a skin as colorfully decorated as that of a gila monster, red and blues shimmering in the sun. Light glinted from the razored knives the allosaurus used for teeth, and its small hands clenched and unclenched as if in eagerness to leap and rend and kill.

But Travis was correct in that the allosaurus didn't seem to be concerned about them. Though Aaron shivered whenever the hunter's unblinking gaze swept over the area where they stood, the dinosaur's concern seemed to be with something hidden in the giant ferns behind it. Once it turned completely around, the great tail sweeping out high for balance, and faced the screen of green with its mouth open, snarling like a cornered animal.

"Should we run while it's looking that way?" Jennifer asked softly.

"I don't know," Aaron said. "Travis? Can you manage a short sprint for cover?"

"Stay still," Travis repeated. "Get ready to run if we need to—head for the cave where the Gairk held us the last time we were here—but not yet. Wait . . . Listen!"

Aaron heard it at the same time: a piercing call like the deep barking cough of an alligator. The call was answered by another, and another. The allosaurus heard them as well. The creature seemed agitated. It snarled again, its tail lashing as it backed away from the wall of ferns and closed to the Gairk village. The calls from the unseen pursuers grew louder and more insistent, and now they could hear a thrashing among the cycads. Aaron found himself as nervous as the allosaurus. Whatever was making the racket was going to burst from cover any second, and he wasn't sure he wanted to be here to see it. "Travis?" Aaron *managed* to get out.

"I don't know," Travis answered. "I've never—"

Then there was no time to do anything. A half-dozen animals exploded into view, tearing aside the last intervening screen of ferns. They looked like smaller, more agile versions of the allosaurus, with longer necks and slimmer bodies about eight feet in length. Their teeth and clawed hands were dangerous enough, but on each foot they had a huge, scythelike central claw, raised slightly from the other toes. The black curve of those claws knotted Aaron's stomach. He could envision what a kick from one of them could do, ripping and tearing someone open.

Aaron recognized them immediately: "Deinony-chus!" Aaron shouted. Deinonychus, like their smaller cousins the velociraptors, were pack animals, hunting in groups and capable of bringing down much larger prey than themselves.

"This shouldn't be," Travis said. "Deinonychus are Cretaceous, not Jurassic."

"After what we've been through, you're going to quibble about a little temporal mix-up?" Peter asked. "Maybe they came through a time storm, or maybe this world just didn't work the same as yours and ours. They're real, and they're here, and that's all that matters to me. Man, *look* at those things!"

Aaron had to admit that the beasts were impressive. They moved in a graceful choreography, spreading out around the clearing and encircling the snarling allosaurus. The larger carnivore turned slowly, its great feet kicking up clouds of dust and its stiff tail lashing as it tried to do the impossible and keep each of the attackers in its sight. The pack would not let that happen. They shifted, darting in and then back just out of the reach of the snapping jaws as the allosaurus lunged at them. They were like a wolf pack, toying with the larger creature, making it waste precious energy and never quite closing in.

They played a waiting game. Like pawns attacking a lone queen on a chessboard, they moved carefully, always protecting each other and leaving the more powerful enemy an opening to attack.

As Aaron and the others watched, fascinated by this dance of death, one of the pack leaped forward and bit at the allosaurus's tail. The great beast made a shrill bellow of pain and whirled around, snapping at the creature whose jaws were latched around its tail. The movement tossed the deinonychus, which went tumbling away. Two others took the opening given them as the allosaurus tried to deal with the rear attack and dashed in to bite at the allosaurus's feet. Blood gushed suddenly as one of them tore off a great chunk of skin and muscle. The allosaurus screamed, a wild terrible sound, and reared and snapped at these new attackers, but they'd already backed away once more.

The pack closed in now, eager. The allosaurus was visibly limping, and a fan of blood spread down from the raw wound, each movement of the dinosaur sending a scarlet spray flying.

Another deinonychus slashed in to bite the tail, and as the allosaurus whipped about, the others attacked as one. The allosaurus roared, bit, and clawed, but the sudden rush and its already weakened leg betrayed it. The limb buckled under the huge bulk as it turned, and the allosaurus went down. The deinonychus were on it in an instant. Now their legs, with the horrible scything claws, kicked at the exposed belly, ripping open great gashes. Blood fountained as an artery was torn, and the crippled allosaurus moaned, nearly invisible under the snarling, yipping mass of the deinonychus pack. The allosaurus's tail whipped once, the ground shaking under the impact, and the deinonychus pulled back. The allosaurus tried to rise, its great jaws snapping shut on nothing, then the eyes rolled back and the creature fell back. The tail thrashed once more, then was still.

The deinonychus moved in to feed.

"Come on," Travis said, breaking the spell that had fallen over them as they watched the hunt. "Now's our chance."

Carefully, then more quickly, the group moved away from the Gairk village, still following the trail of the Mutata. Aaron's breathing didn't settle until they were out of sight of the feeding deinonychus and the Gairk village was hidden behind a shoulder of the cliffs surrounding the small valley. "That was *awesome* nasty," Peter said, breaking the silence. His voice trembled as he spoke. Aaron could hardly blame him; he didn't trust himself to speak at all. "I thought Struth said there weren't any dinosaurs like that in the valley."

"There aren't," Jennifer answered. She kept looking back over her shoulder, as if she expected the deinonychus to come after them at any moment. "At least not normally. Struth said the Gairk keep them out—that's why their village is near the entrance to the valley; they intercept any of them that wander in. But the Gairk are gone now."

"Then it's no wonder the Mutata followed. I don't much care for Gairk, but if they can beat something like *that* . . ." Peter shook his head. "Guys, if there's stuff like deinonychus out there, how the heck are we going to survive?"

No one answered Peter's question. "I thought so," Peter said at last. "Well, if we gotta, we gotta, I guess. I don't know of a safer place, that's for sure."

No one had an answer for that, either.

Not far from the Gairk village, the steep walls of the valley curved together to form a horn. There, the river had cut a deep ravine through the rock. Limestone cliffs, adorned with long ribbons of green ferns, towered above them. The river, wider now from the water poured into it by numerous small waterfalls, ran faster as it emerged from the valley and churned downhill into the broader plain beyond, where in the blue distance they could see it join another, much larger river. Mists shrouded the plain, through which they could glimpse swamps with tall ferns and the occasional graceful comma that was the neck of a diplodocus plodding through the fertile ground. Further on, at the edge of vision, there was the deep azure line of the sea.

And somewhere out there were the Mutata.

"It's beautiful," Jennifer breathed. She was standing near Travis, who leaned against a convenient boulder. The guide was breathing heavily from the effort of making their way over the tumbled, slippery rocks of the valley pass.

"And dangerous," Mundo added. "Or did you forget the Gairk, or the allosaurus, or those nasty little wolf-lizards?"

"I don't think any of us are likely to forget them," Eckels said. "And I'm not anxious to meet any more of them in person, either."

"For that matter, who knows *what* the time storms may have dumped out there," Peter added.

"Okay," Aaron said. "Like you said before, Peter, there isn't any safer place to be at the moment. Let's camp here for the night." The sun was already near the horizon, and the violet shadows of the valley's walls were spreading out over the plain. Aaron didn't think Travis could make it much further, nor was he any more eager than Eckels to be exposed in the open. There was plenty of cover here—the unknown could wait for tomorrow and full light.

"Let's use that area over by the cliff wall," he said. "It'll keep out the breeze. Peter, Mundo, can you get a fire started? We'll set up a watch schedule . . ."

* * *

The campfire spread a comforting halo of yellow light around the narrow pass into the valley, painting the rocks of the steep cliff walls with shifting yellow. Outside, the land was wrapped in starlit darkness, though the sounds of the night animals boomed and chirped and bleated. Aaron walked away from the fire and leaned against the cliff walls, staring up at the dusted canopy of sky. He heard someone approaching, rocks clunking dully underfoot, but Aaron continued to watch the display overhead.

"Pretty, isn't it?"

"Hi, Jen. Yeah, it is. It's something that seems to hit me every night since we left Green Town. Even out at our house, the glare from town pretty much wiped out most of the stars and the sky was just the sky. Here, it feels like I'm staring into some black, deep well with little glowing fireflies in it, and if I fell, I'd keep going forever and ever. It's so *far* . . . Aaron shrugged. "Guess I never realized how small we really are in the scheme of things."

"You're worrying about our situation again."

Aaron had to chuckle. "I don't think I ever stop. I doubt *any* of us ever do."

"You really think we can fix things?" Jennifer asked. Her arm slipped around his back as she leaned in against him. She felt warm and soft. "Or are you just trying to keep the group together as long as you can?"

"No." He breathed in the scent of her hair, pulled her tighter to him. "I really think . . . well, I don't know, Jenny. I'm not sure what to do, but I have this *hunch*. Sometimes, it'll be really clear in my head for a moment, and then I try to grab it and it all slips away again, like a dream. Time traveling makes things so . . . so *tangled*. I keep thinking about how we got dragged into this, and about some of the weird things that have happened, and . . . Aaron shrugged in her embrace. "I don't know."

"You think we're here for a reason," Jennifer suggested. "You think we were pulled into this by some . . . some destiny."

"I guess so." Aaron laughed again, a short bark that had very little amusement in it. "That sounds pretty egotistical, doesn't it? But Tezozomoc thought the same thing. I hope he's right."

"I hope so too," Jennifer said.

Her face was outlined in blue starlight. She smiled at him. There was an expectancy in her eyes that pulled Aaron's head down, and her hand came up to cup the back of his head. Her lips were very, very soft.

Intent on themselves, neither of them had noticed Peter's silent approach. The young man watched Aaron and Jennifer kiss. He said nothing, staying in the shadows of the cliff wall. Only Peter's hand was in starlight, and his fingers slowly clenched as he witnessed their long embrace.

He watched for long seconds. Finally, still in shadow, he turned and walked back to the fire.

5

Hatched Schemes

Aaron awakened to the keening, plaintive cry of pterosaurs, launching themselves from their nests on the cliff face high above them to snare insects flitting through the morning sun. Aaron squinted into the dawn, shielding his eyes and watching the small flying dinosaurs perform their graceful sky ballet.

"Hungry?" Travis asked him.

"Absolutely famished," Aaron responded. "If I were any hungrier I could touch my ribs from the back. What do you have?"

"Anything you want as long as it's fruit," Peter answered sourly from across the fire. Aaron thought Peter's gaze lingered too long on him, like an unspoken challenge, but he ignored it.

"Sounds great to me," he answered. "Toss me something."

Travis underhanded a softball-sized globe that looked like a pear with warts. Aaron looked at it suspiciously while Jennifer yawned nearby. "That's a *ca*-sai," she told him. "Kind of tart, but pretty good once you get used to it. They were Struth's favorite."

"I think they suck," Peter said. He threw his own *ca-sai* rind into the fire, which sent sparks reeling into the morning air. "And I'm going to get real tired of fruit while we're off chasing dinosaurs. I can tell you that now." With that declaration, Peter got up and stalked away from the campsite, going to the end of the pass where he could look back into the valley of the Mutata.

"What's with him?" Jennifer asked.

"I thought it was just losing Chantico," Travis said. "Now I'm not so sure. He seemed pretty moody when he woke up."

"He had a bad dream," Mundo commented. "He dreamed he was here." At Aaron's scowl, Mundo shrugged, his white fur riffling in the breeze coming up from the valley below. "Hey, I had the same dream, too," he said. "Scared the heck out of me." Eckels, nearby, was the only one who laughed, a sound like a dry cough.

Peter's grumpiness seemed to put a damper on conversation. The group quickly finished eating, extinguished the fire, and gathered up their few belongings. "Okay, Mundo, you're on point," Aaron said when they were ready. "Let's go find the Mutata."

"God knows why," Peter mumbled, but he swung in behind Eckels as the group set off.

The hike down from the high pass became progressively easier. Evidently there had been a fair amount of traffic into and out of the valley in the past, for a wide, erratic path had been made by the treading of many dinosaurs' feet—mostly, it seemed, those of the Gairk. The Mutata tracks followed this meandering path down from the tall hills until the slope began to flatten and the realm of the ferns began. By midday, they were hiking through a thick forest of the leafy plants, towering well over their heads. Life was plentiful around them, and Aaron found himself fascinated despite the dangers they were in.

"Look, Jen," he said. "Over there . . ." Aaron pointed at a small dinosaur with blue-green and bright orange scales, no larger than a house cat.

"What?" Jennifer asked. "Is that something special?"

"You know it," Aaron said. "That's no dinosaur I've ever heard of before, one that I'm sure never made it into the fossil record. I've seen, oh, a dozen others that aren't recognizable. Do you understand, Jen?—those are creatures entirely out of the realm of our knowledge. We're the first humans to ever see them, and we get to see *everything*: how they move, the color of their skin and their eyes, where they live . . ." Aaron made a movement with his hands; the dinosaur skittered away, startled. "Man, I learn something new here, every minute."

"So . . . you're telling me that you want to stay here?"

The questions, asked innocently and with such a serious expression, caused Aaron to stop. Travis nearly lurched into him. "No," he said quickly. "It's just—"

"I understand," Jennifer said quickly, laughing at him gently. "It was a *joke*, Aaron. I understand. I really do."

With a sidewise glance at the grinning young woman, Aaron nodded. A dragonfly slid by on cellophane wings, nearly a foot from head to tail. Unseen animals croaked and growled and grunted on every side of them. "There's something here," Aaron said at last. "Something that's compelling. I mean, Otomo's world, Tezozomoc's world, or Egypt or Rome—they were all strange and fascinating, but *this* . . . this is totally alien. We don't belong here. This world wasn't built for us."

"I know," Jennifer told him. She pointed through a break in the ferns to a nearby swamp, where a young diplodocus munched on high leaves. "It belongs to them."

Aaron felt Jennifer shiver with the words, and all the light seemed to seep from the land around them. Aaron suddenly looked at it with different eyes. He put his arm around Jennifer, trying to find some comfort in closeness.

From behind, Peter watched Aaron and Jennifer talking as they walked, and the slow rage continued to build in him, like the coals from the fire last night. Eckels obviously sensed it, for the thin man sidled up alongside him. "Ahh, young love," Eckels whispered. "Touching, isn't it?"

"Just shut up, Eckels."

"It bothers you, doesn't it? Well, it should. She's the only female in this world, Peter, since your cute little Chantico decided she liked her old friends better than you. Think about it: a whole world, and Jennifer's the only woman in existence—and she's already made her choice plain. Where's that leave you and me, huh? You think you can watch that, year after year?"

"What do you mean? We find the Mutata, figure out where they hid the time machine—"

"You're not telling me you've fallen for Aaron's 'Let's Glue The World Back Together' nonsense, have you, kid? C'mon, we both know that's not going to work. Everything's broken, and it's going to stay that way. We need to do whatever we can to make sure we survive in as much comfort as possible."

"What's that mean, Eckels?"

"It means that it's time to look out for ourselves. If Aaron and Jennifer and their trusty safari guide want to go chasing big lizards, let 'em. I don't know about you, but if I'm going to spend the rest of my life in some history that's not my own, I want it to be something that's at least halfway familiar."

"Like?"

"Like maybe Rome—I was making headway there, until our friend Aaron stuck his nose in it. Or maybe Egypt or even Mexico. At least there's *people* there." Eckels stopped. They were well behind the others now, who were barely visible through the intervening screen of fronds. "Well?"

"I don't know . . ." Peter ran his fingers through his tousled red hair, over the ragged growth of beard he'd picked up in the months away from home. *He's right. Aaron's got some crazy idea that's never going to work, and you already know what this world's like. If you're going to be marooned, you don't want it to be here . . .* "I don't know," Peter repeated. "I gotta think about this."

"Fine," Eckels said. The rest of the group was out of sight entirely now, and Eckels suddenly looked fearful. His head swiveled from side to side, his eyes peering at every sound. He began to walk quickly toward the others. "Just don't take too long about it," he called back over his shoulder. "Who knows how long we'll last here."

The land became greener, more tangled, and far more wet as they went on. Mud caked their shoes, and each step was an effort as the ground clung to their feet, releasing them with a loud *squealch* and leaving behind a footprint that slowly filled with water.

Twice during the day, the sky covered over with quick black clouds, and a time storm careened noisily through the landscape, though never near enough for them to see the quick changes. Still, it served to alert them that this world, already dangerous enough, held other dangers beyond those of the land itself.

If that weren't bad enough, there were the insects— most of them larger than their descendants in Green Town, but no less obnoxious and irritating for that: flies the size of red grapes, insistent clouds of midges, biting and stinging swarms of nameless creatures. Mundo waved his hands uselessly at a particularly persistent specimen. The ape was caked to his knees in mud and his black muzzle was wrinkled in vexation.

"This world is *stupid"* he said, exhaling loudly through his nose and swatting at the insect, which buzzed in annoyance and veered off to bother some less dangerous victim. "In *my* world, I *was* the insects, and I knew better than to bite myself. Aaron, are you sure this is worth it?"

"I'm beginning to wonder myself," Aaron admitted. He shielded his eyes against the low shafts of sunlight filtering through the ferns and pointed to his right. "Mundo, there's a patch of higher ground over there. Why don't we head that way? It's getting late and we're going to need a place to spend the night."

"Hey, look at this!" Mundo exclaimed as they approached the rise. "I guess we deserved a break today."

Mundo was grinning as if he'd made a joke. Aaron puzzled over that until he stepped up onto the dry ground himself, stepping over the exposed roots of the swamp plants. "What are you talk—" Aaron stopped.

The vines had covered over most of it, the sign had fallen over, and only half the building was there, but the twin arches of bright yellow plastic were unmistakable. Aaron could see the faint circular trace of the boundaries of an old time storm. This had been here a long time, wherever it came from—time enough for the land to have claimed it as its own. Despite that, Aaron felt compelled to call out. "Hello? Anyone here? Hello?" There was no answer except the rustling of small animals disturbed by the noise.

"I wonder if they have drive-thru service," Aaron commented, shaking his head. "I doubt that anything's left to eat, that's for sure."

"Except for us," Jennifer said shakily. "Look!"

She pointed to the shattered glass door of the vine-snared restaurant. A head was peering out from it—a dinosaur's head, and the teeth in its open mouth were sharp, white needles. Its tongue emerged and flicked over the deadly array. Instinctively, Aaron identified it: velociraptor.

"Everyone be ready to move," Aaron said. "It might have more friends inside. Peter—"

Aaron stopped, glancing around quickly.

Peter and Eckels were gone, vanished. The only person behind him was Travis. Before Aaron could call out for them, a growl from the dinosaur brought his head back around.

He was just in time to see the velociraptor leaping through the air toward him.

6

Divergent paths

Aaron had no time to move. His response to the sudden attack was instinctive, taught to him by months of aikido practice. As the velociraptor flung itself toward him—its mouth gaping, the sharp and deadly long second toe on each of its feet extended, a hissing gurgle coming from its throat—Aaron simply accepted the attack, allowing himself to fall backward with the impact. In a tangle, he and the German shepherd-sized predator went down on the soft ground. The velociraptor, not used to victims who gave it no resistance, went tumbling away from Aaron, who did a back roll and ended up in a standing position. He swayed, feeling pain along his right forearm; he put his other hand on it instinctively; it came away bloody. Sweat was running down into his eyes. Aaron squinted through involuntary tears, blinking, trying to find his attacker.

The velociraptor had struck the metal pole that held the restaurant sign. Even cushioned by the foliage that had wrapped around the fallen pole, the dinosaur was visibly stunned. It shook its head like a fighter downed by an unexpected uppercut. Before it could move, Travis lunged forward with one of the Roman spears. The bronze point impaled the velociraptor to the ground. The creature screamed in pain and defiance, thrashing at the spear with its hind legs and claws as Travis tried to hold it down.

But Travis, weak from his wounds and gaunt from months in various time lines, was nowhere near as strong as he had once been.

"C'mon, die, you ugly thing!" Travis grunted. As Aaron, Jennifer, and Mundo all rushed to help, the velociraptor gave an almost human scream and lurched to its feet, tearing the spear shaft from Travis's weak grasp.

The raptor, free once more though bleeding from the terrible wound in its scaled underbelly, shrieked defiance at them. It snapped once at Mundo, its head slashing forward on the long neck almost like a snake's. Mundo yipped and jumped back. As Aaron desperately tried to clear the sweat from his eyes, the raptor turned to Jennifer. It snarled and gathered itself.

But Jennifer didn't give it a chance to attack. She ran forward herself, grabbing the end of the spear. With a cry, she jabbed the weapon deeper into the dinosaur, pushing and straining. The raptor shrieked and fought, but its efforts only widened and deepened the wound. Jennifer kept pushing, the raptor backing up until its spine touched the trunk of a cycad. Travis came forward now; the two of them continued to put pressure on the spear, and with a terrible crunching sound that Aaron would remember ever afterward, the tip came through the back of the raptor and entered the tree. Pinned like an insect, the doomed creature flailed and tore at the shaft in desperation. Jennifer held on, the wooden spear shaft slippery with the raptor's pulsing blood.

Aaron managed to blink his eyes clear at last; he helped hold down the dinosaur with his uninjured arm. It hissed and spat as red-specked foam flew from its mouth, as the dangerous hind feet slashed air only inches from their faces, as its struggles became slower and weaker. Dying seemed to take the raptor hours, though Aaron was certain that it was actually only a few minutes.

At last, the creature collapsed over the shaft, silent and unmoving. Slumped over with weariness and relief, the three humans and Mundo backed away from the corpse. "You never know who you'll find eating at places like this," Aaron said. He tried to laugh, and then realized that his forearm still hurt. He moaned instead, suddenly sick to his stomach.

"Aaron?" Jennifer said. "Oh my God, you're hurt. Here, lie down. Travis, give me a hand. Mundo, would you get some of the cloth bandages out of my pack? See if we can get a fire started so we can boil some water . . ."

Aaron was content to let Jennifer fuss over him. His head was pounding, and he could barely see. A red film covered everything. He lay back, trying to control his nausea. Jennifer hovered over him, her face concerned. "All right, I'm just going to wipe away some of this blood . . ." Aaron could feel her dabbing at the long wound. He watched her expression, but she had her "doctor" face on—he couldn't tell what she was thinking. "Mundo, I need my pack," she said. Aaron lost sight of her for a moment, then she was back.

She looked down at him and smiled. "You're going to live," she said. "It's a long cut, but mostly shallow. The blood's making it look worse than it is."

"Tell me about it." Aaron grimaced. The world seemed to be returning to a normal color. He tried to sit up.

"Just stay still," Jennifer told him. "Travis has a fire going; I'm going to clean it once we have some water I can trust. Then I'm going to bandage it so the insects don't bother it and it doesn't get infected."

"We can't stay here," Aaron said. "Velociraptors are supposed to be pack animals—they'll be more of them coming around."

"We'll move into the building for now. You aren't going anywhere until I take care of this."

Suddenly Aaron remembered what the attack of the raptor had driven from his mind. "Peter! Where'd he and Eckels go? Jen, we have to go after them."

Jennifer's mouth tightened into a grimace. "That can wait," she told him. "Right now, let's just worry about you. Pete's made his own destiny." Her hands continued to work on him as she talked, soft and gentle as she cleaned the wound and wrapped it. "I just hope he likes what he finds," she said.

"C'mon!" Eckels grated out. He shoved Peter in the back, and Peter whirled and took a swing at him.

"Back off!" Peter dropped into a martial stance and Eckels took a step away. "Listen!"

They could both hear the roaring and hissing of an angry dinosaur emanating from the direction they'd come. Peter, up to his ankles in mud and stinking water, balled his hands into fists. "They're being attacked," he said. "I gotta go back!"

"No way." Eckels shook his head. "Look, kid, you were the one that wanted to cut out. Well, I think that's a good decision, but you can't worry about them any more. If it's a pack of those killer lizards like we saw in the Gairk village, then your being there just means that you'll die too. You're not going to make a difference one way or another."

"They're my *friends*."

"Right. We've both seen how they treat you—or are you having memory lapses, too?"

"All right," Peter answered disgustedly. "I get your drift." Peter stared at the green foliage around him. He could still hear the shrill cries of the dinosaur, and he thought he could also hear Jenny, shouting faintly.

"Hey, by the time we manage to slog through this gunk and get back to them, it'll be over, one way or the other," Eckels was saying. "They're dinosaur meat or they're all right, one way or the other."

"Or they're hurt."

Eckels sighed. "Make up your mind, Peter. We're on our own or we're not. Wherever we go, you can't spend the rest of your life worrying about what happens to them— you might as well go back now if that's what you're going to do. Stay, and nothing changes: Aaron still runs things, and there's no humans in the world but us. Go, and we can make a whole new life somewhere else, in a world we at least partially understand."

"Eckels, you should have been a politician."

The man gave Peter a grin. "I assume that's a yes."

Peter shook his head. The sounds were gone now. Eckels was right about that, at least—whatever had happened back there was already done. Peter couldn't effect the outcome one way or the other. Besides, if they *had* survived, then Aaron had already noticed their absence. "It's a yes," Peter told Eckels.

Peter didn't return the smile on his companion's face. *I really don't like this guy, and I don't trust him. As soon we get to wherever we're going—and that's to Kemet and*

*Chantico, as far as I'm concerned—I'm leaving him
behind, too.*

"All right," Eckels was saying. "Then let's get going."

Peter looked once more at the now-silent screen of
ferns that separated him from the only friends he had
in this world. The doubts threatened to surface once
more, but he shrugged and refused to listen to them.
Instead, he turned and slogged onward, heading back
toward the valley of the Mutata. The going was slow,
and without Mundo to guide them and with the tall
ferns blocking off his view of the land, Peter realized
that it would be easy to become lost. The sun was
sinking rapidly and twilight was settling over the
swamp. They'd only been gone an hour or two, and
Peter realized just how much he'd been dependent on
the others. *I don't care,* he told himself. *I'm as competent
as any of them. More.*

"I thought we'd be back on dry land by now," Eckels
complained. "Are you sure we're going in the right
direction?"

"Yes," Peter told him curtly. "We were in the swamp
for three, four hours, remember?" Peter stopped, one foot
on a tangled maze of roots. They were both a mess,
covered with mud to the waist, their pants and shoes
hopelessly soaked. Without a fire, it was going to be one
uncomfortable night, but Peter didn't see any alternative.
He looked around for a hummock or a little rise,
anywhere where they might be relatively dry, but the
dying, green-gold light revealed nothing but water, ferns,
and a few trees. "Eckels, we aren't going to get out of here
tonight, that's for sure. I think we ought to climb one of
these trees; we can tie ourselves in the branches for
the night."

"You gotta be kidding." Eckels snorted. "Do I look like Mundo? A tree isn't exactly my idea of a safe place to sleep. I say we keep going."

"It'll be dark in a few minutes. We can't walk through this at night."

"We can't be far from being out."

"Maybe not, but if we go wandering around in the dark, we'll be lucky if we don't end up further in. We're waiting for morning."

"Oh, I get it. You're the leader, I'm the peon. We do what *you* say."

Peter gave Eckels a disgusted wave of his hand. "Stay on the ground then. Go ahead and try to find your way out. I'm willing to bet you'll find something that thinks you'd make a great bedtime snack. I don't care; I'll be up here."

With that, Peter jumped up, grabbed an overhanging limb, and pulled himself up. The branch was wide enough to sit on comfortably, and most importantly, it was dry. His pants dripped water like a slow rain.

Eckels grimaced, looking up at Peter. "Give me a hand," he said at last. Peter resisted the impulse to add a comment.

A few hours later, Peter wasn't so sure that Eckels hadn't been right. He started a small fire in a crotch of the tree with moss and some dry twigs that were within reach, but the smoky, fitful flames seemed to only make the chill worse. His pants itched as they dried, and his legs felt like they'd been stuck in a refrigerator for the last week. His ragged Roman sandals never did dry out. He took them off, but he didn't relish the thought of putting them on again in the morning.

The two made a desultory meal of the *ca-sai* in their sacks, and Peter leaned against the trunk of the tree near the fire and fed the embers the last of the twigs and moss, then put his hands behind his head and stared up through the broken canopy of the tree to the sky. He squinted—where there should have been stars, there were fast-moving clouds, the edges touched with flickering lightnings.

"Oh, man. I can't catch a break—" Peter breathed, then pulled himsef up. "Eckels! There's a time stor—"

He didn't have time to get anything else out. The ferns bowed in submission to the tyrant wind, like an invisible wave moving through the swamp toward them. Peter could hear the shrieking whistle as the tree's branches began to sway. Eckels had gone flat on his stomach, hugging the branch. Peter tightened his grip on the trunk as the first blinding lightning flash left afterimages of snake-tongue purple and red in his eyes. *Things* went zinging by them with the thunder, hissing like fireworks, with faerie arms and wrinkled infant faces. One of them bobbed in the air in front of Peter, let out a laugh, and went flittering off in the next gust of wind. Peter had no idea what they were or what world they came from, and in the next lightning flash, they were gone.

To their left, there was a bellow like a demented train whistle, and they could glimpse a tower of craggy stone, with flickering lights in a row of window high up on the summit. Black smoke belched from the top of the building, and the shrill whistle sounded again, this time to be answered by some creature far off in the swamp.

Another lightning, and it was gone. The storm was at its height now, and flashes of other worlds came and went as if thrown on the screen of the swamp by a cosmic slide projector. Peter, hanging onto the tree in desperation, lost count of the lightning flashes, but he could tell the storm was fading as the wind lost intensity and the clouds began to part. The final lightning bolt flared not ten feet from them and thunder followed instantly, hammering against his chest. Peter cried out, unable to see. He blinked, trying to focus in the sudden darkness.

There was *something* moving in the darkness below them. Peter could hear the liquid sound as it moved through the swamp. "Man, that was way too close. Bet you're glad we're up here. Who knows where we would have ended up if we were traipsing around out there," he said.

Eckels didn't answer. Peter turned his head to look at him.

He saw immediately why Eckels hadn't spoken. The man, still hugging the branch for dear life, was staring wide-eyed at a dragon's head that had suddenly appeared through the leaves scant inches in front of him.

"Greetings!" the dragon said.

Eckels yelped, tried to jump up and run at the same time, and succeeded in losing his grip entirely. He fell with a splash into the watery mud ten feet below.

7

Dreams of War

The Nesting Walk was a total disaster.

They lost five Mutata in the first day of the Walk; seven on the second day. One disappeared in the midst of a time storm, as chaos rippled around them and lightning filled the air with the smell and tang of ozone. Two more were killed by tawny, golden brown creatures with furred heads and bodies and great ripping claws on their front paws, creatures that no Mutata had ever seen before—and which SStragh knew must have come from yet another time storm.

But most of them fell to an enemy they knew all too well—the Floraria who shadowed their little herd as they walked through the swamps and then over the hills to where the salt sea licked at the skirt of the world. The Floraria were huge bipedal predators, all jaw and teeth and very little brains—she remembered that the humans called them *Allashaharus* or something like that. SStragh herself nearly was killed in the last attack. Just before the ferns grudgingly gave way to rocks and sand, a Floraria charged them from the cover of the last of the cycads. Lhath hooted a warning, his nostrils flaring at the end of the nasal horn and his spinal frill rising in alarming blues and greens. His spear held in his right hand, he turned to face the onrushing beast as the other Mutata hurried to support him, as SStragh moved to protect Raajek.

The Floraria, its jaws gaping, its truncated, deceptively strong tiny forearms clenching and its meat-stench filling the air, snapped at the spear that Lhath thrust at it, breaking it like a twig. The beast shook its great head, and Lhath, still clutching the spear, went tumbling as the Floraria turned to face the rest of them. Frraghi roared back at it in insane, furious defiance, his hooting sounding thin and high against the bass roar of the carnivore. Frraghi thrust, ducking under the jaws that tried to close around him, burying his spear deep in the Floraria's abdomen.

The Floraria reared back, its roar now one of pain. The other Mutata rushed into the opening. Two more spears found the creature, and it clawed at them as it might at thorns stuck in its side. Spear shafts shattered and broke, but the flaked stone heads remained. Blood streamed from the wounds, and the smell of it infuriated the Floraria. It spun, its muscular tail sending Mutata sprawling, then turned to attack once more.

But SStragh led the next wave, knowing that the best way she could protect the OColi was by killing this monster while it was already wounded. She rushed at the Floraria as it was about to crush Frraghi under its great hind legs. The impact of spear against flesh sent a shock through her whole body, but she only grunted and pushed harder, trying to find the thing's hidden heart. Through the roaring of blood in her ears, SStragh could hear her fellow Mutata trying to find openings, could sense Frraghi rolling away to safety. Then the Floraria's forepaw slammed against her shoulder, the claws ripping long furrows along SStragh's flank. SStragh mewled in pain, but the rest of her companions hit the Floraria at the same time.

The creature decided that this meal was too much trouble. With a final roar, the Floraria turned and fled, blood spattering the ground as it ran.

If the All-Ancestor was just, SStragh decided, the Floraria would die of its wounds later, in slow pain and helplessness. With luck, the beast would become a meal for one of its own.

Afterward, as he pressed the healing *jhafi* weed against SStragh's cuts, Frraghi said nothing. He didn't need to. She could hear his words in his stance, in his odor: *It's your fault that the Gairk aren't here to protect us. It's your fault that so many have died. It's your fault that there are so few of us left.*

The worst thing was knowing that he was right.

"Tomorrow, we'll be at the Nesting Grounds," he said to her. SStragh only nodded. She closed her eyes as the *jhafi* sent its burning potion into the cuts. Frraghi stroked her flank, and she found herself responding to his touch, lowering her stance in acceptance.

"I'm sorry that your first Nesting Walk is this way," he said to her. "It should be a time of joy. But your humans . . ." He stopped, but his scent told the rest: *Your humans have made this a mockery, a debacle. Your humans made the Gairk so angry they left without us, and now we are prey to the Floraria. The Dreaming Storms kill those the Floraria leave behind, and all of us have seen how often there are humans in those storms.* With it, the moment of tenderness was gone. They both knew it. When Frraghi moved away a few moments later, SStragh didn't follow.

Later, as they continued the walk, SStragh moved close to Raajek so that she could guide her through the broken landscape. Her old teacher gave a scent that was a strange mixture of sadness and amusement. "We have lost too many," Raajek said. "The All-Ancestor is looking the other way. The Ancient Path is lost."

"OColi Raajek," SStragh answered softly. "Please don't say these things. There is still hope. With enough egglings and a safe walk back to the valley—"

"Tell me, SStragh," Raajek interrupted, and she sounded like SStragh's old mentor once again. "Do you believe that there will be enough egglings? Do you think that our walk back will be safer?"

SStragh thought of the humans and how easily they lied, how easily they could fasten their hopes to events that were so unlikely as to be near impossible. That wasn't something SStragh could do. "No, OColi," she answered. "I don't."

"Neither do I." Again, the puzzling scent wafted toward SStragh. "At least the Floraria will be well fed."

"OColi!" SStragh hooted in surprise.

Raajek only chuckled. "What, my OTsio, you're shocked by that? What other kind of reaction did you think I could have? I've done what I could for us; it wasn't enough. Now I can only pray to the All-Ancestor that She takes our failing as punishment enough and spares the rest of the world. Perhaps Mutata elsewhere will survive, or the Gairk, or even our slow cousins the Floraria."

"You're giving up, Raajek?"

Raajek turned her blind eyes toward SStragh, smiling sadly. "No. I am only saying what my heart feels. But I am not giving up. I say this only to you, because you are also part of my heart, whether you know it or not."

"OColi . . ." SStragh didn't know how to reply. For a long time, the two of them walked in silence, with Frraghi pacing alongside them at a tail's distance.

The actual Nesting Grounds were shared by several tribes of dinosaurs. The Mutata followed no directions, used no landmarks—the location was imprinted in their souls, in the genetic coding of thousands upon thousands of generations. The sea called them with its rhythmic pulse, with its briny scent of life, and it was to the sea that they came. SStragh had accompanied the Mutata on these walks as a youngling, too immature to lay her own eggs, but following the herd because she must, because it was part of the OColihi, the Ancient Path. SStragh remembered the strangeness of it, the odd pairings of male and female that strengthened as they approached the grounds, the strange scents and sights and sounds. Here was where the ferns and cycads no longer grew; here was the sandy dune where the brooding, pensive Gairk who had always accompanied them would turn aside and go to their own place further north along the shore . . .

. . . and here—with the salt scent strong and almost overpowering—was the final, stone-strewn rise, from which at long last they could see the surf going about the slow business of transforming rock into sand.

. . . except . . .

Frraghi, out ahead of them, sounded a low, mournful note from his nasal horn as he stood on the summit of the rise. The low wail echoed in SStragh's bones; she had never heard anything so sad in her life. The rest of them felt it too, even Raajek. The ancient Mutata straightened, her ragged frill rising with Frraghi's call. "What's the matter?" she said to SStragh, her voice high with concern. "What's going on? Tell me!"

"Wait here, OColi," SStragh told her. "Wait." With that, SStragh ran up the broken slope to Frraghi's side.

There she stopped, as the last faint dregs of Frraghi's sorrow thrummed low.

SStragh looked down at the ancient Nesting Grounds of the Mutata. She remembered how it had been: the white-stained rocks; the crushed remnants of shells everywhere; the mounded sandy hills of the old nests; the bleached bones of the egglings who failed to survive the crucial first days, falling to sickness or to the wriggling lizards who lurked in the hollows of the rocks, waiting for a helpless victim. The nursery had extended down the beach for a day's walk in either direction: all the various tribes of Mutata and—to the north—the Gairk.

That's what SStragh remembered. It was not what she saw.

The ancient Nesting Ground was pitted and scarred. It looked like a thousand time storms had struck here, each leaving its distinctive mark on their world. SStragh could not understand even a fraction of what she saw— she wondered whether Jhenini and the others would have known what these strange parts of buildings and other landscapes might be. They littered the Nesting Ground, taking up space that used to be full of nests and dinosaurs.

Now . . .

The nests were mostly destroyed. Where once a hundred tribes of Mutata had nested there were few, so few. In front of them, the breaking waves lapped not against rock but against the burnished, smooth surface of some tilted, multicolored wall. Close by, a triangle of some smooth, silvery stone set in the middle of a large circle of polished blue crystals reflected back SStragh's image. The bright shape swayed in the wind, seemingly as weightless as the air itself and yet tethered invisibly to the ground.

Not of our world. Not from any world I saw with the humans.

"Frraghi! SStragh!" Raajek called from below. SStragh turned to see the OColi, with the rest of their small band of Mutata looking anxiously up toward them. "What is wrong?"

"Tell her," Fraaghi said softly from alongside SStragh. Her mate smelled of defeat, of resignation. "I cannot. I don't have the words."

"I don't know how to say it, either," SStragh moaned.

Frraghi looked at her now, and she could see the emotions riding in the colors that moved over his skin. "It is your doing," he told her. "Ultimately, that is the guilt you alone must bear. So tell the OColi. Find the words."

"SStragh!" Raajek called again.

"OColi," SStragh started, then the emotions overwhelmed her. "OColi," she said. "It is all destroyed."

The Mutata found what space they could to build their nests. There was no question about that, even among the time storms' litter. They must lay their eggs: the OColihi demanded it. Ritual and habit demanded it. Their very bodies demanded it. So even as they mourned the loss of their ancient Nesting Grounds, even as they found what scraps of it remained, they did what Mutata had always done.

Male and female together built the nest, a careful conglomeration of sand and mud moistened with their saliva. The nest was preferably sheltered from the offshore wind behind rocks and yet open enough that predators could not easily sneak up to steal the eggs.

Then the female would carefully deposit the fertilized, cone-shaped eggs into the nest with their narrow ends down, moving as she did to lay them in a circle. The work exhausted the female, but there was no rest. Not yet. More sand and mud must be placed on top of the eggs. Again the male helped, mounding a thin layer on top of the clutch.

The wind and the sun quickly dried the moist nest, and the sun turned it into a warm oven, where the eggs would eventually come to life. For several days, then, the job of the parents was to protect the nest, for the nesting grounds swarmed with natural enemies: the Claw-Diggers, human-sized lizards who considered Mutata or Gairk eggs a rare and much-prized delicacy; Tunnelers, furry blind moles who burrowed into the nests, breaking the eggs from the bottom and sucking out the sustenance inside. There were Sun-divers, winged creatures whose favorite prey were the eggling dinosaurs, or the bright-eyed Surfling, who would come from the sea at night, tearing into unattended nests with shovel-like flippers to snatch the eggs and take them back to the sea.

These were dangers enough. Now there were more.

SStragh had, of course, known all this. She'd seen the routine during other Nesting Walks, but now, taking part in it for the first time, she realized how much she had missed. As SStragh, with Frraghi alongside her, built her own nest not far from the triangular, floating mirror, her emotions underwent a complex and radical change. The eggs . . .

She had not known that she could ever find them so precious, so valuable. She looked at them, realizing that these were part of her, that each had been touched with her life and Frraghi's life, and that each was a vessel which would soon burst forth, alive and hungry and dependent.

Hers. Her children. Her egglings.

SStragh touched the leathery, warm surface of each egg in turn, marveling. There was suddenly nothing in the world more valuable to her than these bits of her lying in the mud near the shore.

"I remember the feeling," Raajek said behind.

The scent of the OColi came a few moments later, sympathy underlaid with the everpresent rot of her failing body. "OColi," SStragh said. "I never knew—"

"You can't know, not until you feel it," Raajek told her. "Do you remember on the last Nesting Walk how you watched Ilhia after the Claw-Diggers raided her nest and broke all the eggs. You thought she'd gone insane."

"I remember," SStragh said. "Ilhia caught the Claw-Digger as it finished the last egg. She smashed it with her tail, and I've never heard a more terrible sound than the call she gave then, when she saw the ruined nest. She kept stomping on the Claw-Digger's body long after it was dead, shrieking and crying, as if she were going to keep doing it until the Claw-Digger was nothing more than a stain on the rocks. No one could calm her down."

SStragh paused. She looked at her own eggs.

"I understand Ilhia," she said. "I understand."

"No, you don't," Raajek told her. "Not really. And I pray to the All-Ancestor that you never do."

Once the nest was built, neither SStragh nor Frraghi ever strayed far from it. One or the other would make short forays, accompanied by other Mutata, into the fern forest a morning's walk away. There, they'd quickly gather what food they could and hurry back. There was never enough food, but that was expected. They all knew that the Mutata who returned to the valley would be thinner and weaker than those who left. That was the way it had always been. That was the OColihi.

And there were things outside the OColihi as well: Dreaming Storms. They came every day, sometimes more than once. Almost always, they would see the storm gathering above them, the clouds melting like quick smoke, the thunder after the lightning strokes nearly deafening.

SStragh watched the dark clouds form like a mist high above her. Up and down the stretch of beach that was the Nesting Ground, hoots of alarm rose as other Mutata saw the Dreaming Storm begin. Mothers ran to nests; males took up protective stances alongside them.

Frraghi was no exception. He came at a dead run from the dune above, half sliding and half running down the slope toward SStragh's nest. His spear was out, and defiant, he shook it at the sky as the first flash of lightning sent white light glaring. SStragh saw a forest of impossibly tall, thin trees, with strange many-armed beings skittering through the branches. The creatures looked angry to SStragh, with strange black carapaces and glittering claws—just seeing them sent a shiver of fear through her.

But the Dreaming Storm had placed the forest well out to sea, and as quickly as it came, it fell in a cascade of white foam. Thunder boomed, shivering the sand and sending granules tumbling down the slopes of the dunes; the wind brought strange odors that flew by too fast to contemplate.

Another lightning strike came, closer. There were no living creatures this time, but a circle of crystals, all glowing as if flames played inside them, appeared where Lhath's mate sat on her nest. Lhath screamed in fury and frustration, battering at the crystals with his spear shaft. They broke under the assault, and as each facet shattered, a clear, piercing note like a cry was cast to the winds.

A shivering of lightning and Lhath's mate and nest were returned to this world as the crystals returned to wherever they'd come from.

But SStragh had no time to appreciate Lhath's shout of triumph and his scent of joy. The lightning had brought with it another fragment of time line, a pockmarked, desolate circle, one edge of which was no more than a tail's length from SStragh's nest. In the middle of this new landscape, far too close to her, sat an ugly machine, a thing of smoke and metal and fire, a turtle shell of steel with twin treads for feet and a snout that belched fire. The thing clanked and snorted, and it moved toward SStragh and her nest. Frraghi shouted and threw his spear—it clattered harmlessly against the black iron flanks of the fire-turtle and fell to the ground where the treads ground it under. Frraghi ran forward, and as he did so, the thing spat a line of fire from a small nozzle on its side, a searing wall of flame. Frraghi shrieked. His headlong rush nearly took him into the fire, but he managed to stop, staggering, and then backed away from the rippling heat.

The steel turtle, clamoring, rattled forward. Now it was nearly at the edge of its own world, treads churning rock into gravel, tearing at the ground as it advanced. SStragh howled her challenge, her head up as she faced the machine. Part of her screamed to move, to leap aside before this apparition crushed her underneath. *At least save yourself! You can't stop this machine!*

But she could not. She could not willingly allow it to grind her nest, her eggs, under its vast weight. She could not abandon them. Wonderingly, she knew that she would rather die than move. If the machine of the Dreaming Storm would crush her offspring before they were even hatched, it would have to crush her as well.

The treads ripped stone. The turret wheeled around slowly, the snout pointing directly at her. To one side, she could see Frraghi, desperately trying to find a way around the flames that held him at bay. The machine, smelling of grease and oil and death, reached the edge of its own world . . .

. . . and lightning flashed again. The war machine vanished, as if it had never been there. SStragh staggered, almost falling.

"SStragh!" Frraghi called, and then he was there, steadying her. SStragh blinked. The Dreaming Storm had moved on, passing beyond the dunes and into the line of ferns beyond, pieces of other times blinking into brief existence as it went walking on its legs of lightning and roaring with its voice of thunder.

SStragh watched it go, her tail wrapped around Frraghi's legs. She looked at the nest, at Frraghi, at Lhath and Raajek and all the other Mutata.

"I'm sorry," she said. "I'm sorry."

8

The Dragon's Tale

"Ouch!" Aaron hollered.

"Just be quiet and let me finish," Jennifer told him. "You have two options: I either stitch this up or you're going to have a scar the size of Texas on your arm."

"I know, I know. It just feels like you're using California for a needle," Aaron grumbled, but he clamped his teeth together and stayed silent while Jennifer finished the stitching. He had to admit that he admired Jennifer's resourcefulness: the "needle" was a small, curved thorn from one of the bushes around the ruins of the diner, and the thread was pulled from the hem on Jennifer's shirt. He knew that, on his own, he would have simply cleaned up the blood—most likely without boiling the water first—and hoped for the best. He also would have probably died from the resulting infection.

Through the front windows of the restaurant, he could see a time storm raging somewhere not too far distant. Aaron tensed for a moment, causing Jennifer to push him back down on the seat of the booth ("Hold still, will you!") but the stormfront seemed to be moving away from them and the thunder was only a low grumble. "Did anyone see where Peter and Eckels went?" Aaron asked, hoping to keep his mind off the painful tugging Jennifer was doing on his arm.

"I was busy watching the velociraptor," Travis answered. "What about you, Mundo?"

The ape looked up from where he was prowling behind the counter of the restaurant. He held up a bag of hamburger buns, grimacing at the blue-green, lacy mold that covered most of the bag. "Nothing to eat, but we could start a penicillin factory," he muttered, then shook his head. "I don't know," he said more loudly. "Eckels and Peter were behind me, too. Like everyone else, I was more worried about our dinosaur friend than watching them."

Aaron grimaced. "What about the pieces of temporal machinery they carried?"

"They've still got them, or they threw them away somewhere," Travis told him. "And by the look you just gave me, that wasn't the answer you wanted to hear. What's that going to do to this idea of yours?"

"I don't know," Aaron answered. He started to sit up; Jennifer pushed him back down again. "Maybe we still have enough of the pieces to play with—besides, I'm still not sure exactly what it is we need to do. I just know that we can't do it without most of the temporal mechanism Eckels blew up. We might still have enough, but there's no way to tell until we have the time machine."

Jennifer finished the stitching. She patted the wound clean again with a moist cloth, then wrapped it. Aaron caught a glimpse of himself in one of the aluminum surfaces of the counter. The black stitching crossed his arm, tying together the angry red edges of the wound. "I look like Frankenstein. I hope you got the right brain, Igor."

Jennifer didn't seem to be in the mood for jokes. She sniffed in something approximating a laugh, but didn't smile. "You look like you're awfully lucky to me," Jennifer told him. "We all are. That thing could have easily killed us, all by itself."

"You stopped that from happening," Travis told Jennifer. "You know that, don't you? If you hadn't jumped in when that thing tore the spear from my hands . . ." Travis stopped. "Anyway, thanks," he continued. "You're a heck of a lot braver than a couple of other people I could name."

Jennifer only shrugged. "We're all doing what we have to do. Which brings us to the next question—what do we do now? Look for Peter and Eckels, or continue after Struth and the Mutata?"

"Eckels and Peter want to go their own way, then fine," Travis retorted. "We just saw the kind of monsters that are out there waiting. My bet is that they're already—" Travis stopped, seeing the look on Jennifer's face. "Sorry," he said. "I didn't really mean that. It's just wishful thinking on my part about Eckels. Still, the truth is that they obviously won't *want* to be found, so why waste time trying? We all know what they're going to do—find a piece of roadway and go back to Rome, if this is Eckels's idea, I'll bet—or maybe to Kemet on Peter's part, chasing after Chantico."

"Which means that we know where they're heading," Jennifer said. "The only roadway we know about is back in the Mutata valley. That's where they have to go. If we catch them before they get there—"

"*If* we catch them," Mundo said. "They have a couple hours head start, remember. Aaron's hurt, Travis can't move very fast. We're not going to outrun them."

Aaron grimaced. Mundo was right. His arm was beginning to throb, he discovered, and aspirin tablets weren't going to be invented for millennia. He suspected that his aches were going to get worse, not better in the next several hours, and a fast hike in the swamp wouldn't help. Travis was looking thinner and more in pain every day.

"Let's get some rest right now," Aaron told them. "That's going to help us the most. Besides, it's getting dark." He looked at Jennifer as he spoke. He didn't like the thought of abandoning Peter, especially in the company of Eckels, but he didn't see any choice.

In the end, finding the time machine is more important, he told himself, and he hoped that Jennifer understood that as well, even if it was something neither of them would say aloud. *We can't think about Peter or ourselves, not if we want to stop this madness.* "Travis, Mundo, I think you're right. Peter and Eckels have made their own destiny this time; we'll keep following the Mutata trail."

Jennifer closed her eyes briefly at that, and Aaron thought she'd protest. But when her eyes opened, she only nodded.

"I'll take the first watch," she said.

Outside, there was a growling and hissing from close by. Through the restaurant's windows, they could glimpse shapes slinking through the night around the building.

"I think we'd all better stay up," Travis said. "I don't like the looks of this."

As Peter watched, the dragon that had just sent Eckels tumbling from the tree turned to him. In the last flickerings of the time storm, Peter could see the scales on the creature's head, like fragments of mottled aquamarine ceramic tile, and the ruff of purplish horn that formed a collar just below the head. Part of him marveled at the dragon's strange beauty, while the other half wanted to do nothing more than jump after Eckels.

The dragon belched, and a faint puff of steam jetted from its nostrils along with a wisp of flame. Peter pressed back against the tree trunk, waiting for the inevitable jet of fire that would reduce him to a twisted heap of bones and ashes.

"Oh. Terribly sorry about that," the dragon said. Glittering, diamond-pupiled eyes as sharp as knives regarded him in the darkness. "Must've been that sheep I ate last night."

"You *talk!*" Peter exclaimed.

"So do you," the dragon pointed out in a slow, deep voice. In the darkness, wings rustled. "But you'll have noticed that I didn't find it worth mentioning."

Great, Peter thought, *I'm being lectured by something from a fairy tale*. "Sorry," he said, deciding that humility was the best tactic. The dragon was big enough to snap him and swallow him in one bite. "We don't exactly have dragons—especially talking ones—where I come from. Though considering some of what we've seen, I suppose I shouldn't be surprised."

"I'm *not* a dragon," the creature said.

Well, you sure look *like one*, Peter wanted to say, but decided that arguing with something six times larger than himself wasn't a wise move. "Okay, you're not a dragon. Then what are you?"

"I'm a wisp. A nothing. A dream that fades in daylight and returns in the dark. *You* chose this form I wear, not me, and I speak the words in your own head."

"Great. You spout zen poetry, too. You got a name?"

"You may call me . . ." The huge beast paused, its eyelids half closing in thought. ". . . the Midgard Serpent. Or just

'Serpent.' Yes, that will do, though I have myriad other names: Iörmungandr, Leviathan, Tiamat. . ."

"Serpent will do," Peter said. "And you're an awfully impressive wisp, frankly. If you're something out of my head, I have a much better imagination than I thought."

The Midgard Serpent turned its head sidewise, so that one great lidded eye peered at him. Then it drew back just a little. It harrumphed, as if clearing its throat. "Aha! You're the ones, aren't you? The ones that tore apart the walls between the worlds? You're the ones who have been troubling my dreams and making me think of leaving my meditation. I thought there were more of you, but so much has changed, so much is different than what it was . . . It doesn't matter. I've been looking for you and now I've *found* you."

Its eyes narrowed with the word, almost angrily, and Peter found himself pressing back against the tree trunk once more.

"It wasn't me!" Peter cried. "It was Eckels, the other one. He was the one who started this. I just got caught up in it later."

The serpent looked down. Peter caught a glimpse of a clawed, four-fingered forefoot, which reached out and then brought up from the muck a dripping, mud-covered and shivering Eckels. The serpent held the man in its fearsome grip, the talons lightly touching. "Is this an 'Eckels'?" the serpent asked as water dripped from its hand and Eckels wriggled in its grasp.

"No!" Eckels shouted. "It wasn't me. It was Travis. It's all *his* fault!"

"Do you *all* act this way?" the Midgard Serpent asked in a voice full of exasperation. "If I find this Travis, will he scream and point his finger at the next person and say 'It wasn't me, it was him!'? No wonder you haven't fixed the mess you've caused. You're all too busy blaming each other."

The serpent placed Eckels on the branch with Peter. The men glared at each other while the serpent stared at them, its breath washing warm over them. "The truth is, I don't care which one of you caused this," the serpent continued. "It was hard enough to find this place, and I only have a little time here. I'd rather not waste it listening to everyone making excuses. Now, where are the fire-emeralds?"

Peter looked at Eckels, who shrugged.

"Fire-emeralds?" he asked.

The serpent looked at Peter with its head cocked and one eye closed. "Fire-emeralds," it said again, speaking slowly as one might to a child. "They're green. They glow. I saw you with them in my dreams."

"You mean these?" Peter asked. He fumbled in his pack for one of the pieces of temporal machinery. He pulled it out and held the fragment of twisted metal toward the serpent, who hissed and sent curls of steam floating into the night air.

"Ahh,"it said. "Very good. Now . . . where are the rest?"

Peter carried one other fragment: he pulled it out. Eckels had one in his pack, and produced it with a frown. The serpent waited; when neither of the men came up with any more of the fragments, its head reared back on the long neck, breaking off branches and shaking the tree. "That's it?" the serpent asked. "There were more of them in the dream, many more."

Peter looked at Eckels. The man was shaking his head, his dark eyes glaring at Peter. The serpent waited, still hissing slightly, as if a teakettle were boiling in its stomach. "That's all we have," Peter told the serpent finally. "That's all there are."

The lie tasted like sand in his mouth. He tried to tell himself that it really wasn't a lie—*who knows what had happened to the others by now? Maybe they are all gone, carried off by whatever attacked Aaron and the others.* The rationalization didn't make him feel any better.

The serpent's head came back down. The wings rustled, the tail lashed invisibly on the ground below. "Then the dream was a chimera, a ghost of something that once was," it said sadly. "I had hoped . . ."

"What did you see?" Peter asked it. "What *are* you?"

"You really don't know me, then?" the serpent asked. Peter shook his head. The serpent seemed to sigh, then it brought its gorgeous, terrible head close to their perch once more.

"Let me tell you . . ."

I don't remember where I was born (the Midgard Serpent said). That particular memory is lost in the mists, adrift in time. I don't truly have a form that is mine—as I said, I found my present shape within your mind, snatching it from you just before you saw me. Mostly, I sleep, and I dream. I see the shapes of all worlds and all times, and I watch their pageants, their glories and their falls. Many times I watch your people, the humans, who appear in most of the time lines, though in others, you never appear at all. I cruise the waters of a world in which the most intelligent creatures are the dolphins, and they cavort in undersea caverns which they have created by singing to the corals which form them. I see worlds where sentient plants have created cities of green, interlacing branches and where the hives of insects cover miles; where the world-tree has sent its tendrils to the uttermost corners of the world.

I am the Watcher, floating above the worlds, placed somewhere beyond time and the interlinked net of the universe of worlds. I see reflections of myself in the myths and legends of these histories, a corruption of myself which tells me that once, somehow, I was linked to this land and the endless variety of histories that had marched over it.

But until now, even though I could see everything, I could not touch the time lines. Oh, occasionally I could make myself visible—in the dark night—to some particularly receptive individual, and I could make myself heard in other creatures' dreams, but once the sun came, my words and my presence would fade, as if I had never been there.

I always wondered why. I always wondered who had placed me where I was, and for what purpose. I wondered, but there was no way for me to know.

And then, one day, unseen by me, something struck the worlds like a hammerblow, something that put a crack in the jeweled timelines, a crack that grew and widened.

You see, there had always been barriers between the worlds. No one in one time line could see or know about those in any other. But this crack, this fault—the force of it broke apart the walls. At first very little happened, but as I watched, 1 saw the cracks widen and spread, and I saw the first of the dark storms that tore through the walls, mixing the worlds that had never touched before.

I could still do nothing. I could only watch and dream. But . . . in my dreams, I saw the fire-emeralds. I also saw humans, a half dozen of them, and they held the fire-emeralds in their hands. From the point in time where they stood, several time lines grew, reaching outward like a new set of branches from the cut trunk of a tree.

In one of those branches, and *only* in one, I saw the pieces placed together once more. In that universe, the crack healed itself, the walls of the world closing together once more. But in all the others, I saw the fire-emeralds scattered and lost, and the crack continued to widen until it touched each and every time line. As the walls breached, the worlds collapsed into one another, spinning into violent time storms that were vast, continent-wrecking hurricanes. No time line was safe, none too far away to be spared.

The chaos took them all.

After the storms had spent their destructive energy, there was no longer a multitude of histories, no more intricate spiderweb of worlds. There was only *one* world. One history.

And that awful one world that the chaos created . . . A barren, dead ball it was—a lifeless hulk spinning through space eternally empty and silent. That's what resulted from every time line except the one: an utter loss of life.

I was mad with grief, insane with rage—not only for the sheer waste, but for myself as well, who would spend the rest of eternity dreaming over nothing. I gathered my energies, concentrating as I had never done before, focusing on the time storms and the rippling chaos spreading through the worlds over which I watched. I willed myself to fall into the storms, to travel with them until I found the world of the fire-emeralds, the world in which they were all gathered.

I was certain that I knew where to go. I was certain that I knew who I had to find to make it all possible.

I came here.

I came, but I find that this is just another of the empty branches, the branches leading to death. I thought I had come to the one place where I help, where the healing might begin, but no.

Maybe my vision was wrong. Maybe there never *was* one world where the mending could begin. Maybe you weren't the one I was supposed to find. Maybe . . .

But it doesn't matter. This isn't the place. I've failed.

9

Lunch to Go

With the Midgard Serpent's last words, Peter seemed to shake off a spell. He looked around, startled. Eckels was asleep on the branch and the dawn was beginning to touch the edges of the leaves. Even the serpent noticed. "Ahh, the sun," it said. "It's time for me to leave, to return to my eternal dreaming."

"Wait a minute!" Peter yelled at the creature. "What do you mean, it's time? What about the fire-emeralds? C'mon, you gotta tell me what we're supposed to *do* with them. I . . . I lied to you. I know where the other pieces are."

The serpent was shaking its head. The outlines of the beast had gone murky and uncertain, with beads of blue-white light crawling the boundaries of it. Peter realized that he could see through the serpent, as if through milky glass. "I have no time left to speak with you," the serpent said sadly, and its voice was fading as well as the body. "I told you, I'm the creature of dreams. Of dreams . . ."

In a last swirl of light, the apparition vanished like a morning fog. "Wait!" Peter called after it. "You have to explain things to me! I need to know what to do!"

The serpent only looked at him sadly, with eyes nearly lost in the morning mist. "You already know," it said. "All you have to do is listen to the voice inside you—your *true* voice."

"What the heck are you yelling about?" Eckels said groggily, knuckling his eyes. "You want to bring all the dinosaurs in this swamp down on us?"

"The Midgard Serpent," Peter told Eckels wildly. "It's gone. It vanished as soon as the sun touched it."

Eckels looked around wildly for a second, then narrowed his eyes suspiciously at Peter. "Serpent? I don't see any snakes. What are you talking about, pup?—what kind of serpent?"

"The Midgard Serpent. You know, the talking dragon? The one that scared you off the branch last night?" Peter stopped. Eckels was looking at Peter as if he were utterly mad.

"*I* slept pretty well, considering my bed was a lousy tree," Eckels said. "On the other hand, I think *you* were having nightmares."

"Hang on," Peter said. "Are you telling me you don't remember the time storm, the dragon, all its talk about fire-emeralds and cracks between the worlds and the rest?"

Eckels grinned, rubbing his head sleepily. "Oh, I remember the time storm all right. And I remember going to sleep right afterward, too. What's the matter, kid; you eat something that disagreed with you?" Eckels laughed as Peter, confused, ruffled fingers through his red hair.

"Man, I know what I saw. I wasn't dreaming." Peter looked around wildly, causing a large lizard perched on the branch near him to go scampering for safety. "It must have done something to you, Eckels, something that made you forget."

"Right." Eckels was still grinning, furrowing his thin face. "Let me ask you this: what's more logical, that you had a nightmare, or that you were having a conversation with a talking dragon who also had the power to make me entirely forget he was here, but then didn't bother to do the same thing to you? C'mon, kid. Be reasonable."

"Eckels, I tell you it was here." Peter brushed at Eckels's sleeve, stiff with dried, congealed mud. "Look at yourself—see how muddy you are?"

"I was slogging around in a swamp all day, if you recall. How the heck am I *supposed* to look. You're covered in mud, too."

Peter shook his head, looking around desperately for other clues. "There—see how that branch is snapped off? The serpent did that when he brought you out of the mud."

"With both of us climbing around here in the dark, a broken branch is pretty weak evidence. Sorry."

Eckels reached down. Their three pieces of temporal machinery were laid out on the widest part of the branch. He put one into his pack. "C'mon. Let's get going. The sooner we're out of this swamp, the better."

"Wait! That's it!" Peter told him. "The pieces—what are they doing out?"

"We *took* them out, remember? You wanted to see which ones we had, so we'd know which one to put in the roadway."

"No, the serpent made us show them to him. It said all the pieces had to be together . . ." Peter's head was spinning. Eckels was so convincing. It *was* insane to think that the Midgard Serpent had sprung from a time storm and talked to him. It was crazy to believe that it was anything other than a nightmare. But . . .

If the serpent is right, then you're the one who ends every-thing. You heard it: without all the pieces, the crack can't be repaired, and Aaron was talking about how he thought he knew how to fix things . . .

"You coming or not, kid?"

If you go back now, there's at least a chance you can find them again. If you go back to the valley, it's over. You'll never see Aaron or Jennifer or Green Town again. Never.

"Peter! Hey!"

Peter shook his head stubbornly. "We're not going to the valley, Eckels. We're going back."

"*What!* Are you entirely out of your head!" Disbelief pulled at Eckels's face like putty, narrowing his eyes and digging deep ruts in his forehead. "Hey, we *left* them, left them for good. I ain't going back there. No way."

"Then you're going on alone," Peter told him.

"Why?" Eckels demanded. "Is this because of your stupid *dream*, kid? Is that what you're telling me—you're going to go running back to your friends because of some nightmare?"

"Eckels—"

"Hey, I mean it." Eckels cut him off with a wave of his bony arm. "Look *around* you, boy. You see all this muck? You smell the swamp and see the lizards crawling around? That's *reality* you're looking at. So open your eyes and take a breath and forget those dreams. You want to live this way for the rest of your life?—which isn't going to be very long if we stay here, anyway. Is that what you want?"

Peter hesitated. Part of him screamed that Eckels was right, that the serpent had only been a dream brought on by exhaustion and lack of food, but the creature's words seemed to continue to echo through him. *"Listen to the voice inside you . . . I was certain that I knew who I had to find to make it all possible . . . Listen to the voice inside you . . . inside you . . .*

Peter took up his pack. He put the other pieces of the broken temporal mechanism inside it. He dropped down from the branch into the shallow water of the swamp, ripples spreading outward from where he landed. He watched them, dark rings growing wider as they moved away from him.

How many parallel worlds branch off from this decision? he wondered. *Where do they lead and how do they end?*

"You'll never know, Pete," he answered himself aloud. "And you only get to see one, so you'd better go the right way."

"What?" Eckels asked, half falling, half climbing down the tree after him.

"Nothing. Just talking to myself."

"Yeah?" Eckels sniffed. "When you start answering like that, it's time to worry." He shifted the pack on his back and pointed west. "Best I can figure, the valley's that way. Let's hit it; I can't wait to be on dry land for a change."

Eckels started to walk, then seemed to realize Peter wasn't following him. He stopped and looked over his shoulder. "C'mon, kid."

"I'm not going that way," Peter told him. "I made a mistake. I'm going back."

"I thought we went over that."

"We did. I don't agree with you."

Something between anger and fear crossed Eckels's face. His voice changed from a scold to a wheedling plea. "Kid, you can't do that. We can't split up, not me and you. One person doesn't stand a chance in this place. We need each other."

"Then come with me."

"Because of what some dream-thing said to you?" Eckels said, scoffing.

"Yeah," Peter said. "That's exactly why." He turned and began slogging through the muck, returning—as best as he could tell—the way they'd come the evening before. He didn't look back, didn't wait to see whether Eckels was following or not.

Somehow, a few seconds later, he wasn't surprised to hear Eckels scurrying after him.

"Hey! This looks familiar!" Peter shouted a few hours later. "Look—there's the restaurant." He slogged through the shallow water toward the rise where the ruins stood. "Aaron!" he called. "Hey, Jennifer!"

There was no answer. He reached dry ground and stood there, hands on hips. He wanted nothing more than to see his friends emerge from the building, waving to him. "Aaron?" Peter called again. When nothing happened, his head dropped.

"Ahh, guys, I'm so sorry," he whispered. "I never should have taken off like that."

"Take a look at this, kid," Eckels called from the far side of the rise. Peter crossed to where the man was standing. There, someone had pinned the contorted body of a dinosaur to a tree with a spear. Scavengers had been at the animal—it was already nearly skeletonized, but there was no mistaking the ferocity of the dinosaur's teeth or the large curved claw that was the second toe of either foot.

"This doesn't look good," Eckels said. "Look how the ground's all kicked up, and there's a lot of blood around here. Must've been one heck of a fight. Remember that uproar we heard? They killed this one, but there must have been other dinosaurs around—they didn't get all of them."

Peter felt his resolve harden. He took a deep breath, then yanked the spear from the dinosaur's remains. Shouldering it, he headed toward the restaurant.

"Look, kid," Eckels called after him. "I wouldn't. There's nothing you want to see there. It didn't work out; let's go back to our original plan."

"I have to know," Peter told him.

The sense of fear and uneasiness increased as Peter approached the building. The large plate-glass window near the entrance was shattered, glass scattered all around the interior. He couldn't see anyone inside. "Aaron? Jenny?" he called softly as he stepped over the jagged shards still remaining in the window.

No one answered. Nothing moved in the shadowy interior. He knew they'd been here—someone had set a campfire going in the center of the restaurant; when he bent and touched them, the ashes were still warm. Behind Peter, glass crunched underfoot as Eckels stepped into the building.

"I don't like the looks of this," Eckels said.

"Shut up. Look around—they might still be here. They might be hurt."

"Or dead," Eckels muttered, loud enough that Peter heard it, though he pretended not to. "Sure, kid. Sure." Eckels sniffed in disdain. A few moments later, he called to Peter. "Hey, take a look at this." Peter came over quickly. Eckels was standing in front of a booth. There were pieces of red-stained cloth scattered on the table, and red-brown droplets had splattered the seat. "Somebody lost a lot of blood right here," Eckels said. "Doesn't look good." He prodded the piece of cloth with his sword point. "Isn't this a piece of what Jennifer was wearing?"

Peter had recognized the pattern, but he wasn't going to admit it. "I don't know," he said. "I'm not sure. There's no body, though," Peter said. "They must be okay." He didn't sound convincing, not even to himself. There was a raw, empty feeling in his stomach. He was afraid to look further, afraid that he'd find Aaron or Jennifer lying still and silent on the floor—afraid that he'd find worse than that. His imagination produced a hundred scenarios, and none of them were good.

"So there's no bodies," Eckels said. "Whatever killed them could have dragged them away, or scavengers could have taken care of that."

"Keep looking around, and keep an eye open for whatever attacked them," Peter said.

"You don't have to remind me about that," Eckels retorted, but he moved away from the booth, heading toward the rear of the building. Peter prowled the counter area, then checked the kitchen. Ten minutes later, he was certain that—whatever had happened to Aaron and the others—they weren't here. He and Eckels met in the front of the building.

"They're still alive," Peter said. "I know it."

"Yeah? What makes you so certain?"

"You find any packs or greenstones?" When Eckels shook his head, Peter spread his hands wide. "That's why I know. Scavengers might drag off bodies, but they aren't going to be interested in pieces of temporal machinery or any of the rest of the stuff we're carrying."

"Unless their packs were still on their bodies when they were killed," Eckels pointed out.

"No. We'd have found *something*. They were here, but they've moved on, that's all. We'll have to follow them."

"*You* follow them," Eckels said. "If this mess hasn't convinced you, it has me. I've had it with lizards and dinosaurs and ferns. There's no future in this place; I'm going to make my home in a world I can halfway understand. I'm going back."

"No, you're not," Peter told him. "We stay together. The pieces of temporal machinery stay together."

"Yeah? Who told you that—your dream dragon? Well, *my* piece of machinery is going to activate that roadway back in the Mutata village and get me back to Rome, and it's staying with me." Eckels's fingers tightened around the hilt of his sword. "Now, if you'll be kind enough to step out of my way . . ."

Peter only shook his head. "I mean it, Eckels."

"So do I, kid."

With that, Eckels stepped forward, brandishing the sword. Peter immediately dropped into a defensive stance, his spear pointing at Eckels's chest. The man suddenly yelled, and as Peter thrust at him, Eckels swung the sword. The blade met Peter's spear shaft a foot behind the head; with a sharp *crack*, the front end of the spear went pinwheeling off. Before Peter had a chance to turn, Eckels took another step, swinging the sword wildly back the other way.

Peter ducked, but the flat of the sword struck him full force on the side of his face. Fireworks went off in his head, a blinding, dazzling display of light that narrowed quickly to a cone and then dwindled into the distance. Peter could feel himself falling, but he couldn't seem to move his legs or put his hands out to stop the fall.

The floor of the restaurant was much harder than he would have believed, and finished what Eckels's blow to his head had started.

The last thing Peter remembered was lying there staring at Eckels's filthy boots right in front of his eyes.

10

Reunions

"We're close. Very close," Mundo said. His nose wrinkled as he sniffed the wind. After a day of walking through a forest of cycads and tall ferns, they'd reached a rocky, sand-laden plain dotted with small brush. They could all smell the briny scent of the sea, but Mundo seemed to be able to pull more from the smells around them. "There! I just caught a big whiff. Gan you smell that? That's the Mutata."

Aaron sniffed gently—too much motion would send his head throbbing again. Reflexively, he touched the bandage on his arm, then pulled his fingers away quickly when they touched a sensitive area. "No, I don't smell it. We'll take your word for it, Mundo."

"You humans have truly lousy noses," Mundo commented. "Makes me wonder why you even kept them, evolutionarily speaking." He pointed to a rise a mile or so away. "They're over that ridge, I'll bet. Near the sea." The ape grimaced, looking at the desolate landscape around them, pockmarked with the circular wounds of a dozen or more time storms. "Doesn't look like the safest place in the world, either," he said. "So what do we do now that we're here, boss?"

Everyone was looking at Aaron. *I really don't know for sure*, he wanted to say. *I didn't have a plan beyond finding them—and I wasn't actually sure we'd get this far.* But the leader in Aaron wouldn't let him admit his uncertainty.

He looked at Travis, leaning heavily against a cycad; at Mundo with his filthy, matted fur; at Jennifer, who watched him with a combination of trust and worry. They were all exhausted, and the thought of running into the kind of reception Aaron suspected the Mutata might have for them wasn't exactly pleasant.

"We'll camp out here in the ferns for the moment," he said. "After dark, Mundo and Jennifer can check out the Mutata—they should be semidormant then—as safe as they're going to get, especially if there are Gairk around, too. Meantime, let's get some rest and food."

A few hours later, Aaron watched the sun setting over the ridge. The last heat of the day warmed his skin as the golden, dying light washed over him. "It's pretty," Jennifer said. She came up behind him, putting her arms around him and pulling him into her. They stayed that way for a long time, just watching the sun ease its fiery bulk down into the unseen places beyond the sea.

"I love you," Jennifer said. "Do you know that?"

"Yes," Aaron answered. "I do. I hope you know it, too."

"Yeah, I do," she whispered, and her lips brushed his neck. They didn't say anything else until the sun had disappeared and the ridge was a solid black curve against the rose and violet sky. "Aaron—" Jennifer began, and stopped.

"What?"

"I . . . I just have a feeling about tonight. I don't know—maybe it's because we've already lost Peter and Eckels.

I don't know how Struth is going to react when I ask her for help. Even though I think of her as a friend, she's still Mutata, and so much has changed. She may decide to turn me in, or she just might kill me herself . . ."

"None of that's going to happen," Aaron told her. He turned so they faced each other. In the waning light, her eyes were bright and worried. "You'll be fine," he told her. "I trust you, and Mundo's the best guide we have right now, with Travis half lame. After all we've gone through with her, I trust Struth, too. Once you know where the time machine is, come straight back here. I'll make sure Travis is ready to go."

He could feel more than hear Jennifer's long sigh. "I guess we're doing all we can do," she said. "I just hope—"

Aaron stopped her words with a kiss.

"Just keep hoping," he told her when their lingering embrace ended. "That's all we can do."

SStragh placed her hand on the thin layer of sand covering the nest. The grains were still warm with the day's waning heat. "Here," she told Frraghi and Raajek. "Put your hands here."

Frraghi guided Raajek's hand down to the nest, then he placed his own hand alongside SStragh's. Frraghi straightened a moment late with a snort. "They're moving," he said in wonderment.

"*Geedo*," Raajek told him, with an amused sound in her cracked, ancient voice. "What did you think they would be doing, Frraghi?" Raajek kept her hand on the nest, her mouth slightly open as she relished the tiny pulsing below, as the movement of the embryos rocked the eggs' casings. "Males never understand," she told SStragh. "They're always so amazed at the simplest things."

"I'm amazed myself, OColi," SStragh answered. The wriggling of her offspring called to her. She imagined that the egglings could feel her in return, that her warmth reached down into the shells and comforted them. "They'll be breaking free in a few days." She imagined that moment—the stubby eggtooth on their snouts cracking open their prisons and letting them claw their way to the light. SStragh smiled at the thought, and her stance was wide and open, accepting of the moment. "Despite it all, OColi, there will be egglings on this strange Walk. Lhath's nest is stirring too, and Diosai's."

Raajek didn't answer, but Frraghi's scent had gone dark and protective, and SStragh watched him, the last rays of the sun outlining the knobby scales of his head. "Yes," he said. "Despite it all. The OColihi is stronger than even the Dreaming Storms."

Raajek gave the nest a last gentle touch, then straightened with a plaintive moan from her nasal horn. "Oh, these bones are getting so old . . . I'm happy for you, SStragh. I truly am. But I wish I could share your optimism."

"OColi—"

Raajek waved SStragh silent, her scent signalling a faint rebuke. "I can *feel* it," she said to SStragh and Frraghi. "I can feel the chaos growing closer, and I'm afraid that very few egglings will return with us. Too few . . ."

"You *know* this," SStragh asked her old mentor. Raajek shook her aged snout.

"No, I don't know it," she answered. Then her scent changed once more, and she patted the sandy earth of the nest affectionately. "And I'm probably wrong. Your nestlings feel strong, SStragh—like you. Like Frraghi. I will be glad when they break free and we can return to the valley away from this . . ."

Raajek stopped, sniffing the wind. SStragh knew that even without eyes, Raajek could sense the strangeness the Dreaming Storms had placed all around them.

Raajek didn't finish her thought. Nodding to SStragh, she let Frraghi lead her away to the scree of rocks the OColi had made her temporary home. SStragh watched her go with a deep sense of affection. Then, as the light faded in the west and the first stars appeared, she snuggled down on her nest to await the morning.

"Careful," Mundo hissed to Jennifer. He pointed to a round patch of glassiness that gleamed a cold blue in the starlight. "That's nothing natural—it came from one of the time storms. Smells like Eckels's old socks, too."

Despite herself, Jennifer smiled. In the darkness, Mundo's face was a blur of darkness in the midst of his white fur, but she could imagine the ape's face, wrinkled in disgust. "You have a way with images," she told him.

"Eckels has a way with body odor," Mundo replied. "Just don't fall into anything while we're climbing over these rocks."

The two of them made their way up the ridge. Peering over the edge of a jumbled mass of stones, they could see the Nesting Grounds spread out below them on the falling landscape, leading down to where the phosphorescent surf licked at the stubborn rocks of the shore. The scene was scarred with the acne of a hundred time storms and littered with patches of ground and artifacts from alternate time lines. "Look at this," Jennifer whispered. "What a mess . . ."

The Mutata had made their scattered nests wherever they could. The scene looked nothing like the orderly Nesting Grounds Struth had once described for Jennifer. This was instead a place under siege. Jennifer had to believe that only the chains of long evolutionary habits—the Mutata's *OColihi* or Ancient Path—had made the Mutata stay here. Jennifer peered into the darkness, trying to find a form she recognized among the mostly dozing Mutata.

"At least I don't see or smell any Gairk," Mundo said alongside her. "That's one thing in our favor."

"Do these smell like the Mutata we know?" Jennifer asked him. Mundo looked at her with one eyebrow raised.

"They smell like every Mutata I've ever met. And every Mutata I ever met was from the same tribe. So I can't really say for certain, I guess."

"Okay, okay . . ." Jennifer raised up. A few of the Mutata were moving slowly about, but most had settled down on the nests or were snuggled next to their mates. Occasionally, one of them would trumpet a series of notes in a minor key that would echo sadly among the hills to be answered by a Mutata further down. Jennifer wondered what they were saying.

"They're praying to the All-Ancestor," Mundo said. When Jennifer looked at him, irritated that the mindreading ape was skimming her thoughts, Mundo shrugged. "Sorry. I just can't help myself."

"Then read this, you turkey," Jennifer told him, and closed her eyes.

"I'm not a turkey; I'm an ape—" Mundo began, then a moment later, he sniffed indignantly. "And here I thought you were a polite young woman," he said. "Hey, isn't that Fergie? Over there, near where the hill curves out."

Jennifer looked toward where Mundo was pointing. It looked like Fergie, though it was difficult to tell at this distance. There was another Mutata, no doubt a female, sitting on an earthen nest near him, but with the darkness and the shadows, Jennifer couldn't tell who it was. "All right," she said. "Let's head over that way. Carefully . . ."

It took them some time, moving over the broken ground, to come near the area. They skirted a circle of broken concrete that looked like part of an expressway, though the lines painted on it were chartreuse, not white, and the lanes were too narrow for any cars that Jennifer knew. They came near a broken structure that looked like a giant honeycomb and smelled of sweet, pollen-laden flowers; they darted behind a leaning wooden statue twenty feet high that depicted a bird-headed man with three eyes and a fierce expression.

After what seemed like an hour or more, they were finally standing on an outcropping above the nest. Mundo held Jennifer back, his strong arm gripping her shoulder. "Wait!" he husked out. "Don't you smell it?"

"What?"

Mundo sniffed again. "Ozone. I think . . . yes, look there . . ." Mundo pointed to the line where the sea met sky. A fast-moving rank of clouds blotted out the stars there, and underneath the black ramparts, swift lightnings lashed the frothing tops of wind-driven waves. Faintly, they could hear the first premonitions of thunder.

"Time storm," Mundo said. "Coming fast."

"Then we don't have time to waste," Jennifer told him. She crawled to the edge of the outcropping and peered down. The nest sat near a strange triangular metal sculpture that hovered in the air slowly turning, defying gravity. And the Mutata on the nest, her long head just rising as if from a disturbed sleep . . .

Jennifer recognized her at once.

"Struth!" she called out in Mutata, trying not to let Fergie or any of the other Mutata hear her. "Struth, it's me, Jennifer."

But Struth looked at her, and in those large, beautiful eyes, Jennifer saw no friendliness at all. "You!" Struth barked loudly, rising. "*Yeie!* I won't let this happen!"

"Struth!" Jennifer said, but the Mutata had snatched up her spear.

"*Yeie!*" the Mutata said again—as thunderclaps cracked and the sky behind her flickered with mad electricity. She brandished the spear in her right hand. "You should never have come here, Jhenini, for now I must finish what I should have finished long ago."

With that, Struth rose from the nest and charged.

11

In the Eyes of the Storm

The dream had been so terribly, terribly vivid . . .
SStragh was standing alongside the ruins of her nest. The
eggs—*her* eggs—were broken and dead, and there were
human footprints everywhere in the dirt around them. A
wind was screaming something that sounded like words,
only the thunder made it difficult to hear them and the
lightning blinded her. For an instant, SStragh thought
that she glimpsed a figure riding the storm—a dinosaur,
perhaps, but one with wings. The strange being looked
down at her and spoke, and the words came out
encapsuled in orange fire.

"Those who break can also mend," the apparition said,
and vanished again in a clap of thunder. "And those who
can mend need you."

SStragh gazed at the ravaged nest and she screamed in
fury and despair. "Why?" she called out, not knowing if
she was crying to the wind or the storm or the flying
dinosaur or the humans who had taken the lives of her
egglings. "Why?"

The only answer was the lightning and the grumbling
words of thunder.

. . . words of thunder . . .

SStragh came awake with a gasp. Looking out to sea, she could see the time storm coming, the sharp scent of the lightning riding the winds before it. Underneath her, she could feel the eggs in their nest, and for a moment, that reassured her.

Then a voice brought back memories of the dream. "SStragh!" someone called from the rocks above and behind her, speaking in a horrible, strangled accent. "SStragh, it's me, Jhenini."

"You!" Struth said. "*Yeie!* I won't let this happen!"

"SStragh!" Jhenini cried out, but the memories of the dream and the urge to protect her nest were far stronger than any bonds SStragh had ever forged with the humans, even Jhenini, who was the best of them. Her spear was nearby. SStragh picked it up.

"*Yeie!*" SStragh told the human again. "You should never have come here, Jhenini, for now I must finish what I should have finished long ago." SStragh heard the words coming from herself even as she marveled at them. Part of her—the part that once followed Raajek's new path—cried out: *No! That's Jhenini! She's your friend!* But the voice was very small and tiny against the surging power of instinct and SStragh's need to protect her eggs.

SStragh raised herself up even as Frraghi turned to see the cause of her commotion, and started toward the human.

And the Dreaming Storm broke.

A forked tree of lightning erupted between SStragh and Jhenini. She could feel the electricity's heat on her scales and smell the ozone. The thunderclap sent her sprawling. Half blinded, SStragh squinted through rolling afterimages and saw that the strike had knocked Jhenini and Mundo down also.

"SStragh!" Frraghi yelled, and his voice sounded as if it came from some immense distance away—SStragh was half deaf, as well. "Look out!"

SStragh looked. And she trumpeted in alarm and fear.

There were *eyes* in the storm.

A huge circle of sand so red it looked as if it had been soaked in blood had appeared not a tail's length from SStragh's nest. And on that circle there stood a figure who might have stepped from the mythical world of the All-Ancestor. The creature was built with the upright stance of the humans, but there any resemblance ended.

Towering as high as the lowest banks of thunder-heads, its clothes were shreds of gray vapor. Glowing, phosphorescent eyes gleamed angrily from a head shaped of blue-black clouds which roiled and pulsed, tiny lightnings flaring within it. It opened its mouth and a hurricane wind burst forth, a primal, wordless roaring louder than the thunder. Though the clouds wrapped around it, SStragh could see its massive chest like a mountainside, and its legs were twin cyclones, churning the scarlet sand underneath it. Glowing white-blue storm-fire pulsed through its body; its hands—tipped with talons that gleamed like the burnished *mhetal* SStragh had seen in the human worlds—clapped together and a fireball burst from them, spitting and hissing as it exploded against a nearby dune. SStragh could hear Mutata screaming and bleating in panic. The apparition tilted its great head and stared down at them, and there was nothing in those glowing eyes but death.

SStragh hurled the spear at it, like a twig thrown at a mountain—the storm-beast pursed cloud-lips and exhaled: the spear went tumbling end of over end away.

SStragh hooted in despair. There was nothing she could do. She prayed, prayed to the All-Ancestor that the next stroke of the Dreaming Storm would come and take away this horrible creature. Prayed that it would not move away from its red circle before the Dreaming Storm took it back from where it had come. She had forgotten Jhenini and Mundo, had forgotten everything except the Beast.

Please, All-Ancestor, hear me . . .

But it seemed that the All-Ancestor could not hear SStragh above the roar of the storm. The whirling tornadoes of the storm-beast's legs bent; the massive body turned.

It took a step, stepping past its scarlet boundaries. In the wind of its movement, the triangular sculpture alongside SStragh's nest went flying away. And with that step, that first awful step, the storm-beast came down directly on SStragh's nest.

SStragh screamed, a sound of torment that sounded raw through her nasal horn, a wail so loud in her head that it drowned out the clamor of the storm and the dream-beast.

"*Yeie!*" she shouted in denial, but the beast only chuckled with its wind-breath as it smashed earth and eggs underfoot. As the cyclone ripped away the stones SStragh and Frraghi had so carefully placed around the nest, as it flung dirt and shell fragments everywhere, the sight tore open SStragh's heart as well. She saw Frraghi attack from one side, saw the creature tear Frraghi's spear from his grasp, saw lightning come from its hands and send Frraghi hurtling backward, wounded.

SStragh could bear to watch no more. Desperately, she charged herself, barehanded. She didn't know what she intended to do; she attacked with full knowledge that there was no way she could hurt this thing. She only knew that the mother's fury in her burned so hot that it would, it *must*, sear the dream-beast's cloudy flesh, and her anger was so strong that it would burst out of her if she didn't use it.

SStragh charged, throwing herself at the wind-driven leg that had crushed her unborn offspring. She hurled herself into the tomadic chaos, hoping to cause the creature at least some little pain before it killed her.

Darkness greeted her. The great winds picked her up; sand scoured her face, wind-thrown rocks thudded against her body. SStragh wailed as she was tossed like a leaf in a gale, whirled around and around, tumbling helplessly, and then was suddenly thrown away from the coiling tornado.

SStragh landed heavily. She had only a moment to mourn her terrible losses before the darkness took her.

Jennifer had never seen anything so awe-inspiring as the apparition the time storm had brought. The dark storm giant with glowing eyes was more horrible than anything she had yet seen in the myriad time lines they'd glimpsed. Just looking at it made her heart pound in her chest, made the blood pulse louder in her temples than the storm itself.

From their vantage point above the beach, Jennifer and Mundo watched it step from its circle, saw it demolish Struth's nest, and then witnessed the hopeless, frantic attacks of Fergie and Struth. When Struth was hurled head over tail from the creature, Jennifer cried out. "No!" she screamed, the same futile denial Struth had shouted.

And the storm creature looked at her.

Looked at Mundo.

"Mundo! Run!" Jennifer said, but even as she prepared to flee, she saw that Mundo was staring transfixed at the vision, his muzzle tilted upward to look at the storm-beast's head, his mouth open.

"Mundo!" Jennifer screamed.

"I know you," Mundo said softly, almost inaudible under the storm-beast's winds.

"What? You mean that's from *your* world? Is that . . . is that the thing that Aaron said destroyed the compound back in Green Town?"

"Yes," Mundo answered, still rapt in the vision of the monster. "From *my* world. Part of *me*." Strangely, tears were welling in the corners of Mundo's eyes. "And I know its pain," he added.

As if it had heard Mundo's words, the storm-beast howled. The sound of a thousand thunderstorms boomed and rang in its voice. The storm-beast stared down at them, and then it bent down, its lightning-wrapped hands reaching.

"Run!" Jennifer shouted again, and threw herself aside, but Mundo did not move. The ape stood there, his fur whipping in the winds, stark white against the ugly backdrop of the storm-beast's cloud-wrapped body. The storm-beast's hand wrapped around Mundo, lightning crackling as its huge fingers closed around him. Mundo shrieked, but even in the painful sound, Jennifer caught a sound of satisfaction in the ape's voice. She started to get to her feet, thinking that—somehow—she might be able to pry Mundo loose from the storm-beast's grip, but Mundo shook his head and held a hand out to stop her.

"No, Jennifer!" he shouted. His fur was smoking as energy flickered around him. "Don't worry about me. I know him. I *am* him. Jennifer, I'm sorry, but this is what

I want, what I've wanted ever since I left my home. He can take me *back!*"

"Mundo!"

"Tell Aaron I'm sorry, Jennifer. Tell him I hope it works out, but you'll have to do it without me. Don't you see? This is my *chance!*"

The beast held Mundo up in front of its face and its gaping mouth of cloud. Mundo held his hands out as to embrace the creature, and the storm-beast spoke again, small cyclones writhing from its mouth like tongues. Mundo pointed urgently toward the circle of red sand.

"Quickly!" Jennifer heard the ape say. "We have to be there before the time storm takes it away again!"

The storm-beast grunted and turned. Jennifer could feel the time storm gathering itself for the next lightning strike. She was certain that the storm-beast would lose this race, that the time storm would bring the next piece of alternate reality here and take away the red sand forever, marooning the beast and Mundo forever.

She wasn't sure what would happen then.

One step, another. Mundo was shouting at the creature, exhorting it to go faster. The circle of sand was only a step away. The storm-beast moved . . .

. . . and the time storm loosed another bolt. Jennifer screamed and tried to blink away the afterimages. "Mundo!" she cried.

There was no answer. Where the circle of colored sand had been, there was nothing but the normal landscape of the Nesting Ground.

Mundo and the storm-beast had won their race. The two of them had found their way back into their own world and time once more, and they were gone. Jennifer found that, even in the midst of the destruction caused by the storm-beast, she was crying in happiness.

12

Making Decisions

Jennifer didn't have much time to contemplate Mundo's departure in the hands of the storm-beast. The lightning strike that had taken away the storm-beast had left behind another remnant from the alternate time lines—a sputtering, wing-shaped vehicle sitting on a slice of roadway, from which two featherfaced and inhuman riders stared in confusion.

The storm did not keep the image there long. As the wind ruffled Jennifer's hair and the cloud boiled overhead, the storm moved on, the next stroke of lightning appearing well behind Jennifer. Already, the clouds were thinning and the thunder fading to memory.

It was over. "Mundo . . ." Jennifer breathed. "I hope you're back home, back where you are everything and everyone. Be happy, Mundo." Then she shook away the spell of the time storm and looked around. Everywhere in front of her there was destruction, the storm-beast's legacy. Around the Nesting Ground, Mutata were standing up, looking dazed.

Jennifer saw Struth, laying on her side not far from her crushed and broken nest. Frraghi was down not far from her. Jennifer remembered Struth, and how her friend had greeted her—*Run!* part of her screamed. *Run while you can. Get out before they notice you!* She started to turn and obey that inner voice, but there was another compulsion in her, a stronger one.

She's hurt, and no matter what, she's your friend. With a sigh, Jennifer scrambled down the small cliff of rocks to the rocky ledge of the beach and ran toward Struth.

Struth was still breathing. Jennifer quickly ran her hands over the Mutata's body, prodding, searching for broken bones or other injuries. Despite some superficial cuts, Struth appeared otherwise uninjured, though Jennifer had to admit that her knowledge of Mutata anatomy was shaky, at best. Struth was beginning to regain consciousness, fluttering the lids over her large, brown-gold eyes.

"Struth," Jennifer whispered as the Mutata tried to rise. "Carefully, now. Easy . . ."

Jennifer helped Struth get to her feet, though beyond the first glance, Struth didn't seem to take much notice of the human. She limped over to the ruins of her nest and stood, staring down. "My eggs . . ." she said, her husky words burdened with more sadness than Jennifer could believe a voice could hold. "My children . . ."

"Oh, Struth, I'm sorry. I'm so sorry." Jennifer's own eyes filled with tears in sympathy. "I wish . . ."

"Why did you come here?" Struth asked. She was staring down at Jennifer, and Jennifer was suddenly very aware of the sheer mass of Struth's body, of how the Mutata towered a good foot taller than Jennifer, of the stubby claws on her hands, of how the thick, powerful tail swayed as if Struth were about to strike with it.

And most of all, she saw the utter lack of humanness in Struth's face, which suddenly seemed more cold and lizardlike than before. The wide-set eyes glared at her from either side of the long, curved nasal horn, the nostrils flaring.

Jennifer took an involuntary step back. "We . . . I mean I . . ." she began, stuttering. "We need your *help*, Struth. Aaron . . . he thinks he knows how to fix the rifts between worlds."

"Can he fix *this?*" Struth asked, her hand waving over the broken shell fragments and torn earth of her nest. "Can he bring this back?"

"Struth—"

Struth took a step toward Jennifer, who retreated. "Can he give me back the lives of my egglings?" Struth thundered, punctuating her words with furious trombone blasts from her horn. "Can he take away all the pain that you humans have caused? Is he the All-Ancestor, that he can do that?"

Another step, and again Jennifer retreated. "Struth, please!" Her hands were out, pleading. *That's a human gesture,* someone was saying inside her head. *Struth doesn't understand it* "No, we can't do that, but we *can* save the Mutata. We can bring normalcy back to your land so that the next time you go on the Nesting Walk, you *will* bring back younglings. Struth, I promise that."

Step. Retreat.

"You have promised things over and over again. Why should I believe you now?" Struth gave another blast of sound. "You humans have no honor, no OColihi. You will say anything to avoid death, even when you hear the All-Ancestor calling for your soul."

"Struth . . ." Jennifer's spine bumped against the outcropping. Struth continued to move forward, and she pressed back against the rock. "Struth, it's *me*, Jennifer. If you know me at all, you know that I would never want to hurt you, that I'd never deliberately lie to you. Struth, you are my *friend*—I know you don't really understand that word, but I want you to try. I also know that you're hurting right now and I wish I could help, but there's nothing I can do about that. Please, don't throw away the chance to save your people and your world because of your loss. I need you, Struth. All the Mutata need you."

The plea came from Jennifer in an ever-increasing rush, as if she could stop Struth's advance with the sheer flood of words. Struth took another step, then hesitated. Her eyes narrowed. "What do you need from me?" Struth asked. "What are you asking *this* time?"

"We need to know where the time machine is. We need to know where Raajek and the others have hidden it."

Struth snorted. "So that's it? You want the time machine so you can escape and leave us, so you can go back to your own worlds and leave us helpless." Her tail twitched, her hands closed into claws.

"Struth," Jennifer said desperately. "You know me better than that. Remember, long ago, after I saved his life, I agreed to give myself to Klaido, to let him kill me without protest. I would *still* do that if I thought that there was no way to repair things or if everything was hopeless. I would do it now if it would ease some of your pain."

Jennifer took a breath and stood away from the cliff wall, her hands down at her side. "Strike me if you think I'm lying to you, Struth. Take me in payment for the lives of your egglings, and I will walk with their souls to the All-Ancestor."

Struth glared and hissed. She turned sidewise, the tail lashing. Jennifer knew that a blow from Struth's tail would crush ribs, would send her helpless to the dirt where Struth could kill her with one more strike. Struth made a sound of anger, and Jennifer closed her eyes, waiting for the tail to whip around.

A moment later, she opened her eyes again. Struth was still glaring at her angrily, but the tail had relaxed and her finger had opened. "I have seen enough death today," Struth said. "I am tired of death."

"Struth . . ." Jennifer rushed forward and hugged the Mutata, throwing her arms around the warm, hard scales. "Struth, you must hurt so much . . ." Pulling the Mutata's head to her, Jennifer whispered fiercely. "The only way we can end this is with your help. I need you, Struth. We all need you. Tell me where the time machine is."

But it was Raajek's voice who answered her, not Struth. "So the human has come back, and she has brought the Dreaming Storms with her. At last we can give Jhenini's soul to the All-Ancestor and find peace again."

Jennifer looked up, startled, to see Raajek, Fergie, and Lhath arrayed behind Struth. Jennifer gasped, looking around desperately for a way to run. "Grab her, Struth. Don't let her escape again."

Struth's hand suddenly closed around Jennifer's arm. She tried to pull away, but the hand only tightened its grip. She looked at Struth pleadingly, but there was no sympathy in her face.

No sympathy at all.

Peter woke up with a head that felt like a truck had run over it. His temple was throbbing. He reached up with his hand and felt a knot there the size of a tennis ball. "*Ouch!*" he exclaimed. "Man, that's tender . . ."

He opened his eyes. He was lying on the restaurant floor. There was blood spattered on the tiles around him. Groaning, Peter got to his knees, taking a slow inventory of his body as he did so. Nothing seemed to be broken. One hand on a booth table to steady himself, he managed to get to his feet. In the windows, he caught a glimpse of himself. The knot on his forehead was purple and swollen, and he must have hit his nose on the way down, since blood was smeared from one nostril all the way across his cheek. "You're a mess," he told his reflection. The reflection grimaced back at him.

"Eckels!" he shouted, then groaned again as the effort sent waves of pain flooding through his head. "Eckels! You lousy coward!"

His shouts sent a few small lizards scrambling for cover near the counter, but Eckels didn't answer. Peter slumped into the booth and sat cradling his aching head in his hands, taking stock. He didn't know how long he'd been out; he supposed that he was lucky Eckels hadn't simply killed him while he was unconscious.

From the limp look of the pack on the seat alongside him, though, Eckels *had* taken the two pieces of temporal machinery that he carried. "Okay, Pete," he told himself. "It could be worse. You're alive. There's still some food in the pack. You must have been out most of the night, 'cause it looks like it's starting to get light in the east, but you're as secure as you're gonna get in this place. What was it the Serpent said—'listen to your true voice'? Well, listen. Now, what are you going to do?"

He didn't have an easy answer for that, and his throbbing head didn't make contemplating things any easier. "C'mon, Pete, think . . ."

You really want to find Jenny and Aaron again. That's where you want to be, but you don't know where they are. On the other hand, you know exactly where Eckels is heading, but you don't really want to be with him . . .

Peter groaned. He seemed to remember hearing the thunder of a time storm during the night, and that reminded him of the Midgard Serpent. He still didn't know if the creature really existed or not, but the words it had spoken about the different time lines kept coming back to him.

"In one of those branches, just one, I saw the pieces placed together once more. In that universe, the crack healed itself, the walls of the world closing together once more. But in all the others, I saw the fire-emeralds scattered and lost, and the crack continued to widen . . ."

"Listen to the voice inside you . . ."

"All right," Peter said. "If Eckels makes it through the path, he's going to take all the greenstones with him. If that happens, there's no way Aaron's plan—whatever the heck it is—can work. And right now I'm the only one who has a chance to catch Eckels. And I'm the one who—ouch!—has the score to settle with him."

Peter glanced at his reflection in one of the unbroken windows; and there was something new in the eyes that looked back at him: a maturity and resolve that was almost frightening in its intensity.

"I guess you do have that inner voice, after all," he said.

The reflection smiled grimly back at him.

Travis came up alongside Aaron as he peered out toward the sea. False dawn was beginning to color the eastern sky, and Aaron didn't think he'd slept more than an hour or two during the night, worrying about Jennifer.

"Hey, son, they may have had problems finding Struth. For that matter, they may have been greeted with open arms and decided to spend the night. You can't worry about it. Your job is to stay here so Mundo and Jennifer can find us again when they get back."

"I know," Aaron answered. "But that time storm last night was a big one, and it came from right over the ridge."

"There's nothing you can do about that. We have to wait."

"We should have all gone—man, if you weren't hurt . . ."

Travis didn't say anything to that, and Aaron knew that the safari guide had been hurt by what he'd just said. "Travis, hey, I didn't mean that the way it sounded. I know you're doing all you can just to stay up with us, and we wouldn't have gotten through half the scrapes without your help. So—"

"You don't have to apologize, Aaron," Travis said, but there was a tightness in his smile. "I understand what you're feeling. I also know I've been holding you guys back."

Travis coughed, one of the deep, hacking attacks that were coming more and more often to the man, and when he turned and spat, Aaron saw the blood that flecked the saliva. Through the night, Travis had moaned and turned in his sleep, and he could barely get out of the bedroll in the morning. The wounds on his legs, when Aaron rewrapped the bandages, looked ugly, and Aaron was certain that the blue lines creeping up the guide's thighs were a bad sign. Travis ate virtually nothing and Aaron could count the ribs on the once-muscular man's chest. He had never recovered from the wounds given to him by the allosaurus that had chased him into Aaron's world in the first place, and the series of worlds which had followed had each taken their toll, with the time storm in Rome being the proverbial last straw. The Travis who stood beside Aaron now was only a shadow of the person he had been when they first met.

But he was still proud. He shrugged off Aaron's hand and shook his head. "No," he said. "I don't need a nursemaid. Not yet." His scowl caused Aaron to back away a step.

"Sorry. I just thought . . ."

Travis's expression softened slowly. "Yeah. I know. Sorry—I guess I'm a little touchy too, huh?" Travis sighed, a rattling breath that sounded liquid in his chest. He stared out to where they'd last seen their two companions. "The least we can do is take a look, just to make sure. That ridge should give us a decent vantage point. What'd'ya say?"

Aaron smiled. "I say let's take a look."

Aaron walked behind Travis as they walked the quarter mile to the ridge and then moved up the steep slope, ready to catch Travis if he fell but careful to let the man find his own way over the broken ground. It took them twice as long to reach the ridge line as it would have taken Aaron on his own, but at last they stood on the height where the sea breeze tossed their hair with salty fingers. They could see the gleam of the sea spilling out to the horizon, the sun glinting from the moving wavetops. From where they stood, the ridge fell quickly down to a long, sloping plateau of rock and sand that edged a half mile or more out to where another sharp embankment made the final drop to the beach and the surf tumbling against the shore. "I don't see any Mutata," Aaron said. "Travis?"

Travis was shading his eyes from the sea glare, looking to his right down the slope. "There! Down a bit, near where the ridge curves out," he said, then: "I don't like this."

"What?"

"Didn't Mundo say he didn't smell any Gairk?"

"Yeah," Aaron said, squinting at the cluster of dinosaurs he could see in the distance. Then, with a hissing exhalation of breath, he saw what Travis meant. Mixed in with the Mutata were the figures of taller dinosaurs, and sun glinted from the copper breastplates they wore. "Gairk," Aaron breathed. "Oh, no. Jennifer . . ."

Without another thought, he started to scramble down the steep slope.

13

A Race Against Time

Jennifer knew that she was in desperate trouble when Raajek, despite the fact that it was the middle of the night and most of the Mutata were groggy and slow, dispatched two young Mutata with a message for the Gairk. By dawn, a contingent of Gairk had arrived and were meeting with the Mutata OColi.

Jennifer knew she was the topic of discussion.

She was left bound with thin vines well away from the remaining nests, guarded by a Mutata who refused to answer any of her questions, and who kept his spear in the right hand. That alone told her she was considered an *iado*, an animal and nothing more, a curious monkey who could make sounds that resembled language. The guard glared at her and looked as if he'd be happy to kill her well before the Gairk and Mutata had reached a decision on what to do with her.

Struth came to her just after dawn. She took the spear from the guard and lifted her spinal frill in a gesture of command. "You are relieved, Dhorin," she said. "I will watch the human now, until they come for her."

Jennifer didn't say anything until the guard, with a last glare at her, turned and left. "I take it that 'until they come for me' means that the decision's been made," she said at last.

"*Geedo*," Struth answered flatly. Jennifer thought that Struth looked exhausted, as if the events of the night had taken every last reserve of strength she had. The colors of her scales were muted, and the skin under her eyes was dark and sagging. Her voice carried the pain of loss in every word. "Raajek has claimed the honor of Giving you, over the objections of the Gairk OColi, who wanted you killed as a troublesome *iado*, in the Gairk manner."

"I suppose I should be grateful for that."

"The Gairk way would have been very . . . *painful* for you." Struth shifted the spear she carried from her right to her left hand. "Raajek would slay you quickly, with honor."

"Somehow that's not really comforting." Jennifer sighed and wriggled in her bonds, which were cutting into her wrists and ankles. "Struth, I am truly sorry for what happened to your nest. I wish . . . I wish there were some way I could have stopped that from happening. I'm sorry it's ending this way, but I want you to know that I still think of you as a . . . friend." Jennifer used the English word, since there was no analogue for it in Mutata.

"Friend . . ." Struth rolled the word on her tongue, her voice sad. "I don't think I ever really understood the concept of that, Jhenini."

Despite the situation, Jennifer found herself smiling. "I think you understand a lot more than you think, Struth."

"I do not understand you humans. I do not understand why you refuse to stop fighting, why you cannot accept that the All-Ancestor has broken the OColihi and is calling an end to my world and yours. It's not just you— I saw it in the other human worlds also."

"I suppose that's our nature, Struth. We fight, we go down kicking and screaming and protesting. We keep trying to find a way to fix things even when it looks hopeless."

"What would you have done with the time machine, Jhenini?"

"We would have kept fighting. We would have tried something else to fix the time rifts."

"It wouldn't have worked," Struth said.

"Maybe not. Even probably not. But we think there's a *chance*, Struth. How can you give up when there's still hope?"

"Is there hope for you?"

At that, the full weight of her situation came down on Jennifer. Her stomach turned, and she fought down the return of the fright and nausea that had been her companions since her capture.

"I don't see much hope, no," Jennifer said, and she pressed her lips together to hold back the cry that wanted to escape her. "But I won't just accept this, either."

"Somehow, that is what I knew you would say," Struth answered. With that, she took a step toward Jennifer. Her spear point prodded Jennifer's abdomen, and Jennifer, helpless, closed her eyes, biting her lips so that she would not cry out when the blade ripped into her. *At least die bravely, as a Mutata would,* she told herself. *Show them that we're as good as they are.*

But instead of the agony of a spear thrust, she felt the edge of the spear slide between her bound hands, the razored edge of the obsidian point sawing back and forth as it sliced through the vines holding her. "Struth? Struth, what are you doing?"

"Be quiet, Jhenini. Let me do this."

After Struth cut her loose, Jennifer crouched on the sand, trying to rub life back into her numb hands and feet. "Why, Struth?"

Struth, her bulk shielding Jennifer from the Nesting Ground, answered slowly. "All night, while Raajek, Frraghi, and the Gairk were talking, I could not stop thinking about . . . about my egglings. I thought—and this was, I think, an almost human thought, Jhenini. I've been infected by your beliefs, I'm afraid—I thought that if I did not at least try to end this chaos, that still more egglings would die, and more mothers would feel as I feel now, and that then my egglings would have died for . . . for *nothing*."

Struth's face was bright in the light of the sun, just easing itself over the ridge and the line of cycads beyond. "I didn't want that, Jhenini. I didn't want their deaths to be without meaning." Struth rose, and her scales brightened. "I know where the time machine was hidden," she said. "I will show you."

"Struth!" Jennifer said, and she rose to embrace the Mutata. Her legs, still tingling from their confinement, betrayed her and she fell headfirst into the sand, laughing.

Struth watched Jennifer, who caught a wisp of the scent she knew meant that the Mutata was puzzled. "I will *never* understand humans," Struth said again. "You rejoice at the strangest times." Struth drew herself up on her hind legs and glanced around. "And now we must go, before we're seen. Hurry, Jhenini."

Jennifer didn't need any more encouragement. Scrambling to her feet and ignoring the needling pain in her legs, she put her back to the Nesting Grounds and scrambled up the embankment in front of her. Struth followed, her heavier body causing small rocks and pebbles to go crashing downslope. Jennifer climbed desperately, expecting at any moment to hear a Mutata cry alarm behind them. She was panting by the time she reached the top, pulling herself up and over with exhausted arms. She reached down and pulled Struth up with her. The Mutata, not as well built as a human for the task, half rolled over the edge like a walrus in heavy surf.

Jennifer helped Struth to her feet; then, crouching, they looked back over the beach where the Mutata were tending their too-few nests. Jennifer heard Struth sigh, and she placed a hand on the Mutata. "You can still go back," she said. "I'd understand."

Struth shook her head sadly. "*Gheodo*," she answered. "I cannot do that. The All-Ancestor has called me away with the cries of my egglings."

"Then let's go," Jennifer said.

As she stood, as Struth rose alongside her, they both heard a sudden uproar from the beach. Jennifer looked down the embankment to see Frraghi and a Gairk approaching. Frraghi had stopped, and he was pointing his spear directly to where the two of them stood, outlined—Jennifer suddenly realized—against the sun. A blast from his horn shivered the morning sky, and Jennifer gasped with the sound.

"Come on, Struth—run!" Jennifer turned and fled.

Aaron realized that he'd left Travis behind, that he was alone as he rushed toward the Mutata and Gairk. He didn't care. The wind roared in his ears as he ran, and the feeling in the pit of his stomach told him that Jennifer was still alive and in danger.

He found out quickly that he was right. Even as he moved, skidding and almost falling down the incline, he saw a distant, achingly familiar human figure coming up over the last embankment before the beach, followed quickly by that of a Mutata. They seemed to look back over the edge a moment before turning and running.

"Jennifer!" Aaron called. "Hey, Jen!"

Jennifer saw him then, and angled toward him, sprinting pell-mell through the broken landscape with Struth close behind her. A few minutes later, he pulled her into his arms with a cry of joy. "Jenny! Are you okay? I was worried . . . Struth—is she coming with us? Where's Mundo?"

Jennifer only shook her head into the barrage of questions. "No time," she told him breathlessly. "They're right behind us!"

"Who?" Aaron began, then saw the answer to his question coming over the embankment: a contingent of Gairk and Mutata. "Oh, man . . . I'll bet they're not coming to wish us luck!"

"No one's going to take that bet," Jennifer panted. "Move!"

They ran. Aaron looked back over his shoulder as they approached the ridge line. Frraghi and the other Mutata were falling behind, but the Gairk were gaining. Sun sparked from their copper armor, and they gave loud cries as they ran, swinging their *broaii*.

Travis had made his slow way down the cliff wall of the ridge to meet them. He glanced back at the pursuers, then back up at the tall ridge above them. "I don't think the Gairk can climb that," he said. "Too steep."

"It's too steep for Struth, too," Jennifer said firmly, her hands on her knees as she tried to get her breath. "And I'm *not* leaving her."

"Jenny—"

"No." The word was emphatic, and combined with the look on her face, Aaron knew that any argument would be futile. "All right," he said. "Then let's keep moving.

Maybe we'll find a break in the ridge we can get through." He didn't say what he was thinking: *If the Gairk don't get to us first.*

Tirelessly, the Gairk sprinted over the landscape, perhaps a quarter mile behind them. Aaron doubted that the dinosaurs would tire first in this race, and now that Travis was with them, they were slower than ever.

Jennifer was talking to Struth as they ran. She nodded to Aaron. "Struth says that there's a pass through the ridge line a little bit ahead. She'll show us."

"Great," Aaron said. *And what do we do then?* the cynical voice inside him asked. To that question, he didn't have an answer. He could almost imagine the warm breath of the Gairk on his back. "Run!" he yelled to all of them. "As fast as you can!"

The pass Struth brought them to was a narrow, twisting divide between steep limestone cliff walls fifty feet high. They darted into the narrow passageway, hurrying over the tilted, flat rocks. Jennifer was helping Travis, who was limping badly and wheezing. Aaron knew that the man couldn't keep up this pace for very long. He also knew that if they abandoned the man, he would die. The Gairk would make sure of that. "Go on!" Aaron exhorted his companions, but even as Struth, then Jennifer and finally Travis, emerged from the pass, Aaron could see the first of the Gairk at the other end, its snarling, angry snout open in a display of fury. The Gairk saw Aaron at the same time and gave a roar before charging forward again.

Aaron knew that it was over. He knew that even if they continued to run, the first Gairk would catch them in a few minutes, and they were helpless against its strength. Aaron looked at Jennifer, helpless, wondering what to say.

And he saw, very near her and right at the edge of the cliff, a glint of something metallic. "What?" he said, and despite the sound of the Gairk thrashing through the tumbled rocks of the pass, he ran over to the spot. "Oh my God," he whispered, looking down.

Lodged between rocks was a samurai sword, hilt downward, the blade rusty and corroded. The weapon looked as if it had been sitting out in the weather for months—the cotton wrapping of the hilt was frayed, the brass fittings dark with corrosion. Tied loosely around the guard of the sword was a plastic-coated wire, like an electrical cord, and attached to the cord was a brown, brittle piece of paper. Aaron plucked the paper from the cord. The edges broke apart like an old autumn leaf as he unfolded it, and he could barely read the strangely familiar handwriting, almost as faded as the paper:

PULL ME!

"Aaron! Come on!" Jennifer was yelling. She and Travis were already halfway across the meadow to the cycads.

Aaron picked up the cord, sliding it off the blade. The cord trailed over the rocks and up the cliff wall. The Gairk were nearly through the pass now.

"Aaron!"

Aaron yanked at the cord. He could feel resistance at the other end, high up on the cliff. He pulled again, harder this time, and nearly fell backward as the other end suddenly broke loose from whatever had been holding it.

With a rumble and a crash, boulders began to fall, slowly at first, then gathering momentum and bringing other rocks with them. The whole pass filled with their dust and clamor, and through it, Aaron could hear the cries of the Gairk. The avalanche seemed to last for a long time, though Aaron knew that it was only a few seconds. Then it was over, the last few pebbles falling to bounce from the great rocks that now filled the narrow pass.

From the other side, they could hear the furious growls and bleats of the Gairk.

Jennifer had come running back during the uproar. Now she looked at the sword Aaron was holding in his hand. "How did that happen?" she asked Aaron. "I don't understand."

"I think I do," Aaron answered, staring at the sword. Casting an eye at the ridge, he added: "But we can't stay here. They'll find a way over or around it soon, and I don't think we want to be here when that happens. I'll explain later. Let's get out of here while we can."

14

The Logic of Time

"I don't get it, Aaron," Jennifer said.

The group had paused to rest in the midst of an intertwined grove of cycads. "We can't run forever," Aaron had said only a few minutes before. "I don't care if they're only ten minutes behind us. Travis can't take the pace, and neither can the rest of us."

Jennifer looked back through the branches, half afraid she'd glimpse beaten copper gleaming in the sun, then back at Aaron. The young man kept turning the samurai sword before his face, gazing at it as if it were some religious object. "You're telling me that you know we're going to get to the time machine because you found the sword. You believe that the sword means that we must have used the time machine to put it there, just to get us out of the jam we were in. Doesn't that totally foul up the idea of cause and effect?" Jennifer grimaced. "I mean, you're saying that we are going to go back to put up a trap because we know it's already there. Which comes first?"

Aaron glanced up, but he didn't say anything, the sword on his lap. "It depends on how you look at time,"

Travis answered for Aaron. He coughed and took several breaths before continuing. "From the standpoint of that tree over there, we came here and placed the trap *before* we needed it, then we went away and came back years later and stumbled across the perfect solution to our problem: the effect preceded the cause. The problem is, with the time machine we can loop ourselves back in time. We can look at events from *outside* the normal flow of time, and it all makes sense from our viewpoint."

Jennifer was shaking her head. "But still . . . What about freedom of choice? Does that mean that we *have* to go back in time? Are we forced to set up the trap and put the sword there so Aaron can see it? I mean, even granted that we *did* find the sword and the trap, what if we all decided to just take off for some other place and forget about setting up that little trick for the Gairk? We couldn't do that without creating a nasty little paradox, because we already *found* the sword. For that matter, what if we never *get* to the time machine? What if the Gairk catch us first?"

"Obviously the Gairk don't catch us," Aaron answered. "We get to the time machine."

"At least *one* of us does," Travis pointed out. He coughed again, holding his sides. He was still breathing hard, even though the rest of them had mostly recovered from the long run. "Look, Jenny, I understand your confusion. On the other hand, this does tell us that someone, sometime, finds the time machine again. I think that also explains how you found the tranquilizer needle just when Struth needed it: you or someone else *put* it there, knowing you were going to need it."

Jennifer laughed. "Great—so our future selves twist back in time to help us out now. It seems to me that it would have been a lot more effective for us to simply pop back here and pick ourselves up."

It was Travis's turn to shake his head. "Not possible," he said. "That *would* be a paradox. You can't exist in two places at the same time. Time itself won't let you do that—if you try, something always happens. Try *too* hard, and . . ." He shrugged. "Well, that's what Eckels did when he forced his time machine to go back and meet itself, and the explosion *that* caused is how we got into this mess in the first place. You have to be very careful about how you go about messing with the past—remember, it was a lousy *butterfly* Eckels stepped on, and it changed my whole time line."

"Still . . ."

Travis lifted a hand with a smile and interrupted Jennifer's protest. "That's why Aaron won't keep the sword, either."

"What do you mean," Aaron said, looking up suddenly. He was wiping the blade with his shirt; it was glinting wickedly in the sunlight. "I'm not getting rid of this. No way."

"I didn't say you'd get rid of it. I said you won't *keep* it—time won't let you."

"Time won't *let* me?" Aaron repeated. "I don't care what time says. I'm keeping the sword. It's my good luck charm."

"You can try. You won't succeed," Travis insisted. "The Mutata put the sword in the time machine after they took it away from you. Once we find the time machine, all of a sudden we'd have the sword and its future self all in the same place."

"That's it," Aaron broke in. "We're all confused enough already. And if we sit here talking all day, we'll never get to the time machine, no matter who put the sword there."

Almost grumpily, Aaron got to his feet and began walking away. A few moments later, Travis, Struth, and Jennifer followed. Aaron thrust the sword into his belt.

"After what's happened, I'm keeping you," he told it. "Paradox or not."

Even so, he kept his hand on the hilt, just in case the weapon might vanish like a dream.

* * *

By the time the sun was directly overhead, Peter was still in the swamp, though he felt that he must be nearing the edge of the morass. He was wet to his armpits from having stepped into what he thought was another shallow lake, which had instead turned out to be quite a bit deeper. He'd swallowed some of the dark, murky water, which immediately made him think of Jennifer's warning about drinking from unsterilized streams, no matter how pristine they appeared—and that started him worrying about every twitch of his stomach afterward.

He kept telling himself that he recognized landmarks, that he was on the right track back to the Mutata valley— but he didn't even manage to fool himself. One fern, one cycad, one low lake looked the same as the next. Peter navigated mostly by the glimpses of the sun between the leafy fronds. He looked for signs that Eckels had come this way, but he'd lost the man's track before he was even out of sight of the restaurant.

"Obviously, you're not any competition for the Deerslayer," he told himself, rubbing his bright red hair as he stood in a small clearing. Flies the size of ping-pong balls whizzed by, and a dragonfly on which a small cat could have hitched a ride alighted on the ground nearby, its gossamer wings a blur. "But then, neither's Eckels. Man, he could be *anywhere* in this mess. And so could I."

Peter sighed, squinting up at the sun. "Well, standing here talking to myself isn't going to accomplish anything. As Eckels would probably say: 'Move it, kid!'"

Peter pushed himself away from the cycad he was leaning against and pressed on. He'd gone a hundred yards or so, skirting the edge of a pool, when he heard something crunch underfoot. He looked down to see his shoe covered in a mess of yolk and eggshell—he had stepped on a small nest hidden in the leafy low ferns that covered the lake shore. "Oh, man . . . Peter started to complain. "That's going to be a pain to get off—"

He stopped. He had the impression that someone or something was watching him. Suspicious, he looked around. "Eckels?" he called out cautiously.

No answer. Peter still couldn't shake the impression of eyes gazing at him. Peter scraped the worst of the mess from his shoe. The lake was a fairly large one, but it looked relatively shallow and was pocked with hummocks and small islands. Peter wondered whether wading across it might not save him time, since by his reckoning the edge of the swamp lay somewhere beyond it.

"Might as well," he muttered. "Can't get much wetter than I already am." He took a step into the water.

A sudden, violent swirling stirred the surface a few yards to his left. Peter stopped, halfway through his step. Where the ripples were centered, a pair of bulbous, slitted eyes were sitting on a bumpy log. Peter took a step back toward the shore, and with the motion, the water foamed white as a muscular tail thrashed the shallows and wide, snaggle-toothed jaws gaped open.

Peter half fell backward onto the bank as the jaws snapped water where he'd just been standing. The thing that rushed dripping from the water as Peter scrambled to his feet was instantly recognizable: an alligator, eight feet long and angry. *Alligators and crocodiles are modern-day remnants of the dinosaur age*, Peter remembered Aaron saying once. *They're living fossils. We've found fossilized remains of them further back than you can imagine, all of them looking just like their modern cousins.*

It seemed that Peter had found one of those living fossils, and an angry would-be mother at that. The alligator didn't seem inclined to listen to an apology for stepping on her nest, either. She slithered out of the water onto the bank, hissing like an overheated tea kettle, and Peter decided that the best tactic was flight. "You can't outrun me," he told it. "I was on the track team."

He quickly found that, if he'd been racing alligators, they would have beaten him to the finish line every time. The gator, despite its ungainly look, moved rapidly through the ferns in pursuit. In a very few seconds, it was nearly on him again. In desperation, Peter leaped to the right as the alligator snapped once more. Peter felt a sharp-edged tooth snag the cloth of his pants. He tore loose with a grunt, and the alligator came to a stumbling halt before turning to lunge after him again. Peter moved left; the gator turned with him, but Peter noticed that it didn't turn as quickly as it moved.

"So that's it," he said. "You're a fireball in the straight, but you're lousy at turns. Okay, let's see how you deal with this."

Peter ran again, but this time changed direction in a zig-zag pattern evey ten steps. The angry reptile tried to follow, but stumbled on the first turn, hissed angrily, and stopped.

Peter didn't stop to determine if the alligator had given up the chase. He kept moving. It was an hour before he stopped jumping every time he stumbled across a fallen cycad trunk, but the sun was still well above the horizon when he pushed through a screen of ferns and saw the tall hills of the Mutata valley in the distance. He was well south of where they had entered the marsh, but the pass was visible in the blue, hazy distance between the crowns of the largest hills. He scanned the landscape for signs of Eckels. He saw no one, but Eckels could easily be hidden anywhere in the rolling, rising terrain, or could already be mounting the broken trail that led into the valley.

"What now?" he asked himself, but he already knew the answer. He'd committed himself to going back to the valley. If it was a mistake, it was too late to undo. Taking a deep breath, he pointed himself at the valley and started off.

The swamp had been humid, but at least it had been shaded. Here, out in the open except for scattered treelike ferns, the sun was merciless. Peter was sweating before he'd walked an hour, and by the second, he was desperately thirsty.

"Man, I never thought I'd actually miss the swamp," he muttered after, for the hundreth time, images of lakes and sparkling creeks danced tantalizingly through his head. He shaded his eyes against the brutal light. He was rewarded with a promising glint at the bottom of the small hill on which he stood. A tiny creek wandered down from the tall slopes girdling the Mutata valley, gurgling and foaming as it moved among the rocks. Giant horsetails and fans of lacy green adorned the banks; small lizards sunned themselves on the flat rocks in the creekbed, and small fish darted in the rippling shallows where the water pooled.

Shaded by the taller ferns and cycads, the small valley was one of the more picturesque sights Peter had seen in this world. He hurried down toward the beckoning vision. He didn't know if he could wait the half hour or so he'd need to make a fire and boil the water. He licked his lips, imagining how the cool water would taste . . .

"*Mrrruugh!*" The bleating cry came from behind him. Peter scrambled to his feet, startled. A dinosaur was glaring at him: the creature was five feet tall and twenty feet long, with a bony, tortoiselike plated back, an armored head, and a long tail with what looked like a lumpy bowling ball on the end. Peter took a step away from the dinosaur; it advanced, its tail twitching.

"Ahh, come on," Peter said to it. "I'd be a lousy dinner. Too many bones." Peter retreated again, his foot splashing into the creek. The dinosaur continued to advance, faster this time. Peter swung his head quickly left and right, looking for somewhere to retreat. A tall fern beckoned: *You can make it. No way this thing can climb.*

"I hope you're as slow as you look," he told the dinosaur, then turned and ran. The animal bellowed once more and Peter heard it trundle after him in loud pursuit. Peter didn't waste time looking back, though he could feel the skin of his spine tingling with the premonition that at any second the dinosaur would be on him. He leaped for the tree, grunting from the impact as he hit the trunk, then desperately shinnying up the slanting limb. He was ten feet up before he dared to look down again.

The dinosaur was at the bottom, staring up at him, its front legs up on the trunk. It gave another of its loud bleats and then sat, its hind legs folding underneath it, looking for all the world like an armored dog guarding a treed cat.

"Great. Now what?" Peter asked himself. "You're up a tree, and Godzilla Jr. is sitting underneath it." He gathered his breath. "Go *away!*" he shouted at the dinosaur. "Go on! Get out of here!"

The dinosaur just looked at him.

"This looks like it's going to be a long wait," he said.

15

Falling Waters

"Go on!" The call came faintly from somewhere ahead of them. "Get out of here!"

"My God, that sounds like *Peter!*" Jennifer exclaimed, looking at Aaron with a sudden, bright excitement in her face. Her hair swayed as she turned. "Peter!" Jennifer called, cupping her hands at her mouth. "Where are you!"

"Jenny? Hey, Jenny! Over here!" came the answer to their left. The group moved quickly through a screen of ferns with Aaron in the lead. He stopped suddenly, and Jennifer nearly ran into him. They could see Peter, clasping the branches of one of the tree-ferns like a bright red-topped fruit, while a large, surly-looking dinosaur prowled the base of the trunk. Aaron, to Jennifer's surprise, began laughing. Travis, limping up well behind everyone else, also chuckled.

"What's so funny, you two?" Jennifer asked, frowning. "None of you would find it particularly amusing to be trapped by a hungry dinosaur. Come on, we have to figure a way to deal with that thing."

"Jen, that's an ankylosaurus," Aaron told her. "Also known as the 'fused lizard.' It's a walking tank, I'll admit, but it's also a strict herbivore. The poor thing wouldn't eat Peter no matter how hungry it was. Pete was probably just trespassing in its territory, and it was trying to chase him away."

The ankylosaurus was glaring at the new intruders now. It growled, gave Peter a final angry glance, then headed deliberately toward Aaron and the others, its tail wriggling threateningly and raised high. "Whooah! On the other hand," Aaron said with trepidation in his voice, "maybe it's better to be safe than sorry. I'd hate to be hit by that wrecking ball of a tail. Come on, back up, guys."

Aaron retreated, but Struth didn't follow the rest of them. Instead, the Mutata took an advancing step toward the ankylosaurus, loudly stomping her foot on the ground as she did so. Her spinal frill had engorged and spread out, making her appear even larger than she was. She gave a shrill blast from her nasal horn.

The ankylosaurus hesitated. It turned sidewise, whipping the tail back as if to strike. "Struth!" Jennifer yelled. "Be careful!"

Struth paid no attention to Jennifer. The Mutata snorted at the ankylosaurus. Again, she took a step toward it, loosing another blast from her horn. The ankylosaurus swiveled faster than Jennifer would have thought possible, and its tail slashed the air in front of Struth with a low, menacing *whoosh*.

"Struth!" Jennifer yelled again, but again Struth ignored her. Struth took a deliberate step toward the dinosaur. The ankylosaurus bleated once and backed up, snapping its hooked, toothless beak at Struth. Once more Struth stamped the ground, sounding her own challenge and waving her taloned hands like someone shooing a dog away from their yard, and this time the ankylosaurus took several lumbering steps backwards, nearly colliding with the fern in which Peter was hanging. Struth continued to advance, faster now, and the ankylosaurus evidently decided that discretion was better than valor—it turned its strange tail toward them and ran off along the creekbed.

"All right, Struth!" Aaron yelled. "That's telling it!" Peter dropped down from the tree, landing with a thump on the mossy ground. He looked at the retreating dinosaur and clapped Struth on the shoulder, who snorted and jumped away half a meter. Struth stared down at him with her golden-brown eyes. Peter spread his hands wide to show that he didn't intend the Mutata any harm.

"Hey, I just wanted to say thanks," he said, even though he knew Struth could understand none of the words. "I thought that thing was going to keep me up there all day."

Peter turned to the others. His lips pressed together tightly, and a faint flush crept from his neck to his cheeks. "Didn't expect to *see you* guys here," he said, then shook his head. "Oh, man, that sounds lame. Umm, look . . . Aaron, Jen, Travis: I'm sorry. I blew it. Taking off with Eckels was one of the dumbest stunts I've ever pulled, and I regret it more than you could believe. I'm really sorry."

"Dumb?" Aaron said heatedly. "That's not the half of it. When that raptor attacked, we could have been killed because you weren't there to help us." Aaron swung his arms in exasperation as the color deepened in Peter's face. Aaron was just beginning to launch into his tirade—*If Peter thinks he can get away with an 'I'm sorry' after all this . . .* But Jennifer stepped in between the two of them before he could say more.

"That's enough," she said sharply to Aaron. "Pete's apologized, and he's back. That's enough, and that's all we have to hear."

Aaron started to protest, but Jennifer raised a finger warningly. Aaron took a deep breath, knowing that she was right. *You're just using Peter as an excuse to vent your frustrations. He's your friend, and you've been terrified that something horrible would happen to him. Don't drive him away now—*

It took him several calming breaths before he could get the next words out, but he did. "You're right, Jen. I'm sorry, Peter. I guess . . . I guess I've got my brains stuck in the past. I'm . . . I'm really glad to see you again. I was scared that we had lost you forever, and if I'd taken a few more seconds I would have realized it. Welcome back."

Peter smiled uncertainly and a little shyly at all of them. Aaron held out his hand; when Peter took it, Aaron pulled Peter toward him and hugged him instead.

"I missed you, buddy," he told him.

"Thanks," Peter said, huskily. "And that goes double for me. If I find Eckels again . . ." Peter grimaced. "Speaking of missing people, where's Mundo?"

"Mundo's gone back to his own world," Jennifer answered. Briefly, she told Peter what had happened since they'd parted ways at the restaurant in the swamp. By the time she'd finished, Peter was glancing back the way they'd come as if he expected a band of Gairk to come howling and screaming from over the hill. "What about Eckels?" Jennifer asked. "Where'd he go? And what happened to your head?"

Peter took his turn, giving them a quick synopsis of what had happened to him, though he found himself leaving out the talking dragon. Aaron flushed angrily when he learned that Eckels had taken the pieces of temporal machinery. "And you don't know where he is?"

Peter shook his head. "No. I tracked him into the swamp a bit, but I lost the trail. I know he wants to use the roadway back in the Mutata village, but he could still be wandering around back there, or he could have already gone through. I don't know."

Aaron shook his head grimly. "And we can't waste time looking for him, not with the Gairk hot on our heels. I figure we gained a few hours with our little trick, but if I know the Gairk as well as I think I do, that won't convince them to give up the chase."

Jennifer spoke quickly with Struth, who hooted and pointed back the way they came. "Struth agrees," Jennifer said. "She said that they're going to be angry, and that will just make them faster and more determined to catch us."

"Then we have to assume that Eckels is ahead of us," Travis said. "If not, there's nothing we can do about him."

"We need the pieces of temporal machinery he has," Aaron said. "And we'll get them once we find him. If we don't . . ."

Travis coughed. "Then we'll try it without them."

"Then let's get going," Jennifer said. "The sooner we get there, the sooner we'll know. Come on, Peter—we're glad to have you back."

With that, they headed out once again. The land was rising to meet the tall peaks that surrounded the Mutata valley, the earth crumpled like a sheet of paper into steep hills and valleys, all of which seemed inevitably to run in the wrong direction so that they were constantly having to traverse them. This was hardest on Travis. Aaron noticed that they were having to stop every hour or so to let the man rest and gain back some of his strength, and his limp was becoming more pronounced. He was leaning heavily on a thick walking stick he'd picked up along their trail. Each time they stopped to let Travis rest, Aaron found himself fretting about the time they were wasting, both because of Eckels ahead of them and the Gairk behind.

"Go on," Travis said, after the third or fourth time they'd paused. "I'm a liability; I know it. Why don't the rest of you go on; I'll catch up later."

Jennifer shot a concerned look at Aaron. "No," she said, though she was still looking at him. "We stay together. We're not going to abandon *anyone*. Not now."

"Jenny," Travis said gently, with a smile. "I know when I'm a danger to other people. I'd hate to think that the Gairk caught up with us because I slowed you guys down."

"That's not going to happen, Travis," Aaron told him. "And you can forget about us leaving you here. We're going to need all the help we can get, believe me."

"Aaron," Travis persisted, "I appreciate what you're saying, but I also know the reality here."

Aaron laughed. "Reality? You're going to talk about reality when time storms are ripping the place apart, when we see walking thunder-giants, talking dinosaurs, and worlds where insects are the highest life form? You gotta be kidding—there's no such thing as reality anymore. Now shut up and get yourself ready. We've got a lot of ground to cover before it gets dark."

Travis started to protest, but another coughing spasm cut off the words. While Jennifer went over to minister to him, Aaron moved off a few steps and squinted into the distance, where they could just see the rugged pass into the Mutata valley high above them.

"You've really changed, Aaron."

Aaron didn't look back. He continued to scan the rocks and cliff walls. "What do you mean, Peter?"

"I don't mean anything derogatory. I just mean that you've grown up a lot in the last few months. Somewhere along the way, you . . ." Aaron looked back to see Peter shrug and give a wry, twisted grin. "Well, you became an adult."

"So have you. I like the beard."

Peter grinned and rubbed his stubbled chin. "Yeah, yours too. But it's more than that. I've watched you; you really are the leader here. It used to be Travis, but since he's gotten sick, you've taken over. Jennifer, too—you've both . . . gotten stronger somehow—not physical strength but here. Inside." Peter tapped his chest. "I think that's the problem I had with you. I was jealous of you and Jenny, and of what you've become." Peter gave a self-deprecating sniff. "I guess I have some of my own maturing to do yet."

Aaron smiled at his friend and clapped him on the shoulder. "I think you just finished the process," he said. "Now all we have to do is figure how to get to the time machine before the Gairk get to us. Come on up this way."

Aaron led Peter to the top of a rise. A time storm had left a small, crumbling tower of carved stone there. Aaron couldn't read the hieroglyphics carved on it, but the figures—four-armed, with bulbous eyes and snouts—were definitely not human.

A remnant of another time, another place that shouldn't have existed. Aaron grimaced, then followed the narrow, spiral ramp—obviously not built for their kind of locomotion—to the summit of the edifice. Peter followed and stood next to him as they gazed over the low wall at the top.

Aaron pointed back behind them. In the distance, they could see a group of small figures moving through the flatland near the marsh. "Gairk," Aaron answered to

Peter's unasked question. "I noticed them a few hours back, while we were climbing another one of these cliffsides. Jennifer saw them too, I know. Luckily, Travis didn't notice them or he'd really be insistent about leaving him behind."

"How close are they?"

"I don't know," Aaron answered. He shrugged. "Maybe two, three hours, maybe a little more. They're faster than we are through most of this, but they're definitely much slower at night than us. I'm afraid, though, that they'll gain on us quickly once we're through the pass and back in the valley again."

"What can we do about them?"

Aaron shrugged again, and accented the gesture with a sigh. "You know, I don't have the foggiest idea. None at all." Then he grinned at Peter wryly. "I think the best thing we can do is just keep running."

"Sounds like a plan to me," Peter answered.

"Aren't you glad you found us again?"

"I'm ecstatic. I guess I should have taken off with Mundo instead of Eckels, eh?"

Aaron laughed, and with the sound he felt some of the darkness leave him for the first time in days. "Come on," he said. "Let's see if Travis is rested enough. We've got a long way to go yet. We'll see who's faster: the Gairk, or us."

You will never understand the humans.

That mantra kept reverberating through SStragh's head as they moved through the pass back into the Mutata valley. She didn't understand why they hadn't submitted to their fate when the Gairk had nearly caught them, and she still wasn't quite sure how Jhenini's mate Aaron had managed to send the rocks tumbling down to fill the pass. She didn't understand why they kept running when the Gairk were so close behind them once more. She didn't understand why Trahvis, the one whose inner sickness made SStragh's nose wrinkle, didn't simply lay down as a Mutata would and let death take him.

She wondered why none of them realized that he would not live much longer.

In the two and a half days since they had fled the Nesting Grounds, there had been a hand and a half of Dreaming Storms, and SStragh could not understand why the humans didn't see that the boundaries that held the world together were ripping entirely apart, and this plan of the humans must fail.

But then SStragh didn't really understand why she herself had agreed to help Jhenini and the humans.

The humans are a sickness, she told herself. *They have infected you. You are not human, but neither are you entirely Mutata. Not anymore.*

Another storm was coming, SStragh realized. She could smell it, even though the humans had not yet noticed. SStragh remembered the storm beast that had come from the Dreaming Storm to crush her nest and her eggs, and the aching loss rose in her again.

My egglings, gone. I gave them warmth, gave them life, and I could feel them when I tended the nest. Another few days and they would have hatched, blind and hungry. My children. Another generation of life—gone now, gone because the Ancient Path is broken. Can you really believe the humans can bring it back?

They were nearly through the pass now, and SStragh could see spread out ahead of them the green, lush valley that was her home. It gladdened her heart to view it once more, even though the storms had riddled it with circles of desecration. More storms had struck since they'd left, she saw, and the circles were far larger, many steps across. Soon, she thought sadly, they will be large enough to cover the valley itself. And then what?

She hooted sadly, a wail that echoed among the stones.

"What's the matter, SStragh?" Jhenini asked, moving closer to the Mutata.

"A Dreaming Storm is coming," SStragh told her. She pointed overhead, to the strip of sky that could be seen between the craggy limestone walls of the pass. "See, the clouds are already beginning to gather."

Jhenini glanced up and saw the quick, boiling mass of gray-black clouds that touched the peaks above them. "Another one," she sighed, then called out in her own language to the others. They talked quickly, an exchange of which SStragh understood nothing, then Aaron began half running out of the pass, down toward the valley and the trees.

SStragh wanted to tell him that hurrying would change nothing: the storm would find them or not—but he could not understand her. Bleating in soft frustration, SStragh followed the humans down the narrow path as the wind swirled and raised dust at their feet.

The day darkened around them as they ran, and lightning was flickering bright tongues before they'd gone a hundred steps. The first crack of thunder beat against SStragh's chest, and she stopped with a squawk of dismay. A stone wall had appeared directly in their path, and from it, human faces were peering out between cracks in the stone. Someone yelled high up on the wall, and all of a sudden a rain of sharp arrows erupted from the openings in the wall, accompanied by the sharp twang of bowstrings. SStragh bellowed a warning, but the next lightning strike of the storm came at the same moment: Wall, men, and arrows all vanished in the same instant.

Something howled from high up on the ledge of the pass. SStragh wheeled around to see a creature formed of achingly bright light, like the fires the Gairk used to melt their ores, only this brightness was shaped like a bird and had gleaming eyes of red. It shrieked again and spread its burning wings, leaping from its perch. Light traveled down with it, a swift illumination that brushed along the wash of stone and rock as it glided down. As they all involuntarily ducked; the flame-creature swooped overhead. SStragh could feel the heat of its passage, a searing presence and a wind of heat as it stroked its wings and rose again. SStragh followed the strange thing's rising flight, up into the Dreaming Storm's vortex, where lightning flared once more.

SStragh could feel the storm gathering its energy, and she knew that this flash would bring the final apparition, the one that would remain behind as the Dreaming Storm quickly dissipated.

The lightning, when it came, was blinding. The arcing electricity touched ground immediately in front of them, the thunder ripping air in the same instant. SStragh cried out in pain, blinded, and she heard the humans shout in their own language. Jhenini screamed something, pointing. SStragh, through storm-blinded eyes, saw a vision in front of them that made her trumpet in shock.

Towering before them was a column of blue water, like a wind-tossed sea fifty feet high and utterly filling the pass, a tower of liquid transported here from some other world's ocean and held back by . . .

. . . nothing.

Even as SStragh realized that, she saw the base of the column bulge and collapse, and then the entire structure fell apart, the tower sagging into a torrent, a tsunami that foamed and battered at the pass walls, roaring toward them with its own rumbling thunder.

The humans were shouting. As one, they all turned to run, but there was no time and nowhere to go. SStragh didn't run. Instead, she faced the onrushing wall, knowing that there was no escape from it. She tried to find in herself that instinctive acceptance of fate, the calmness of the OColihi.

If this is my time, All-Ancestor, I come to you gladly.

SStragh closed her eyes.

The water hit her like a thousand charging Gairk.

16

A Death in the Family

Oh man, not AGAIN. . . !

Aaron supposed that he shouldn't have been surprised—given that the world was seventy percent ocean, it was actually surprising that this hadn't happened *more* often.

The wave that had hit them in Rome had been nasty. This was worse, taller and wider, and with them trapped in a rock-walled canyon.

Aaron had once boogie-boarding on a family vacation to South Carolina. He'd thought he'd been doing fairly well, managing to stay up on the board fairly well after his first few tries. Then a particularly large wave came along and he got caught in the breaking tip. The board had flipped and gone one way, and the wave seemed to reach out and pull him down, tumbling him along the sandy bottom of the beach. For what seemed like an eternity, the surf pounded and pummeled him, as he took in water and flailed helplessly, trying to get out of the wave's grasp and find the surface. He was almost in a state of total panic when he was finally deposited—disoriented, waterlogged, and sore—on the shore. Afterward, he'd asked how he should have handled the wave. Everyone's advice was the same:

"Turn your back to the water and just go with it! Don't fight it!"

Aaron barely had time to shout the warning to the others when the wave unleashed by the time storm hammered him down. The churning wave flipped him and instantly bore him under. It was shockingly frigid and he tasted salt water—*from an artic ocean*, an oddly detached part of him thought—and he tried to make himself into a ball. His ears filled with the bass roar of the water, white water foamed around him as he was thrown forward. He felt his shoulder glance off something hard; light flickered past his closed eyes. He was moving at incredible speed back through the pass walls now, unable to control his movement, entirely at the mercy of this raging flood, feeling rocks and boulders caught up in the cascade striking his back, his legs, his arms. He slammed hard against the floor of the pass, and he opened his mouth in an involuntary gasp that took in a mouthful of choking, cold seawater.

Aaron knew that he wasn't going to survive much longer. He desperately needed air, and the wave might smash him headfirst into a boulder at any second. Adrenaline fueled his panic and he began to flail, trying to swim even though he had no idea which way was up, refusing to die passively. *If you're going to kill me, I'm not going easily*, he told the wave.

And suddenly, as if it had heard his defiance, he was free. The wave was past him, most of its energy spent, leaving Aaron deposited dripping wet and spread-eagled on his stomach in a scree of small rocks. He choked and threw up water, then took a long, gasping, desperate breath, his mouth wide as he gulped at the sweet air. His eyes burned with the salt; he shivered under his soaked clothing. His backpack had snagged on a boulder a few feet away, but the samurai sword was gone, taken in the flood. He moved his limbs experimentally; everything seemed to work.

He slowly levered himself up, blinking. The surging water had carried him further than he would have believed—he was lying at the opening to the Mutata valley pass, a half mile or more from where they'd been. He didn't see any of his companions.

"Jenny!" he called. "Peter! Travis! Struth!"

"Over here!" Peter answered from behind screening boulders to his right, then, more faintly from further down the pass, he heard Jennifer's voice. "I'm here, Aaron. So's Travis."

Aaron got to his feet shakily. He could see Peter doing the same, and Jennifer helping Travis up. Everyone looked to be scratched and bumped and bruised. "Anyone badly hurt?"

Peter shook his head; Jennifer shrugged. "Banged up, that's all. Sore." Her hair hung in wet strings around her face and she pushed it out of her eyes. "Where's Struth? Has anyone seen her?"

A trumpeting hoot came from behind Aaron, and he turned to see Struth limping toward them—since she was heavier, the sudden flood hadn't carried her as far.

"Struth, you okay?" Aaron called to the Mutata even though he knew that she wouldn't understand him, but the dinosaur appeared to pay no attention to him at all. She was still bleating and hooting furiously, pointing at something beyond Aaron. "What's she honking about?" Aaron started to ask Jennifer, but the words died in his mouth as he turned to her. Below them, at the base of the steep slope leading to the pass, the newly uncloaked sun was glinting on the copper helmets and breastplates of a band of Gairk.

They ran as best as they could, limping from the bruises and scurrying over and around the boulders the time storm's flood had left in the pass. Already the air burned in Aaron's lungs, and he knew it was worse for Travis, who was lagging behind, refusing to let anyone help him. "We've still . . . got fifteen, twenty . . . minutes on them," Peter grunted out as they ran. "Where's . . . the time machine . . . hidden?"

"In the cave . . . where you and Jen . . . met Eckels," Aaron answered. Aaron glanced back. Travis was far behind now. Reluctantly, Aaron raised his hand and called for a brief halt to let Travis catch up and to allow all of them to rest. Involuntarily, he looked back up at the hollow between the rampart cliffs of the pass. Somewhere between those walls, he knew, the Gairk were running, their ugly snouts full of human scent, re-energized by the knowledge that their prey was just ahead.

Peter was standing with his hands on his knees, his chest heaving. Jennifer sat, her forehead resting on her knees. Even Struth appeared tired, her tail dropping to help support her weight as she stood. Travis stumbled up and collapsed, lying on his back coughing and wheezing. The man looked awful. Jennifer went over to him, offering him water. Aaron watched, wondering how long they could keep up this pace.

"The Gairk are going to be awfully fast now," Peter commented, as if reading Aaron's thoughts.

"Yeah, I know," Aaron answered softly. His gaze was still on the pass, where the sun danced on rocks. Each glint made Aaron's pulse jump. "It's gonna be close."

"No kidding." Peter took a deep breath and slowly exhaled, leaning over again. "Well, we're not going to outrun them by standing here."

Aaron nodded. "Jenny, how's Travis?"

"I'm fine," Travis answered before Jennifer could say anything. He got to his feet, shrugging off Jennifer's hand, though he bent over quickly with another coughing fit, and his legs wobbled as he stood back up. Behind the man, Jennifer shook her head to Aaron, her eyes worried and her lips pressed tight. Travis sniffed and forced himself to stand upright. "Let's get moving," he said. "I'm all right. Don't worry about me."

"Good," Aaron said. "Eckels's cave is five or six miles away, as I remember. Let's take it at a walk for a little bit, anyway. The Gairk are going to be slow coming down off the pass, so I think we can afford to pace ourselves."

That was a lie and Travis knew it as well as anyone, but no one seemed to want to point it out, preferring to relish the false security the words gave them.

Aaron led them on and down into the lush growth of the valley, where at least the foliage prevented them from seeing or being seen by the Gairk. They stayed to the paths made by the Gairk and Mutata, alternating between walking and jogging. Aaron's muscles ached with the exertion, and he knew the rest of them were in the same shape. Under the cycads and tall ferns it was at least cooler, and the sound of the river drew them on. Before long, they came to the empty Gairk village. There, Aaron called for another rest period. They sprawled out, spent. Jennifer threw herself down next to Aaron, and he pressed her hand. She returned the pressure with a faint smile, turning to him and stroking his face once. "Hey," Aaron said. "Hanging in there?"

"Yeah." She squeezed his hand again. "I'm worried about Travis, though. This pace . . . I just don't know if he can keep it up."

"There's not much further to go."

"He doesn't have much left, either." Jennifer lifted up, her face quizzical. "What's Struth doing over there?"

"Where?"

"By the path . . ." Jennifer got up and went over to the Mutata, who was bent over, sniffing at the ground near the path through the Gairk village. "What is it, Struth?" she asked in the Mutata language. Struth sniffed once more, then lifted her head and settled into the stance that Jennifer knew was that of an elder addressing a younger.

"The other human," Struth said. "He came this way. See, that is his footprint. It carries his scent." She pointed at the path, where Jennifer could see a half-moon depression.

"What's going on, Jen?" Aaron asked. Jennifer relayed what Struth had just told her. Travis, his face gray with exhaustion, limped over and crouched down over the area, scanning forward along the track.

"Struth's right," he said. "I might have missed it, but Eckels has been through here. See—there's another footprint, and another over there . . ." His long forefinger pointed.

"How long ago?" Aaron asked.

"A day or more ago, I'd think. Look here—he stepped on a fern leaf here, breaking it apart, and the broken stems are brown and dry. Jennifer, ask Struth—she might be able to tell by the scent."

Jennifer spoke quickly to Struth, who replied at length. "She says it was a while ago; the dew has destroyed most of the scent—it's very faint."

"That's bad news," Peter said, coming up behind Travis. "If he passed here that long ago, he could easily be back in the Mutata village by now. How long's it going to take him to go through the portal?—a minute or so." Peter grimaced, smacking his fist into an open hand. "He's gone, Aaron. Long gone."

For a moment, Aaron felt his friend's despair. Then a sudden idea came to him. "Maybe not," he said.

"What do you mean?" Jennifer asked.

Aaron shook his head. Travis was looking at him; when they made eye contact, the man shook his head, just the barest movement. "Let me think about this," Aaron said. "There's still a chance. Right now, we can't afford to worry about Eckels. One way or the other, he's made his own destiny. We have to worry about us right now." Aaron straightened. He clapped Struth on the side. "Come on. Let's get moving. I don't like this place."

Within an hour, they all knew it was hopeless.

"Gairk!" Everyone heard Struth say the word. They saw the Mutata lift her snout into the breeze that came from their backs, and she suddenly peered back the way they'd come, her spinal frill rising and her stance going wide. A strange, wild scent arose from her.

"Jenny?" Aaron said.

"Give me a moment. Let me ask her." Jennifer spoke rapidly to Struth, then turned back to them. Her face was pale, her expression sober. "She says the scent's heavy. She says we'll be hearing them any moment. They're coming fast, through that stand of cycads."

Aaron took a deep breath. They were very near Eckels's cave, moving among a series of deep limestone ravines. The cycads were downslope, a hundred yards away. *So close . . .* "We can still make it," Aaron told them. "We *will* make it. Come on!"

But even as he said the words, they heard the trumpeting challenge in the distance and the faint dull clamor of bronze against bronze. "Oh, man . . ." Peter moaned. "They're *really* close . . ."

"Run!" Aaron shouted, and they scrambled up the hill. They'd only gone twenty yards or so when Aaron, glancing back, saw Travis stumble and fall. Jennifer stopped and went back for him; sighing, Aaron did the same.

Jennifer didn't have to say anything. Aaron could see the splashes of red over Travis's shirt front and the scarlet on his lips—the man was hemorrhaging internally. Travis coughed, and more blood came up. He managed to reach a sitting position, and shrugged off any attempt to help him up any further. "No," he said. "I can't. You have to leave me now. There isn't any choice."

"Travis—" Jennifer began, but the man only shook his head and smiled at her.

"I'm sorry, Jenny," he told her. "You've been a good doctor. I wouldn't have made it anywhere near this far without you, but you've done all you can." He smiled again at her before turning to Aaron. "From here, I could hold them back for a long time." He paused, and his eyes searched Aaron's. "*If* I had one of the rifles from the time machine," he added.

"If," Aaron said.

Travis would not let Aaron's gaze drop. "What would be good is if one were sitting right over there, behind that block of limestone. Right there, Aaron. A rifle there wouldn't be too exposed. It could easily sit there for days without any trouble." Travis's intense gaze held Aaron. His eyes pleaded for understanding.

It could easily sit there for days . . .

"Travis, I don't know—" he began, but Travis raised a hand to stop him.

"You *do* know," he told Aaron. "You understand what I'm saying and you know I'm right."

Aaron bit his lip, uncertain. The clamor of the pursuing Gairk was growing louder. "Aaron, you have to do it," Travis said. "If you don't, you're killing all the rest of you. That's the hardest part of being a leader—knowing when to cut your losses."

Aaron closed his eyes. *I can't do this*, he wanted to say, but something deeper down, something formed of steel and crystal, held back the protest. He looked at Travis, at the steady, unafraid look in his eyes, and he nodded. "I understand," he said. "Jenny, come on. We have to go."

"Aaron, we can't . . ."

"We can, and we have to." Crouching down in front of Travis, he took the man's hand. "You've been a good friend," he told the man. "I wish it had turned out differently."

Travis gave a chuckle that turned into a cough. After the spasm passed, he wiped his mouth with his sleeve, leaving a trail of red across his cheek. "So do I," he said. "But it hasn't."

"Good luck," Aaron said.

"Remember, Aaron," Travis told him. "Behind the limestone block."

Aaron nodded. Taking Jennifer's hand, he went back to the others. "Let's go," he said. "We don't have much time."

"Travis?" Peter began.

"He's staying," Aaron said, so firmly that Peter only nodded. "Now, let's run!" They fled, scrambling up the hill and down again into another ravine.

A few minutes later, they all heard the sharp, percussive bark of gunfire from behind them.

"What the—" Peter began, but Aaron only shook his head and urged them on.

"Just keep going. There's nothing we can do. Travis is doing it all."

"Where'd he get the rifle?"

"I'll explain later. For now, just run."

They ran. For several seconds, the gunfire echoed among the stones. Then, all too abruptly, it ended.

17

Past Mistakes

"Aaron, we have to go back. Travis—" Jennifer looked back wildly over her shoulder.

"If we do that, we waste everything he's done," Aaron told her. "He's dead, Jenny. We both know it, and we both know why he did it."

"Travis may have killed all the Gairk or driven them off. He could just be lying there, hurt."

"That isn't what happened. There were at least a dozen Gairk, and they're trained warriors. Travis knew that, too. He just wanted to hold them back as long as possible."

"Aaron—" Tears started in her eyes. She stopped, and Aaron took her arm. He touched her cheek, felt the wetness there, and felt the same moisture in his own eyes.

"Jenny, I hate this as much as you do. But this was Travis's gift to us. You know as well as I do how hurt he was. This . . ." Aaron couldn't speak for a moment. He took a long, slow breath. "It's the only way he knew to help us, and he has. He's given us time."

Jennifer shook her head in quick denial. "I know," she said. "It's just . . ." Aaron could see the sad fury in her eyes, the realization that they had no choice. "All right," she told him, sniffing and wiping at her eyes angrily. "Let's go."

A few minutes later, they stood at the entrance to Eekels's cave. The Mutata had sealed the opening with a rockfall from the hillside above. Tumbled boulders and dirt cloaked the jagged mouth of the cave. Aaron could see where they'd first enlarged the opening to get the time machine in, then covered it over.

"We're going to need some poles or something to use as crowbars and levers," Aaron said. "Peter, you check over in that stand of ferns—anything long and sturdy will do. Jenny, explain to Struth what's going on and get her to give us a hand. This is going to take a bit, and we don't have long."

They dug furiously. Peter returned with several large tree limbs, crudely chopped down with his sword. He and Aaron pried away the boulders with the poles, levering them away from the cave mouth. Struth was a dynamo, her small front arms moving constantly while Jennifer dug alongside her using a sword as a spade. Finally, as the largest of the boulders finally rolled aside, they could see a long, dark crack. Jennifer scrambled up the scree of stones and dirt and twisted her body until she could see into the cave beyond. "It's there!" they heard her call, her voice muffled. She eased her way back out, covered with dirt but grinning. "The time machine's in there. It looks fine. Hurry! Let's get the rest of this barricade out of the way."

Aaron's fatigue seemed to fall away with Jennifer's words. All of them worked with renewed energy. The crack widened steadily until they could all see the time machine gleaming in the sunlight streaming into the cave mouth. "Great," Aaron said. "Let's work on widening the opening so we can—" He stopped.

"What?" Peter asked. Jennifer glanced at him, quizzical.

"Look," Aaron told them, pointing at Struth. The Mutata had lifted up her head, staring at the path leading to the cave with her nostrils fluttering as she sniffed. Her color had deepened, and her stance had gone wide.

"Struth?" Jennifer began to ask, but then there was no need to ask what troubled the Mutata. A hundred yards away, a trio of Gairk burst from the cover of cycads, their armor bright in the sun, the blades of their *broaii* swinging threateningly in their hands. They saw the humans and Struth at the cave entrance, and their leader gave a loud bellow of triumph, pointing his *broaii* at them. The Gairk, their taloned feet digging clods of loam from the ground, charged toward them.

"Into the time machine!" Aaron shouted. "Move!"

They ran. Aaron stumbled over the loose rock; Peter reached down and pulled him up. Jennifer reached the vehicle first. She slapped the hatch contact—as it hissed open, she pushed Struth in and hurried after. A few seconds later, both Aaron and Peter piled in. Aaron had time to notice several fragments of temporal machinery piled near the hatch, with the samurai sword given to Aaron by Otomo placed on top. As the hatch shut behind them, Aaron pulled himself into the driver's seat and powered up the machine. The control panel extruded itself from the wall in front of him.

"The opening isn't wide enough," Peter reminded him.

"It's going to have to be enough," Aaron answered grimly. "Man, they move too *fast* . . ."

The Gairk were nearly at the entrance. Lights flickered on around the vehicle, and a low whining growl came from the motors. They felt the time machine sway as Aaron maneuvered it to face the opening and the onrushing Gairk. "Hang on, this is gonna be rough,"

Aaron told his companions. At the same time, he slammed the acceleration control all the way forward.

The engine wailed in protest and the lights dimmed. The surge of acceleration pressed Aaron back against the seat, and the vehicle slammed into the rocks on either side of the opening, flinging him forward again. The time machine canted sidewise to the left, metal scraping against stone with a high screech. Struth went sliding into the side of the cabin with a howl; Jennifer groaned as her shoulder smashed into a bulwark. The time machine shuddered, held fast in fingers of stone. Aaron pulled the accelerator back, then shoved it forward once again. The vehicle protested the abuse, bucking and shrieking, but they were still held. The Gairk began to approach cautiously. Again, Aaron shoved the accelerator forward. "It's no use," Peter said. "We're stuck."

Aaron didn't answer. The Gairk leader stood in front of the time machine. They could see his mouth open in a roar, the needled teeth exposed. He raised his *broaii* high above his head, them brought it down on the windshield. Aaron ducked, waiting for the shower of glass; the thick pane bowed and a star of cracked glass appeared, but the pane didn't break. Grimly, Aaron pulled the accelerator back and shoved it forward again, as if by the strength of his arm he could lend it power. The Gairk raised his *broaii* for another strike, one that Aaron knew would leave the window in shards.

With a metallic groan and a shudder, the time machine broke through. Suddenly released, it leaped forward like a seed shot from between two fingers. It struck the lead Gairk, throwing the dinosaur back several feet as Aaron brought the craft to a quick halt. "Aaron . . ." Peter pointed left. The other two Gairk hadn't even given their downed leader a glance; they closed in, ready to continue the attack. "Aaron, let's keep moving."

Aaron touched the trackball, moving a pointer on an inset screen. "Systems check," he said aloud and a neuter, alto voice replied.

"Calibrations just within tolerance. Support systems functioning. Warning: Power systems at only fifteen percent."

"Aaron!"

Aaron didn't even hear Peter. He was engrossed in the controls, trying desperately to remember how the software that controlled the vehicle worked. It came back quickly. He clicked on a sequence of screen buttons, then moved the pointer to the large one that said Set and Initiate.

He tapped the button alongside the trackball.

There was a low whine that rapidly built in pitch and volume, like the banshee scream of a jet engine at takeoff.

Outside, the Gairk hesitated as the metal beast that had eaten the humans suddenly roared like no animal they had ever heard before. But the noise was only noise, and they had their orders from the Gairk OColi. With a trumpeting challenge that rivaled the sound of the metal beast, they swung their *broaii* in concert, ready to smash open the metal thing and take the humans who they could see inside.

But their *broaii* struck only air. There was a sudden cold wind. The metal monster and the humans were no longer there.

They were assailed by nausea and cold. Midway through the jump, there was a loud *thump* that caused all of them to jump, startled, and then the whine of the temporal machinery cycled down to a mutter.

"Where—" Jennifer began, then stopped herself with a chuckle. "No, I guess I know *where* we are. *When* are we?"

"Two days ago," Aaron answered. "Everybody get in your seat and buckle in. Jenny, tell Struth we're going to be taking a quick ride, so hold on."

The frost from the short leap back in time was slowly dissolving on the windows of the time machine. They were still outside the cave mouth, only the Gairk were gone, vanished as if they'd never been there. Aaron swung the time machine around. Hovering above the ground on its repulsors, they began moving away from the cave with the vehicle bobbing and bouncing like a car with broken shock absorbers, following the path they'd taken. "Where are we going?" Peter asked.

"Taking care of some past business," Aaron answered cryptically. "You'll see what I mean in a few minutes."

Not long after, they were on the slope where they'd left Travis. Jennifer felt a tug of grief at seeing the place again, knowing that in a few days, this would be the place where they would lose a good friend. Aaron stopped the craft. Going back to the weapons rack of the time machine, he pulled one of the rifles from the hold-down, checked to make certain that it was loaded, then opened the door to the vehicle.

At that moment, everything suddenly fell into place for Jennifer: the cryptic comments, the hints, the strange behavior. "You're leaving the rifle for Travis. That's what he meant when he said it would be nice to find a rifle. He was telling you to come back and leave him one."

Aaron nodded, his face grim.

"Why can't we go back and get *him*, then? Why can't we move to the Gairk village, and pick Travis up when we walk through?"

"Because we didn't." Aaron wasn't looking at her, and that made her angry. He almost seemed impatient.

Jennifer stamped her foot on the decking. "No," she said firmly. "I won't accept that, Aaron. We can't pick up Travis because we *didn't*? What does that mean?"

"I understand," Peter said before Aaron could answer. "At least I think so. We didn't see a time machine arrive and pick up Travis; therefore, we're not going to do it now. If we *had* done it, we'd all remember it."

"That's part of it," Aaron said. "Jenny, I really don't like this any better than you do. If we went and rescued Travis, the paradox of our being there, where our past memories tell us we've never been, would cause another rupture in the timestream. I'm afraid that the time storms would become stronger and more frequent, and we might not be able to repair the damage. That's what Travis told me, anyway—if something never happened, it *can* never happen, or the strain on the time stream is just too much—it's what blew up Eckels's time machine in the first place. But I'd hang all that if I thought we could get Travis and still do what we need to do. But I don't know that we can. There isn't much power left in this craft at all, and we still have some jumps to do and some ground to cover. We can't move around too much in time, or we'll never get back home."

Aaron hefted the rifle. One corner of his mouth lifted in a faint smile. "Let's see what we have left once we've done everything we know we have to do," he told her. "If there's still power, then we can go back and get Travis. Hey, if we can go back in the past, it doesn't matter if we do it right now or twenty years from now, right?"

The answer didn't really satisfy Jennifer, but she couldn't think of any argument against it. "All right," she told him.

Aaron quickly ducked under the hatch and went outside. Jennifer watched him as he carefully placed the rifle near the limestone block where Travis would—in two days—collapse. When he came back, the door hissing shut behind him, he slid into the pilot's seat with a grim look. Jennifer took the seat alongside him. He wouldn't look at her, and when she put a hand on his shoulder, she could feel the muscles tense underneath her fingers. "Hey," she said. "It's not your fault that he died."

"I feel like it is," Aaron answered. "Putting the rifle out there was like putting the last nail in his coffin."

"He asked you to do it, remember? And you said it just a minute ago—we didn't rescue him, so we can't."

"I know. I still don't have to like it. I miss him, Jenny. I really do. He pulled me through some rough times, and we all owe him our lives." Aaron leaned in against her briefly, hugging her, and she drew him close, comforting him as she might her brother. He stayed in her embrace for long seconds, then reluctantly drew away again.

"Let's go on," he said. "There's somebody we have to meet."

Aaron moved the craft along the Mutata paths until they came to the Gairk village once more. He maneuvered the time machine into a thick growth of ferns just past the village, opened the door, and shut down the power. "We're waiting here," he said.

"For Eckels," Peter added.

"Right." Then, to both Jennifer and Peter's unasked question: "There's no paradox involved in picking up Eckels. Travis knew that; that's why he didn't worry about Eckels. He knew that once we had the time machine, we could find Eckels. We know he got this far, so this is where we're going to meet him."

Peter grinned at that, wickedly. "Eckels is going to be one surprised dude. I'm gonna *love* this."

They didn't have long to wait. It was no more than a few hours later that Struth, on lookout at the edge of the village, gave a soft hoot of warning. Not long after, Eckels came striding into the village, sweating profusely in the afternoon heat, with both he and Peter's packs slung over his shoulders. Peter stepped out from the ferns into his path.

"Hey partner," he said. "I think you have something of mine."

Eckels gasped as if he'd seen a ghost and nearly dropped the packs. "Peter!" he exclaimed, his cheeks gone pasty and bloodless. "This is . . . ummm . . . really a surprise. I thought . . . I mean I hoped . . ."

"You thought I'd be dead by now."

"No," Eckels said quickly, glancing furtively around as if searching for the best way to run from the muscular youth in front of him. He still had the sword shoved into his belt, Peter noted, and Eckels's hand stayed very close to the hilt. "That's not it at all. I . . . I went back for you, after we had the argument. I did. I was sorry about what happened and I wanted to make sure you were all right."

The man's voice gained confidence as he elaborated on the lie. "In fact, that must be how you managed to get here first," Eckels continued. "Sure . . . we must have missed each other in the swamp, and you went on while I went back. Anyway, I'm glad we hooked up again." He gave Peter a tentative grin. "Partner."

"You're a really lousy liar, Eckels."

With Peter's words, the grin sagged and vanished. Eckels scowled, his thick eyebrows hanging above his eyes like thunderclouds. "I don't like your tone, kid. Especially when it looks like I'm holding all the cards. I have the pieces of temporal machinery, and I have the only weapon."

Peter continued to smile, which deepened Eckels's frown. He pulled the sword from his belt, brandishing it. "Get out of the way, kid, or I'll finish what I should have finished back in the restaurant."

"And what's that, Eckels?" someone said.

Eckels nearly sprained his back swiveling around to see where the new voice came from. Aaron stepped out from the ferns cradling one of the rifles from the time machine. Jennifer emerged from behind a cycad to Eckels's other side. Eckels spun, looking as if he were going to make a dash back the way he'd come, but Struth was standing on the path behind him.

Eckels dropped the sword. It clunked dully on the ground.

"Look, guys," Eckels said. "You can't blame me. I was doing what any of you would do if you thought there was only one way to stay alive."

"I don't think so," Jennifer told him. "I don't think any of us qualify as that much of a coward." She held out her hand. "The temporal machinery, Eckels. Now."

"Hey, you gotta let me keep at least one of the pieces. After all I've gone through, I think I've paid for them—"

"Shut up, Eckels," Jennifer told him, and the quick fury in her face silenced him. "Paid for? You don't know how expensive those pieces were. You have no idea at all. They've been paid for, all right, but not by you. Give us the temporal machinery, Eckels. *Now.*"

Eckels dropped the pack on the ground. Glowing shards of green metal tumbled out. Eckels's expression had gone from scowl to a pleading, almost comical half-smile. "Look, I'm sorry," he told them. "I really didn't mean any harm to any of you. Hey, if I had, I'd've killed you, Peter, right? So what are you going to do with me?" Eckels's eyes suddenly narrowed. "Where's Mundo?" he asked. "Where's Travis?"

"Mundo found a way back to his world," Jennifer told him. "And Travis . . . He . . ." She looked at Aaron, desperately. "He's waiting to be picked up," she finished.

Aaron couldn't bear to contradict the pleading in her gaze. To avoid it, he turned his attention to Eckels. "As to what we're going to do with you," he told the man, "I don't really know."

"You can't leave me here," Eckels cried. "You have the time machine. You can't leave me stranded."

"Why not?" Peter asked. "That's what you were planning to do to us. Worse, I don't think we can trust you, Eckels. I don't think we can afford to turn our backs on you without worrying about a knife from behind."

"Come on," Eckels pleaded desperately. "If you leave me here, you might as well kill me. I won't have a chance. You wouldn't do that. I know you all. Please." Eckels sagged, falling down on the path. "Please," he said again.

They all looked at each other. Struth hooted as if puzzled by this strange human interaction. "He's right," Jennifer said, voicing what they were all thinking. "You know he's right."

Aaron nodded toward Peter. A flush had risen on his neck, rising all the way to his cheeks. "Pete?"

"Leave him, and he can't hurt any of us again." His words were clipped, and short, and as sharp as daggers. His gaze never left Eckels.

"Leave him," Jennifer answered softly, "and we all have to live with knowing what we did. You think that's not going to hurt?"

Peter turned to her. "Jen, he's dangerous."

"He's human," she replied. "We can't punish him for that. How many mistakes *have you* made, Peter?"

Peter gave a shout of pure anger and spun around. No one said anything. Eckels watched him, still sprawled in the dust. Peter's shoulders lifted, dropped again, and he turned back to them.

"All right," he said. "You're right, Jen. We can't leave him. But I'll tell you this—he's made all the mistakes he's allowed. Next time, I make sure it's the last."

18

A Gift of Blood

"Where did you find the hypodermic, Jenny?"

"About here, I think."

They'd walked back to the Mutata village, pushing the time-traveling craft rather than riding in it. Even floating on its antigravity repulsors, the heavy machine was difficult to get moving, though it continued to travel easily once it was in motion. Stopping it or turning it, however, was another matter. They were all sweating profusely by the time they reached the village that evening, and without Struth's extra strength, the task would have been impossible. They'd seen three time storms during the day, but all had luckily struck well away from them. Still, Aaron made sure that the rifles were always accessible, not knowing what visitors the time storms might have left behind.

"You're not planning to push the time machine all the way back to the Nesting Grounds, are you?" Jennifer asked Aaron. She pulled a towel from the vehicle and mopped her face before sinking down gratefully into the shade of one of the white-domed buildings of the village. Eckels, breathing hard, went pacing over to the piece of floating roadway, with Peter and Struth following closely behind him.

"I just want to save every last erg of power in the thing," Aaron told her. "I don't know how much it has left, or how much we're going to need. If we don't have to use it, we won't," he answered. "I don't relish having to shove the thing over the mountains and across two days of plain. Even I'm not that stupid." Aaron grinned at her.

Jennifer tossed her towel at Aaron. Pulling it off his face, he laughed, and she chuckled with him. "You know, that's the first time I've heard you laugh in a long time," she said.

"You too."

"I think . . . Well, since we actually managed to get the time machine, I'm beginning to think we have a chance. Thanks to Travis." The mention of the man's name sobered them both and their quick hilarity vanished. Jennifer caught her breath, remembering the last time she saw Travis—the pain on his face, the sober acceptance of his death written in the lines on his face. "Come here," Jennifer said. "Just hold me, would you? I need . . . I . . ."

Aaron took two quick steps toward her. Opening his arms, he pulled her into him. They hugged, saying nothing, for long minutes. Finally, Jennifer pulled away from Aaron. Rubbing at her eyes with the back of her hands, she sniffed. "Thanks."

"Any time. I needed it, too. We haven't had time to mourn him, but I promise, once this is over, we will. We all need it."

Jennifer nodded. Standing, she looked at the empty village around them. "Now what?"

"I say we rest. In the morning, we'll take the time machine back—and we'll drop off your medicine."

SStragh could not hold back the low, disconsolate call that resonated from her nasal horn. The mournful sound emerged unbidden as she gazed at the *OColihi-ka*, the Temple of the Ancient Path. The sacred space had been violated by a time storm, part of the structure vanished into the void and replaced by something that looked neither human nor Mutata: a tangle of transparent cylinders as long and thick as her tail, meeting at all sorts of odd angles and extending twice as high as the *OColihi-ka*. The whole assembly glowed a soft, pale yellow in the twilight. SStragh could not decide whether it was an artifact built by some strange beings or something entirely natural in the world from which it came, but she did feel a satisfaction in knowing that it wasn't human. Humans appeared in most of the varied worlds of alternate time, and they were responsible for far too many oddities.

SStragh moved into the temple itself. The sacred nasal horn of the All-Ancestor was still there, and the long sacrificial knife with its keen blackstone edge lay alongside it, though one end of the case of polished blackstone in which they both rested had been sheared away by the crystalline logs.

SStragh reached in and gently removed the horn from its nest of mammal-down. She had only seen the fabled horn before; she had never touched it. As a professed disbeliever in the OColihi, Raajek had never been one to attend the rites held here; as Raajek's student, SStragh had also avoided the place. The bonelike structure, an ancient fragment of a Mutata nasal horn and reputedly that of the All-Ancestor herself, weighed almost nothing.

At the broken end of the horn, near where it flared into the high Mutata nose-crest, part of the smooth, hard exterior had decayed away, revealing the labyrinth of hollow spaces inside that made up the bone matrix. The bone was stained red-brown, the result of season upon season of rites, when Mutata blood was given to the All-Ancestor to bring Her blessings.

In that, SStragh realized, the Mutata were not so much different from some of the human societies she had seen.

The oral history passed on from OTsio to student through the ages said that this horn had been found on the site of the temple when the first Mutata had come into the valley. Finding the ancient remains had been the sign for which SStragh's long-dead ancestors had been searching, and they immediately determined to establish their settlement at this place. Raajek, like every other OTsio, had regaled SStragh with the tale, though Raajek had added, skeptically, that she believed the tale to be apocryphal.

"The All-Ancestor is a spirit, a belief," she had said. "The horn is probably that of some unfortunate Mutata who wandered here before our own ancestors and was eaten by Floria, nothing more."

SStragh had believed that also. Yet she found that actually holding the horn gave her an odd lightheaded feeling. Afraid she might drop it, she placed the unthinkably old remains back in the case. She thought about the humans' machine, which could go back in time, and she wondered what she would see if they went back to the time before the ancestors.

Are you really the All-Ancestor, she asked the horn. *Or would I just see some unfortunate Mutata, a nameless wanderer killed alone by some predator?*

"SStragh? What was that thing you were holding?"

Jhenini's voice came as a shock; engrossed in her own thoughts, SStragh had not heard the human enter the *OColihi-ka*, and the breeze was blowing her scent away. Even though she knew that Jhenini would probably miss the subtlety of her stance, SStragh raised herself into a teacher's position and changed her scent to that Raajek used to use when she spoke to SStragh as a youngling. "It is the horn of the All-Ancestor. A sacred thing for us."

"Oh? Let me see . . ." Jhenini moved past SStragh and peered into the blacks tone case. She reached down to touch the horn.

"*Yeie!*" SStragh bellowed. "No, you cannot!"

Jhenini snatched her hand back as if she were afraid that the horn might burn her. "I'm sorry," she said, then raised her chin, showing SStragh that she was sorry and submitted to her anger—the gesture looked silly with humans, but SStragh appreciated that Jhenini would at least make the show of obeisance. "I didn't know."

"Humans always think they own everything," SStragh huffed, then softened her scent and stance, letting her frill collapse once more. "I am sorry, too," she said. "I am just angry, looking at this." She pointed to the glowing tangle of beams that had broken the temple. "I am angry that there is nothing I can do to stop it."

"We *are* going to stop it."

"Do you really believe that, Jhenini? Do you *really* believe it?"

"I—" Jhenini stopped, and SStragh could smell her uncertainty. "Yes, I believe that," Jhenini said, but even though the words were forceful enough, the odor of her doubt colored the statement. "We can. We have enough of the pieces of the other time machine. Once all the portals to the other time lines are closed and the shards of the broken machine are back in Travis's world, then the Dreaming Storms will end."

"You know this is true?"

"I have to believe it is," Jhenini answered. "Because if it's not—"

Jhenini didn't need to finish that statement. SStragh had only to look around her to see what would happen. She had only to remember her nest and the eggs crushed under the storm giant's feet. If it didn't work, then the Ancient Path of the Mutata was over.

As if to lend weight to what Jhenini had said; they both heard the rumble of a distant time storm, even though the sky above them was sprinkled with stars emerging from the twilight. Jhenini shuddered at the sound, as if cold. Through the broken sides of the building, they could see the storm, striking the rim wall of the valley. In the lightning flashes, distant, strange worlds came and went.

"I don't know that I can believe you, Jhenini," SStragh told her.

SStragh looked down again at the horn of the All-Ancestor. She reached down and pulled the knife from the case. The glittering, glassy edge of the weapon was as dark as the coming night. SStragh saw Jhenini's eyes widen, and she took a step back from SStragh. "SStragh," Jhenini said, and her voice trembled. "What are you doing?"

"What I should have done long, long ago," SStragh told her. "I have never given the All-Ancestor what She has asked for. I will give it to Her now."

"SStragh!" Jhenini's voice was nearly a shout. The human looked around wildly, realizing that SStragh was between her and the exit of the temple. "After all we've been through, after all you've done, you can't. Not now. Not when we're so close."

SStragh held the blade before her snouted face, admiring the workmanship, the flaked edge that was so fine, so sharp. The wooden handle was carved with intricate symbols of the All-Ancestor, and SStragh thought she could feel the power of a thousand past ceremonies throbbing in the weapon as she held it. The knife ached to be used; it cried to open flesh.

SStragh raised it up.

"SStragh!" Jhenini cried again, cowering.

And SStragh brought the blade down. Slowly, with a long intake of breath, she opened a shallow gash on her own arm. As the blood started to flow, SStragh went to the case and let the slow, thick droplets rain down on the All-Ancestor's horn, and SStragh prayed. She prayed that she had chosen the right course with the humans, and that they would indeed help restore the Ancient Path.

"SStragh," Jhenini said, watching. "I thought . . . I'm sorry."

"You humans never understand," she told her. "You think everything is about you. It is not. I have lost more than you can imagine."

"SStragh . . ." She could feel the heat of Jhenini's body next to her. A hand stroked along SStragh's flank—a human gesture that meant nothing to the Mutata, though SStragh didn't protest. She watched her blood splash down on the horn, slowly, drop by drop. In the darkness, she couldn't see the color of the blood, but she could smell its salt scent.

"You don't really trust me, Jhenini," SStragh said. "After all this, you still don't know me or understand me."

Jhenini seemed to have no answer to that.

Blood dripped on bone.

Across the valley, the Dreaming Storm muttered, thundering curses to which the land had no answer.

19

Past Times

"Everyone ready?"

Aaron glanced over his shoulder at his companions, all—with the exception of Struth—strapped into their seats in the time machine. Peter gave Aaron a thumbs-up; Eckels just looked glum. As usual, Aaron had no idea how Struth felt, but Jennifer, in the seat alongside him with the paper-wrapped hypodermic of adrenaline in her hand, echoed his own sentiments. "The sooner we do this, the sooner we get home," she said. "I'm ready."

"That's good enough for me," Aaron said. "Remember, everyone, this one has to be quick and quiet—there are going to be Mutata around." With that, Aaron clicked the controls and the low, familiar whine began to build.

As Aaron well knew, the limitation of the time machine was that in Struth's world, it could go no further back in the past than the moment it had arrived. That meant that to drop the hypodermic at a point before Jennifer used it to save Struth's life would also mean going back to a time when the Mutata were actively hostile toward humans. Aaron had carefully set the machine to re-emerge from the time stream at night, when the

Mutata were mostly inactive, but there would be guards to deal with. The worst problem was that because of the time differential between the various time lines they'd been through, none of them were entirely certain as to when events in Struth's world had taken place. They'd have to trust to luck and fate as much as anything.

It should be right. Aaron told himself. *After all, Jennifer did find the hypodermic, and none of us remember hearing the Mutata talk about a time machine showing up in the middle of the night. That means we're going to be successful, doesn't it?*

Unfortunately, the inner voice wasn't very persuasive. Another, more cynical one kept intruding. *You of all people know that history can be changed. Presto, there's a little change and BOOM! everything's different. Forever.*

Aaron knew the cynical voice was right. They'd seen far too many strange historical twists to believe that history was something immutable, unchangeable. History handed out no guarantees, ever.

Solemn-faced, he watched the world beyond the windows fade into the gray-black nothingness of between-time as the temporal machinery wailed, as the nausea of time travel sent his stomach to doing push-ups and the chill of the void dotted his arm with goosebumps. Aaron leaned back, waiting to be deposited sometime two years before.

Something seemed to slam into the side of the time machine. As Aaron, startled, yelped and Struth hooted, the time machine canted over sideways. Aaron lunged for the controls. An ethereal, unseen fist pounded the other side of the craft, sending them all back the other way. Eckels cursed as he was shoved from one side to another of his seat. "Aaron!" Jennifer cried. "What's going on?"

"I don't know," Aaron answered, fighting the controls shivering and jerking under his hands.

"This hasn't ever happened before." A glob of fiery-red liquid smeared itself across the windshield, throwing off liquid sparks. Through the mist, they caught glimpses of a smeared tapestry of worlds: swamps; mountains; the surging gray waves on some ocean; bright-colored geometric buildings; herds of six-legged, coarse-maned beasts, their breaths a fog in the air . . .

"That's a time storm!" Peter called out from behind Aaron. "They're tearing up and down the whole time stream."

Aaron didn't have the breath to answer. The controls had a life of their own—keeping the bouncing craft steady was like trying to hold a kite in a tornado. He heard Struth rebound off a bulwark with a thud and a shrill bellow; in the seat alongside him, Jennifer was tossed side to side, her hair flying as she gripped the edges of her seat with fingers gone white with strain. Aaron's own fingers were just as pale on the stick, hanging on as if he were going to tear it loose from the panel. The temporal machinery screamed in mechanical agony—readout dials on the control panel had gone red and somewhere an alarm shrilled.

"Warning," the androgynous voice of the on-board computer called, eerily calm in the tumult. "Approaching tolerance limits. Shut down."

"I can't, you idiot!" Aaron yelled back at the computer. "I'd love to, but I can't."

"Shut it down, you fool!" Eckels screamed. "Listen to the computer—you'll kill us."

"No!"

"Tolerance limit exceeded," the voice answered, unshaken. "Automatic shutdown sequence engaged."

"No!" Aaron shouted. The time machine was bouncing as if running over a gravel road. His voice shivered with the motion. "You can't do that."

"Shutting down," the implacable voice told them, and the whine of the temporal mechanism began to cycle down through the octaves. With it, the bucking of the craft began to subside and the time storm within the void faded back to the normal emptiness. The cold and nausea subsided, and the blackness on the windowshield began to lift.

An aching quiet settled around them.

"It could be worse," Aaron said. "At least we came through during night time."

Jennifer had rushed back to Struth, who was grunting and complaining in her own language. "What happened?" Jennifer asked Aaron.

"I think Peter had it right," Aaron said. "The whole fabric of time is ripping open. Remember the bumps when we went back a few days to place Travis's rifle?—this was a lot bigger jump, and a whole lot rougher. I don't know if we could make much of a longer jump right now without the storms tearing the machine apart." Aaron sat back in his chair. Every muscle of his body ached, and the ringing in his ears was louder than the temporal mechanism's wail had been. His fingertips trembled from the residual fatigue of holding the control stick.

"The computer shut us down," Peter said. "So when *are* we?"

"Good point," Aaron said. "I don't know. Computer— date check."

"2201, May 15, 01:05," the voice answered.

"Right," Peter said sarcastically. "2201—what, of the Jurassic? I think your friend needs some recalibration, Aaron. The vibrations shook it all up."

"No, it's confused because it's from another time line. We're about a year and a half back—not as far as we wanted to be." Aaron muttered a soft curse. "I have no idea if this is far enough, or where we—our earlier selves, anyway—are at this point."

"Then we just have to trust that we're okay," Jennifer told him. She was still with Struth, checking the Mutata, but Aaron could tell from her face that the dinosaur seemed to be unhurt except for assorted bruises. "We stick with the plan we have."

"Jenny, that could be tragic if we've set down at the wrong time."

"I don't see any choice," she told him.

"She's right," Peter echoed.

"Let's go back." Eckels spoke, and when they looked at him, the man spread his hands wide, palms upward. "Hey, you're all spouting off your opinions. That's mine. We got to the time machine, and that's what you were all after, right? I don't see why you have to go back and do all this, not when it's exposing us to more risk."

Aaron spun in the pilot's chair and jabbed an angry finger at Eckels. He kept his voice low, but the intensity surprised even him. He could see Eckels flinch and turn away, unable to hold his gaze. "Why? Let me tell you. Because we've already damaged history enough. Because every time we make a change in the past, we foul up the future. You remember that, don't you, Eckels? You remember a certain butterfly and the trouble it caused? You remember what happened afterward?"

Eckels wouldn't look at him. Aaron could see jaw muscles jumping in the man's thin face as he stared at the floor. "Yeah. You do. That's why we do it this way— because that's the way it happened. You understand? Eckels? Eckels, you hear me?"

Eckels tilted his face up, his eyes narrowing as he glanced at Aaron. "You *have* changed, haven't you, kid?"

"I guess so."

Eckels nodded. "Okay. I understand."

"Good. Then we're all on the same page here?"

Another nod. "Yeah."

Aaron took a deep breath, forcing the anger out of himself. *He's as scared as the rest of you. He can't help it the way he reacts: he can't help that it isn't the way you'd respond or the way you'd want him to be.* "I want to make one small change," Aaron said. "I think I should go with Jenny to place the hypo."

Jennifer shook her head. "No. We talked about this. I'm the only one who knows where the hypo has to go. You're the only one who can handle the time machine—you have to stay here. I'll go with Pete."

"What's the matter, Aaron?" Peter said, and even though he kept his tone light, Aaron could sense the edge behind it. "Don't trust me?"

There was nothing Aaron could say to that, not without offending Peter. He knew what had prompted him to try to change the plans at the last minute: Travis. He kept seeing the dying man in his mind, and hearing the aching silence after his gun had stopped firing.

You never really understood that this wasn't some strange fictional adventure. You never really understood that there are no rules, and there is no unwritten law that says that you or Jenny or Pete can't die. You can. You might. And you're scared. You're scared that something will happen and you won't be there, and you're going to find that you've lost another friend.

"All right," he said. "Just hurry back."

The breeze was cool—Jennifer blamed that for the goosebumps that prickled her forearms as she and Peter left the time machine. It took a few seconds for her eyes to adjust to the dimness: the moon was a mottled half-circle playing hide and seek with low silver clouds. In the shifting illumination, she could see the clearing where the chunk of white plastic roadway floated, a hundred yards away.

"This isn't what we were supposed to see," Peter whispered.

"I know. We must be somewhere just before we return from Nipponjin. The Mutata brought the roadway back to the village already, but we haven't come back through—right now we're somewhere in Mexico, Egypt, or Rome."

The original plan would have them arrive several months earlier, when this clearing would have been empty. That would have made the task easy—the only danger would have been a chance encounter. They'd not expected this.

"There's a Mutata standing on the other side of the clearing," Peter told her. "Lean a little to your left and you'll see him through the cycads."

Jennifer did as he instructed. The Mutata, in armor and with a spear clutched in his right hand, was very near the roadway. From the dinosaur's unnatural stillness, Jennifer suspected that he was asleep. "That's Lhath," she told Peter, "but I don't think he's awake."

"The wind's blowing away from him, too," Peter said, holding up a wet index finger. "Looks like luck's running with us. C'mon . . ."

Moving as silently as possible, the two moved through the ferns and cycads toward Lhath and the roadway. As they were about to enter the clearing itself, Peter suddenly crouched down and put a finger to his lips. Jennifer saw the reason for his caution immediately: one of the Komodo dragon-like guard lizards was snuffling in their direction, its head cocked quizzically as it listened.

Peter leaned over and whispered into Jennifer's ear. "I'll take care of the lizard; you drop the hypo before Lhath wakes up. And use the rifle if you have to." Peter tapped the weapon strapped across Jennifer's back.

Jennifer didn't answer, but she already knew that she wasn't going to use the rifle. *I can't*, she wanted to tell him, *because I already know I didn't. I've seen Lhath in the future, and I know he's alive.*

Peter slid quickly to her right. As he moved, leaves rustled, and the guard lizard snorted, its bright, reptilian eyes tracking. It waddled quickly across the clearing, its nostrils flaring and growling deep in its throat. Peter moved away from the clearing, at an angle back toward the time machine. The guard lizard took the bait, plunging into the thickest of ferns with a doglike bark as it pursued Peter. Lhath stirred. One eye half opened lazily, but when nothing more happened, the eye closed again. His color and stance never changed, the frill stayed collapsed and close to his spine.

Jennifer stood and ran, stooped, across the clearing. She passed close to Lhath. As she dropped the hypodermic in its cellophane wrapping near the base of the cycad where her past self would one day find it, there was a percussive cough from near the time machine, followed by a loud yelp.

Jennifer turned to run back to Peter and the others.

She stopped. Lhath, his eyes all too alert and open, was staring down at her. He'd snuck up behind her, unheard.

"Human," he hissed. "So one of you has come back, at least. And without Struth to help you . . ."

Lhath whipped the spear point down. "Lhath," Jennifer said. "I have a Far-Killer." Backing away from the Mutata, she pulled the rifle from her back. "You've seen what it can do. Stay back or I'll use it." She pointed the rifle at Lhath. The grip was warm in her hand, the trigger curled invitingly around her finger.

"I'm not afraid of your dishonorable death," Lhath scoffed. "But *you're* afraid. I can smell it." Lhath snorted. She took a slow step forward. Jennifer backed up, but found she could go no further—the roadway was directly behind her. Lhath drew back his right arm, and the spear tip glistened in the moonlight. "I Give your soul to the All-Ancestor, human," he said.

Jennifer couldn't pull the trigger, even though the barrel pointed directly at Lhath's chest. She couldn't, even though she could see the cold, flat stare of the Mutata and she knew that nothing, nothing would hold him back.

She couldn't.

With a cry, she reversed the weapon, holding it by the barrel like a baseball bat.

She swung.

Jennifer had always been good with sports. She'd played hardball on the mixed boy-girl teams in Little League, but had given up the game for soccer and tennis in high school. She'd never taken a better cut at an opposing pitcher's fastball than what she did now. Even as Lhath started to thrust his spear at her, she stepped into his attack. The heavy wooden stock of the rifle slammed into the side of the Mutata's head with a sound like a club hitting a full paint can. She felt the impact all the way through her shoulder to her back, and the stock of the rifle went off into the night doing cartwheels.

Lhath howled. He dropped the club and both hands went up to his face. Blood streamed through his clawed fingers. His head canted, and one eye glared down at Jennifer as if the Mutata could crush her with the intensity of his anger.

And he fell over.

Lhath's fall seemed thunderous to Jennifer. She was amazed that there was no outcry from the village. The sound echoed in her head for long seconds. Then, with a trembling hand, she reached out and pressed two fingers against the Mutata's neck. The pulse was strong and steady, pushing back against the pressure of her fingers. Jennifer let loose a grateful sigh—she'd been afraid that she'd killed him anyway. Standing up, she retrieved the shattered stock of the rifle from where it had fallen; as she did so, she noticed that the barrel of the rifle she was still gripping in her right hand was bent from the force of the impact.

"Guess I should have stuck with baseball," she marveled, looking from the bent barrel to the fractured piece of wood. "I think I definitely hit that one out of the park."

Eighteen days: that was how long it took them to push the time machine to the narrow limestone canyon where Aaron had found the samurai sword and the trap that had helped them escape the Gairk.

Aaron allowed them to power up the time machine only for those places where they couldn't possibly push it themselves. The computer's voice told him that the power was dangerously low, and he knew that there was still at least one time jump to make. During that time,

Aaron lost count of the number of time storms that occurred—it seemed a rare day that four or five of the storms didn't roll through within sight.

When they finally arrived at the canyon, when they'd arranged the rocks and rigged the cable that would send them raining down into the canyon a year and a half from their current "now," Aaron took the samurai sword from the time machine and shoved the blade into the ground alongside the end of the cable. He looped the wire around the blade. Jennifer handed him a piece of paper pulled from one of the manuals in the time machine; still crouching alongside it, Aaron smoothed the paper on his knee and wrote two words: PULL ME!

He stuffed the paper into the loop of cord.

"That should do it," he said, glancing up at her. She saw a silhouette against the sun; he had to squint to see her. Peter, Eckels, and Struth also watched, arrayed around him. "At least it's set up as best as I can remember it."

Jennifer's hand stroked his shoulder. She looked at the canyon, shaking her head. "Strange to think that several months from now, we're going to be running from there with the Gairk right on our heels. I thought for sure we were dead. Poor Travis, he could barely walk . . ."

Aaron rose, hugging her fiercely for a moment. Then he inhaled deeply, taking in the salt tang of the air. "I think we've completed our circle here," he said.

"Then what now?" Peter asked. They were all looking at him, but it was Eckels who was staring at him most intently, with a strange eagerness that caused Aaron's stomach to turn sour. He wondered what the man was thinking, what he was planning.

"We complete the whole circle," he told Peter. "The circle through *all* the worlds."

20

A Deadly Meeting

The eighteen days it had taken them to reach the area of the rockfall seemed insignificant when compared to the trek back, which was largely upslope. It was another twenty-four days until they stood once again within the steep green walls of the Mutata valley. Aaron watched the fuel gauge of the craft with worried eyes, begrudging every minute that they had to power up the engines to glide up a steep hill.

Without the antigrav repulsors, the task would have been impossible; no wheeled vehicle could have made it over such broken terrain, or through such an insane array of obstacles as the time storms had strewn across the landscape. They peppered the face of the world, an acne of destruction. Aaron lost count of the unusual remnants they saw—things too unusual to be anything human, their functions unknown and unguessed.

From their appearances, the time storms were reaching ever deeper into the twisted branches of time, further and further away from the main trunk of reality.

All too soon, Aaron suspected, all the barriers would all be gone, and the various time lines would collapse into one chaotic jumble. When that happened, any hope of repairing Eckels's mistake would be gone.

It isn't fair that this is all on our shoulders, Aaron thought as he looked out upon the Mutata valley once again, awash in patches of wandering sunlight as white cumulus clouds drifted along the sear of sky. *We didn't ask for this responsibility: it was just thrust on us.*

He wasn't sure who he was complaining to. In the end, it didn't matter. They had the burden, and it wasn't going to go away.

It didn't matter whether that was fair or not.

"Here's what we're going to do," Aaron told them as they rested at the top of the pass into the valley. "We can't go back down into the valley now, since we're a year or so back of our last arrival, and the Gairk and Mutata are all there. They'd kill us if they saw us."

"We have guns now," Eckels pointed out. "Let them try."

"I think we've all had enough killing for the time being," Peter answered before Aaron could reply. Jennifer nodded; Struth, who seemed to have had enough of the human chatter, was standing away from them, looking down into her valley. Aaron wondered what the dinosaur was thinking—Struth, of all of them, had suffered through the most changes. He, Peter and Jennifer, or even Eckels, might be lonely and might feel cut off from their lives, but they at least had the comfort of each other, and nearly all the worlds in which they'd been thrown had held people like themselves. Struth had none of that comfort.

"I agree with Peter," Aaron said. "That's why I want to move us UpTime again, back to our 'present' here. The Mutata and Gairk will still be in the Nesting Grounds."

"Except for those Gairk that are still left," Peter added. "You know, the three that got by Travis."

Aaron nodded. "We'll just have to take our chances with them. We'll deal with them if they become an issue."

"What about the problems we had on the last time trip?" Jennifer asked.

"To do what I'm planning, we're going to need at least a couple more time changes," Aaron said. "Again, we're going to have to cope with it, and we might as well start now. It's only going to get worse."

Motioning to the others, he ducked into the time machine, pulling himself into the operator's seat. "Controls out," he said, and the machine extruded the control panel from the wall in front of him. He quickly set the panel for the short jump forward. As the others buckled themselves into their seats and Struth—with Jennifer's help—wedged herself between Eckels's seat and the wall, Aaron's finger paused over the button alongside the trackball.

"Ready?"

Jennifer smiled at him; Peter gave him a thumbsup.

Aaron clicked the button.

The machine whined, the lights dimmed, and the coldness gripped their bones. The trip was rough, the craft tossing back and forth, and Aaron fought for control, not knowing what would happen if he didn't. The joints of the craft groaned with stress, but it was over in a few minutes, and as they came back to their own time, the buffeting slowly ended. When the frost on the windows faded, they looked out and saw the walls of the pass, newly scoured and scarred by the tidal wave that had nearly killed them when they last had been here. Somewhere in the green land below and ahead of them, Aaron knew, Travis was dying, and they were digging frantically to get the time machine out of the cave sealed by the Mutata.

He opened the door of the time machine and turned off the power again. He didn't look at the fuel gauge or ask the computer how much was left—he didn't want to know.

"Okay," he told his companions. "It's time to get out and push again."

In two days, they were back at the Mutata village. Once they were through the pass and into the valley, Aaron had them move off the track between the villages so that they wouldn't have to contend with meeting their past selves. Everything Travis had told him about time indicated that the structure of time itself would make that an impossible task, but he didn't care to take the chance—they knew all too well the consequences of having a time machine meet itself in the past.

A time storm passed the first day of their journey, and the images they saw with it were ones they had seen the day they'd freed the time machine.

It was late the next day when they arrived in the deserted Mutata village. "I'll be glad to get this over with," Aaron said. He was sweating as he pushed the time machine alongside Peter. His leg muscles burned from the effort, his calf muscles tight and hard. The clean, whitewashed domes of the village moved slowly past them. Eckels, Jennifer, and Struth lagged behind, resting from their last shift of pushing. "As soon as we reach the piece of path, we'll get out the piece of temporal . . ."

He paused, noticing that Peter was no longer pushing the time machine, but had instead moved a little away from the craft to stare ahead of them. "What's up?" Aaron asked, straightening and letting go of the time machine, which moved on a few feet and then drifted to a halt.

"The roadway," Peter answered. "It's not there."

"It's *gotta* be," Aaron said, feeling a cold fear settle in the pit of his stomach. "We didn't do anything with it." Aaron ran to where Peter stood, and the coldness spread through the rest of his body, running frigid fingers down his spine. Peter was right—where the fragment of roadway had once floated, there was nothing but empty ground. Jennifer, Eckels, and Struth came running forward, stopping as they too noticed the missing roadway.

"Where could it have gone?" Jennifer cried. "We would have been here yesterday, and the path was here then . . ."

She stopped as a blast from a Mutata nasal horn interrupted her, followed by a rush of the dinosaur's language.

From between two of the nearby buildings, Frraghi stepped out, flanked by a pair of Gairk. He began to speak, his harsh gaze on Struth.

"SStragh!" Frraghi said. "I am disappointed in you."

"Frraghi . . . I thought I would never see you again."

"I pursued you when I saw you running from the Nesting Ground. The Gairk soon left me behind, but I kept following, because . . . because something pulled me on. I had hoped . . ."

Frraghi's scent changed, going strongly sour as his colors faded and his stance widened. "I had hoped that when I saw you last, you were pursuing Jhenini to bring her back for the Giving. I hoped that, but here . . ." Frraghi thumped himself on his muscular chest, where the wounds from the Storm-Beast were just beginning to heal. "In here, the All-Ancestor told me the truth. She told me that you had instead helped the human to escape. How could you do that, SStragh? How could you betray the Mutata that way? How could you do it to Raajek? Is this the way you pay back the death of our egglings? Is this how you repay me for our mating and our vows to each other?"

Frraghi's accusations tore great holes in SStragh's soul, each one a spear thrust to her heart. She nearly staggered from the psychic force of the blows.

"Our egglings are dead, Frraghi," SStragh answered, but she could not force her head down to lend the proper strength to the words. "They are dead like the OColihi, like our entire world—and the only chance I see to avoid that fate is to let the humans try their magic."

"The humans *destroyed* this world," Frraghi raged, stamping his foot so that the ground trembled. SStragh could smell the hostility of the Gairk with him; they were trembling on the edge of attack. "Their magic is the cause of all of this. They are the murderers of our *children*, SStragh. And yet you disobey the OColi when she asked you to Give them to the All-Ancestor. I do not understand this, SStragh." His voice had gone mocking. "Make me understand, mate SStragh. Speak some words that make sense of this madness. I would very much like to hear them."

"I have no words for you, Frraghi," SStragh answered sadly, and let a wisp of cinnamon color her scent as an accent. "There are none. You need faith, and you need trust, and no words of mine could give you that gift. I am sorry for that, Frraghi, because I admire you so much. You are a *friend*."

SStragh used the human word, since there was no word like it in the Mutata language. She marveled at the crystalline sound of the word, at the emotions it evoked inside her.

"What *is fah-rend?*" Frraghi hissed. "Another human thing?"

"*Geedo*," SStragh answered. "Yes. And it is a good thing to be, Frraghi. I wish you could understand that."

"I understand *nothing*." The last word was a roar. "Nothing at all. I cannot understand a Mutata who would betray all her kind."

"I am not betraying them," SStragh said softly, hopelessly. "I am saving them."

"You speak madness again," Frraghi raged back. "This is hopeless." He shifted his spear, right hand to left and back again, and the Gairk bellowed a wordless challenge. With that, SStragh heard movement behind her, and from the corners of the eyes, she saw the two male younglings move on either side of her.

"SStragh!" Jhenini called to her. "Tell Frraghi that Aaron and Peter will kill them if they move. Please—I don't want any more killing."

Frraghi hissed at her, his head craning sidewise as he glared. "I can hear you well enough, Jhenini," he said. "And you've learned nothing about Mutata or Gairk if you believe that we are afraid of dying. I have experienced too much of it to fear it."

The two Gairk, silent during this exchange, had evidently heard enough. One of them gave a disgusted snort, and without further warning, they raised their *broaii* and charged. Twin blasts from the Far-Killers answered, deafening SStragh. With a metallic sound unlike anything SStragh had ever heard before, jagged holes were punched in the chest armor plates of the Gairk. They staggered backward, and the Far-Killers roared once more as blood fountained, spilling bright red carnage. Accompanied by the nostril-twitching scent of the human weapons, the Gairk fell, screaming in agony and despair.

SStragh felt them die. She felt Amath, the God of Death, appear to steal their souls. The sound of the

Far-Killers rang in her ears like the death-bells of the Giving Hall.

Frraghi was standing in shock. The bodies of the Gairk lay on either side of him, bloodied and broken, their limbs twisted in their final death agonies, their mouths open in soundless, deafening cries. SStragh saw Frraghi's spear tremble in his hand. Aaron spoke in the singsong human language, and Jhenini translated: "We don't wish to kill you, Frraghi. If you drop the spear and move away, nothing will happen."

"Nothing?" Frraghi spat, and his free hand waved at the fallen Gairk alongside him. "Is this what humans call nothing?"

"We were only defending ourselves," Jhenini answered, but SStragh saw that her stance was wrong, far too aggressive for the words she spoke. Frraghi noticed it also, for his colors deepened again, and he lowered his head and widened his own stance in response.

"And defending ourselves is all *we* were doing," Frraghi answered. "We are defending our ways and our land. From you."

"Frraghi," SStragh began, but Frraghi thumped the butt of his spear on the ground to stop her words.

"*Yeie*," he growled. "I am finished with listening. SStragh, my mate, OTsioiue of Raajek, listen to me. When I left, Raajek gave me a message. 'If you find SStragh,' she said, 'tell her that I am sorry that I failed her as OTsio. I am sorry that my false OChihi became a part of her. I am sorry that I must order her Given, but for the good of Mutata, I must. You will see to that, Frraghi.' I intend to follow those orders, SStragh. *I*, at least, obey my OColi."

Frraghi took a step forward, his spear snapping down.

"Frraghi," SStragh said pleadingly. "I beg of you, as a mate."

"We are no longer mates." Another step. "Our egglings are dead." Step. "As one of us must be from this moment on." Step, and now Frraghi was close enough to thrust the spear point into SStragh's chest. She lifted her head in submission, not willing to fight Frraghi or run from him. *I place myself in the All-Ancestor's hands . . .*

The Far-Killer in Aaron's hand spat flame, and Frraghi grunted with the impact of the bullet. He took an involuntary step backward, his spear drooping. SStragh cried out, and then Peter's Far-Killer replied. Frraghi dropped to his knees, his chest a red ruin, the spear shattered in his left hand. His mouth gaped, drooling foamy blood.

"It hurts," he said, as if in surprise. "So this is what death feels like. Amath . . ." Frraghi's head dropped nearly to the ground, and SStragh started to run forward. But then Frraghi's head came back up, and for a moment his eyes focused, bright and clear of the pain. "I will watch our egglings for us, SStragh," he told her. "I will hold them safe until you come to meet us."

Frraghi's eyes closed. He collapsed.

SStragh let out a long, terrifying cry of grief.

Struth would not leave until they had placed Fergie in the Giving Hall. Eckels, who had never seen the inside of the Hall, let out a long whistle at the sight: the white walls studded with lacey clusters of brilliant crystals so that they seemed to walk in a glittering wonderland; rows of tiers all around the perimeter of the tall structure; the crater at the center in which the whitened bones of long-dead Mutata lay; the circular platform rising from the center of the bones, linked to the tiers by narrow earthen ramps. They carried Fergie's body up a ramp to the top of the platform, watching as the *jhiehai*—proto-birds whose black, scraggly feathers reminded them of a garish imitation of a funeral director's formal clothes—gathered around the central hole in the roof of the hall, their ugly, bald heads set on long necks craning down at the corpse.

Dusty sunlight lanced down from the central hole, sparking reflections from the crystals and illuminating Fergie's body as if in a spotlight. None of them spoke above a whisper—to speak louder would have breached the inviolate aura of the Hall, like that of a church.

In Fergie's hands, Struth placed the horn of the All-Ancestor, her own blood now brown on the ancient patina. "If we fail, if Mutata never come back here," she said to Jenny and the others, "I want him to care for the horn and keep it safe."

Awkwardly, each of them helped Struth through the rites of Giving. Jennifer and Peter, who had witnessed such a rite once before, tried as best they could to imitate the low, mournful chant of the Mutata as Struth brought the knife and the bowl to the platform—their voices seemed high and thin compared to the remembered powerful drone of the massed dinosaurs. Struth opened a cut on her arm, letting the dark liquid drain into the bowl before pouring it over Fergie's corpse.

As she stepped back, the *jhiehai* fluttered down like a dark cloud to feed, shrieking as they set clawed feet into Fergie's flesh, bent their hooked beaks, and began to tear at the corpse.

Struth watched, impassive, to their human eyes not seeming to show much emotion at all. Finally, she turned back to them, her reptilian eyes dry as always.

"I am ready now," she said. "There is nothing here. Nothing at all."

21

Thunder Redux

Now that it came to it, Aaron found that he had cold feet. *One way or the other, this is the last time we'll ever see this world. We saw so little of it, and a place this beautiful doesn't deserve the bad memories it has for us. Too bad we couldn't have come here under other circumstances.*

"*Regrets are the memories of those who never try.*" Those were his grandfather Carl's words, and remembering them brought back a wave of sadness for his death. "That's one thing I *do* regret, Gran'pa," he whispered. "I wish you and Mom and Dad had never gotten involved in this."

"What?" Jennifer asked.

"Nothing." Aaron straightened. He looked at the others, who were gathered around him and the floating stone, which they'd found in the building Struth called the *OColihi-ka*. Just behind them, the time machine hovered. "I guess we're ready, huh?"

"To get out of this place? Absolutely," Peter said eagerly.

"I'm not sure where we're going is going to be much better."

"I'll take my chances. What's your game plan, buddy?"

Aaron outlined what would happen in the next few minutes, going over it carefully a few times since there would be no chance to repeat. "Got it?" he asked. "Pete, you have the crucial part."

"No problem," Pete said. "It looks like the gateway's sure we're going through, too." He nodded upward at the sky, where the fast, dark clouds of a time storm were gathering. "Unless you like lightning, I'd suggest everyone take cover."

It took a few minutes for everyone except Peter to pile into the time machine. When they were all settled into their seats, Aaron waved to Peter through the windshield. Peter waved back; he crouched and hefted a twisted coil of glowing green metal on the ground beside him. As the clouds masked the sun and the wind sent dust devils whirling around the clearing, Peter ducked underneath the slab of roadway, disappearing from Aaron's sight. A sudden flowering of sparks rippled around the edge of the roadway, and then they saw Peter's arm reappear and beckon to them. "He's got the portal open. Here we go," Aaron said.

He nudged the time machine forward as an impressive display of lightning crackled above them, the sky suddenly so dark that the craft's automatic headlights flickered on, startling Aaron and illuminating the roadway in a bath of warm, yellow light. As the nose of the time machine broke the plane of the roadway, the cold hit them. "Somebody shut the refrigerator," Jennifer muttered. "It feels colder than last time."

Aaron didn't answer, doing his best to ignore the way his stomach was doing somersaults. Frigid blue fire crawled across the glass of the front windows.

Another flurry of sparks erupted in the wake of the aquamarine flame: when the sparks cleared, the mossy green of the Mutata world was replaced by the full lushness of the true jungle—a jungle among whose tangled vines a broken and shattered roadway floated.

Travis's world. Eckels's world.

Eckels, from behind Aaron, gave a guttural cry of recognition.

Aaron spent no time contemplating the scenery. He halted the time machine and opened the hatch, staring back at the broken piece of roadway from which they'd come. The last of the sparks from their passage was fading, guttering on the ground.

"C'mon, Peter," he whispered, "C'mon." There was no answer to his plea. The roadway remained stubbornly empty. "C'mon . . ."Aaron said, a little louder, a little more desperately.

"Aaron?" Jennifer asked. She'd unbuckled and moved silently alongside him. Her arm went around his waist. "Pete hasn't come through yet?"

Aaron shook his head. "No. I was worried about the time differential from the beginning. If it turns out that seconds here are hours there . . ."

"He'll be here in hours, then. But he'll be here."

"I know," Aaron said, but the doubts wouldn't go away as the minutes passed. Aaron ran through what seemed to be a hundred scenarios, each successively more awful. *He could have been hit by one of the lightning strikes of the time storm. Something like Mundo's storm giant might have shown up, or worse, Peter could have been standing right on the boundary between different worlds . . .*

An hour later, Aaron could wait no longer. He unlocked two rifles from the case, handed one to Jennifer and shouldered the other. "You and Struth keep an eye on Eckels. I'm going back to see what happened."

Jennifer looked at the rifle like it was a rattlesnake. "Aaron, stop thinking with your machismo instead of your head. We're *not* splitting up, not now. If you go, we *all* go . . ."

A rumble of thunder and a fury of sparks interrupted her argument. A redheaded youth tumbled out in a Niagara of green and blue flares and the roadway hissed as blue lightning outlined the gateway. Then the light display fizzled to nothingness, and Peter sat up in the middle of the mud puddle in which he'd landed. The glowing green coil dangled from his hand. Aaron helped him up, hugging his friend once he was standing again. "Peter, you had us all worried."

"I was worried, too. Man, I played that a little too close. I pulled out the piece, then tripped and almost didn't make it through. Been here long?"

"Long enough. More than an hour."

Peter brushed uselessly at the dirt and mud on his clothing. "We're going to have one heck of a dry cleaning bill when we get back." He pivoted in a slow circle, taking in the world and stopping when he saw the gigantic carcass of the Tyrannosaurus rex a hundred yards away, now picked nearly clean of flesh by scavenger dinosaurs. "Whooah, that thing must've stood three stories high." Peter shuddered. "This place is spookier than you described. The air could make you drunk, though."

He was right. Aaron had forgotten how oxygen-rich the atmosphere was here, fragrant with the perfume of gigantic blooms and the earthier scent of rich, dark loam. The jungle, as always, reverberated with the cries of its inhabitants. The fronds of the nearest ferns quivered as a small group of hypsilophodons—small and extraordinarily quick plant-eaters with horny beaks and tiny, five-fingered hands—slid away, alarmed by their presence.

Butterflies performed their jittery, colorful ballet above the disturbed leaves, reminding Aaron of how this had all begun, with Eckels's inadvertent crushing of one of those insects.

"It's going to get spookier," Aaron said, clapping his friend on the shoulder again. "Come on, we have an appointment to keep."

"Y'know, it's about time you finally explain to us exactly what it is you have planned," Peter said chidingly as they entered the time machine. "Unless you just don't trust us."

The trouble is, I'm not really sure about this plan. Aaron wanted to say. Jennifer, he trusted implicitly, and he wanted to feel the same about Peter. Eckels, Aaron didn't trust at all, and Struth . . . Well, Struth had her own strange agenda. Aaron still wasn't entirely sure why she had stayed with them. But Peter was right.

"Fine," Aaron said. "This is it, in a nutshell. First, we needed to bring all the pieces of temporal machinery back into this world—they were what were powering the gateways to the various worlds, and they opened the first rips in the fabric of space-time. By bringing all or at least most of the wreckage of the machine back here, we've closed off the main gateways to the other worlds. That's important—it's the first step to cleaning up this mess."

Aaron took a breath. This was where his plan became vague; this was where he was depending as much on luck and intuition as logic. And this, finally, was where he and Travis had disagreed. *And Travis died to give you the chance to try it, anyway. You'd better be right. . .*

Aaron took a breath. He reached out and squeezed Jennifer's hand, smiling at her. "This is the way I think of it," he continued. "We know that time has a one-way flow, at least to us. What happened when Eckels left the path affected everything that happened UpTime from that point, but it *didn't* affect the past. What we need to do is go back into that past, into the minutes just before it happened, and we have to prevent the whole thing from happening."

"And just how do we do that, oh great Time Master?" Eckels said with his usual scowl. "After all, you've done so well so far."

"And it was your fault this whole thing happened in the first place," Peter retorted. Aaron raised his hands, trying to calm things down before it evolved into another argument.

"Listen to me," he said. "There is a way to do this."

"Yeah?" Eckels snarled. "How?"

"The whole problem started when Travis's time safari, with you along, came back to kill that T-rex over there, right?" Aaron pointed at the tented bones hung with pink tatters of flesh that was all that remained of the great carnivore.

"Right."

Aaron smiled grimly. He leaned forward so that each of them heard his next words clearly. "Tell me this, Eckels," he said. "What would have happened if you had arrived and found your T-rex already dead?"

"Initiate," Aaron told the computer, and the terrible cold and disorientation rushed in to take them, while the temporal engine began its banshee wail.

Aaron had thought that the last time jump had been as bad as it could get. Wrong. This one was far, far worse. He thought that some angry temporal god had picked up the craft and was shaking it in its fists. Struth blatted in fear as she was battered against the walls of the time machine; Eckels cursed monotonously and loudly. "Aaron, we're breaking up!" Jennifer shouted at him.

He had no breath to answer. He desperately tried to hold the controls, watching the digital calendar on the control panel that indicated their temporal position. *Just a few more seconds . . .*

Something tore loose behind him with a metallic screech. As Aaron turned to look, he was struck on the side of the head with a steel brace. "Aaron!" Jennifer shouted again. She sounded very far away. He thought he saw her through the end of a black tunnel, her face framed in blond hair that whipped back and forth as if in a wind.

"Jenny?" he tried to say, but his mouth wouldn't form the words, and when he tried to reach for her, he realized that he couldn't feel his arms, either.

The tunnel closed around her face. Her lips were moving, but he couldn't hear her.

Then the end of the dark, dark tunnel collapsed in on him.

Eckels awoke with a groan. He took a quick inventory. The big stupid lizard was curled in the corner of the time machine, its eyes open but glassy and stunned looking. Eckels wasn't entirely sure that Aaron was even alive—it looked like one of the bracing rods for the ceiling had sheared off and hit him—there was a big smear of blood along the side of the kid's face, and he wasn't moving. Jennifer was moaning in her seat, and Peter was out cold next to Eckels, though he could see the chest moving up and down with a strong breath.

If there was ever a moment for him to make a break, this was definitely it.

Quickly, Eckels unlatched his seat harness. Stepping over the trash that had spilled from the wall cabinets onto the floor, he went to the rifle locker, pulling down one of the guns. He checked it—it was loaded. Peter stirred, and Eckels decided that he couldn't waste any more time.

Shouldering the rifle, he darted forward and slapped the hatch contact. It hissed and yawned open, exposing a green world beyond and the curving white expanse of the path, unbroken in this time just before the time safari arrived.

Eckels grinned—it would be easier to move on the path than through the jungle.

He stepped out of the time machine and turned left.

Peter decided that he'd had enough of having his head used for a punching bag. He had the great-grandmother of all headaches, and the entire right side of his body felt like it was one large bruise.

"Peter!"

Normally, he rather enjoyed the sound of Jennifer's voice, but the sound made the headache pound against his temples. Peter groaned and closed his eyes. "Keep it down below a bellow, Jen," he said. "I'm feeling a little on the tender side."

"Peter, Aaron's hurt," she said, and that brought him back. The interior of the time machine suddenly swam into focus around him. Struth was moving painfully near him, and through the open hatch, he was looking out at the same jungle they'd just left. Jennifer was leaning over Aaron, who looked like someone had hit him on the side of the head with a water balloon filled with red paint.

"Oh, God," Peter said. "Jen—"

"Just get me the med kit," she said. "Now!"

Peter scrambled for the kit, pulling it off the wall clips with brute strength. "Here," he told her, laying it on the seat next to Aaron. Jennifer opened the kit and tore open a pack of gauze bandages, using them to pat the long wound Peter could see on Aaron's temple. "Man, Jennifer, that looks nasty."

"Head wounds always bleed a lot; lots of blood vessels close to the surface." Jennifer had gone into doctor-mode, Peter saw. She gave a tight-lipped frown as she probed the wound, and then leaned back with a relieved sigh, which told Peter just how frightened Jennifer had been. "I don't think it's as bad as it looks. The gash is deep and long, but I think the support just glanced off his head."

She opened a bottle of disinfectant and sloshed it over the cut—Aaron groaned as the astringent liquid hit the wound. "I'm going to need some bandages, and I'll have to put some stitches in. Maybe Eckels can tear up . . ." Jennifer stopped. She brushed hair back from her eyes. "Hey, where *is* Eckels?"

Peter felt a fist grab his stomach and twist. "I don't know," he said. They both looked at the open hatchway.

"You'd better find him," Jennifer said.

Now that the time machine had disappeared from sight behind a rough-barked tree whose trunk would have trouble fitting inside a concert hall, Eckels wasn't quite so sure leaving had been a good idea. For one thing, the path ended abruptly a few yards ahead. He should have expected that—Travis would only have laid enough of the floating roadway to accommodate the needs of their hunt—but still it made him pause. Stepping off the path, he knew painfully, would change everything UpTime from this moment, alter everything once again and twist time into a new reality. Guilt made him stop, his hand prowling his narrow chin thoughtfully.

What do you care? You told Travis you were sorry—anyone could have been scared, seeing that monster coming at you. Anyone would have stepped off the path to get away from it. Anyone.

He wasn't certain he convinced himself. He remembered Travis's black stare afterward, he remembered the accusing faces of the guides and the other hunters.

Coward, they all said with the hatred in their eyes. *You coward!*

The trouble was, it was a label he used himself, on those terrible quiet nights when he had to listen to the voice inside himself. He was selfish, he knew that. He could live with his own conceit and his arrogance and his egoism. Certainly he had and would do whatever he needed to do to save his own skin, no matter what happened to anyone else. But "coward" . . .

It bothered him.

That's over now. It's—in one sense of the word, anyway—in the past. You only have two choices—stay on the path, or not.

Eckels frowned. He moved forward to step off the end of the path, to step off the end of Travis's destiny.

But something moved in the jungle beyond. Two immense eyes peered at him from the heights and sent him staggering backward once more.

Peter paused long enough to snag one of the rifles— and to notice that one was missing. Then he was out of the hatch and onto the path. The light was dim and golden-green down here, filtered through ferns, trees, and vines that towered twenty stories above him. The path, pristine and white, meandered through the jungle, hovering just above the ground cover. There was no sign of Eckels anywhere. For that matter, Peter realized, there was no sign of *anything* anywhere. All the lizards and small dinosaurs and small mammals that had been so noticeable when he'd last seen the place were missing, and an awesome quiet hung over the area, as if the jungle were holding its breath.

And then came a sound from behind the house-thick tree to his left, a sound that shivered the very leaves like a wind. A call of fury, a call of unalloyed anger and hunger, the roar trembled Peter's legs and thrummed in his chest. It touched chords of pure primal dread that were eons old, sparked biological responses that were once part of ancestors as ancient as this jungle itself. The reverberating basso challenge snatched away his breath with fingers of sound and left him standing slack-jawed and limp.

Peter wasn't even sure when it ended. He was suddenly aware that the silence had come again and he was standing there with the rifle dangling from nerveless fingers.

He knew where Eckels was, now.

He ran.

* * *

It wasn't fair, Eckels thought frantically. No one should have to face this twice.

The Tyrannosaurus rex, the Thunder Lizard, came forth from the cover of the vines like the regal creature it was. Twin rows of teeth longer and sharper than swords clashed, lungs as powerful as the bellows of a steam engine heaved, and the dinosaur's breath swept over him, bearing the scent of corruption and death. Its head reared back and cocked sideways, so that one lizard eye—a cold eye, an eye of utter self-interest—regarded him. There was no intelligence behind that unblinking gaze, only a predator's native cunning, an appraisal of something potentially tasty.

Eckels fled. He put his back to the horror behind him and pounded down the path.

Behind him, he heard the ground tremble under the Regent of Death's tread. It snarled and moved, covering thirty yards in one awesome stride. Eckels could feel its shadow above him, and the heat of its breath was warm on his back. A moment, he knew, and the great head would snap down like a snake's, uncoiling and striking, and the jaws would close around him.

Eckels slipped and fell. He screamed, knowing he was dead.

A gunshot drowned out his cry.

Peter almost could not find the strength to pull the trigger. He saw Eckels racing down the pathway, and angling toward him from the jungle was a creature radiating terror and breathing fear, something so amazing, so awe-inspiring, that Peter wanted to either stand in shocked admiration or run in sheer panic. The T-rex was taller than his house and yet moved with the effortless, unconscious grace of an athelete. Tan and green scales gleamed, its ludicrously tiny hands clenched as it leapt forward, and those massive pile-driver legs crushed entire small trees underneath. Peter was insignificant in comparison to this, no more than a gnat or a worm.

Then he saw the splash of bright paint on the T-rex's flank: Travis's mark. And he knew that, regardless of what happened, this was the last few minutes of this creature's life, and that if he didn't act now, it would be the last for both he and Eckels as well.

Eckels, looking backward over his shoulder in horror, slipped and fell. The T-rex lifted its terrible head, seemingly to smile with its fanged teeth. In a second, Peter knew, it would strike, and it would feed.

He snapped up the rifle and fired from the waist.

The first shot was followed quickly by two more. The T-rex howled with the shots, rearing back, its thick, tendon-stiffened tail thrashing and snapping off young trees. It screamed, its head back as Eckels screamed with it. A trio of small red spots had appeared on the chest of the beast—they looked insignificant, no more than scratches.

The T-rex shook its head. It hissed and spat, long streamers of drool running in rivulets from between the pointed teeth. One eye regarded Eckels once more, narrowing, and the head lowered.

Still sprawled on the roadway, Eckels fumbled with the rifle. His hands shaking, he took off the safety, brought the weapon up so he sighted down the long barrel, his own brown eye staring into the golden-flecked orb of the T-rex.

He squeezed the trigger.

The kick of the rifle slammed his shoulder into the roadway. His finger still held down the trigger as a wild spray of bullets went whining off into the jungle. The T-rex was screaming now, shaking its terrible head, its right eye a gory ruin. Blood flowed in rivers down its neck. The tail flailed in wild fury, sweeping Eckels backward along the roadway. He scrambled wildly for purchase and finally stopped half off the roadway. The rifle was laying in the middle of the roadway ten feet away. The T-rex roared again, its remaining eye blinking . . .

. . . and it saw Eckels. The dinosaur gave a cry that deafened Eckels and took a step toward him, lifting its powerful hind leg to crush the offending human.

Eckels flung up his hands in useless protection.

Then the other gun barked again and again, and Eckels looked to see Peter standing on the roadway nearby, aiming his rifle and firing over and over again into the chest, into the neck, into the head of the creature.

The tyrannosaurus lurched backward. The clawed foot came smashing down, but not on Eckels or the path. The rex gave a choking gasp, and blood gushed from its mouth.

It fell backward, as massive and impressive as a sequoia, taking the smaller trees with it.

Eckels felt Peter's strong grip on his arm, pulling him to his feet. There was a look in the youth's grim face that he'd never seen before—a strength, a new maturity. "Back to the time machine, Eckels," he said. "Move it! We don't have much time."

22

Farewells

"Jenny!" Peter called as he half dragged and half threw Eckels back into the time machine and shut the hatch behind them. "How's Aaron?"

"I've been better," Aaron answered for himself. Jennifer had just managed to staunch the flow of blood. She pulled a curved needle and surgical thread from the medkit, but Aaron put up his hand. He tried to clear his mind, tried to think through the fog of pain. Struth, Peter, Eckels—they were all there, all alive. That was good. "No time for that, Jenny. The T-rex . . ."

". . . is dead," Peter finished for him. "All taken care of."

Aaron noticed the blood on Eckels's clothing and the terror in the man's eyes, and the strange, severe triumph in Peter's face.

The hatch was open. How long was I out? He shot a glance at the control panel. "Oh my God—it's much later than I thought. I must have—" He stopped. "We have to get *out* of here," he said.

"Why?" Jennifer asked.

"In less than a minute, Travis is going to arrive—the original time safari, with Eckels and everyone else." Aaron turned to the control panel and began changing the settings. "Strap in. If we're here when they arrive, there's going to be another explosion when we both try to occupy the same spot." He grimaced, clicking the trackball's button several times and getting no response. "Computer? What's the matter, why aren't you powering up?"

"Systems not optimal," the neutral voice answered. "Fuel levels critical."

"I don't care. Take us back to these spatial coordinates, two days forward from this point."

"Systems failure imminent."

"Override. Set and initiate *now*."

"Acknowledged. "

The whine of the temporal machinery began again, with a low drone that Aaron had never heard before, as if something were awry with the mechanism. The cold filled the cabin; the disorientation gripped them, making Aaron's head whirl even more with the aftereffects of the blow to his head. The shaking and buffeting of the interstitial time storms hit them almost at once, but this time, Aaron thought they might have subsided somewhat.

Once, there was a sharp bump; when Jennifer cried out alongside him, he shook his head to her, talking through the chattering of his teeth. "Don't worry—that was Travis, passing us on his way back to where we just were." The whine of temporal machinery suddenly cut off in mid-wail, and the lights dimmed. "System failure," the computer said. "Re-entering normal space-time now."

The time machine shuddered like a fish hooked on a line. They were slammed down hard, and Aaron's breath went out of him with an *oomph*. The lights flickered back on, and the frost on the windshield began to dissolve. "When are we?" Peter asked.

Aaron scanned the control panel. "It looks like we're about an hour up from where we were." He frowned, looking at his friends with worried eyes. "That's not good. We're smack in the middle of a timeframe where everyone is showing up here: Travis, chasing Eckels, and me—coming through the piece of roadway from Green Town."

"Except that we fixed all that, right?" Jennifer interjected. "We killed the dinosaur, so Eckels never left the path, and never came back here to create the explosion. That's the theory, right?"

Aaron was looking out the window. Without a word, he unbuckled and went to the hatch, opening it. As he stood there looking at the scene around them, he heard the others emerging behind him.

"The path's still broken." Peter's voice was a husky whisper. "It didn't work."

They had materialized on an unbroken chunk of the floating path, but not ten yards from them was a blackened, torn edge, beyond which the path was missing. "Look," Eckels pointed. The body of the T-rex lay where it was originally killed by Travis, the tree limb that would have caused its natural death draped over it. "Peter and I killed the thing way over there, by that huge tree. What's going on?"

"I think I know," Aaron said. He touched the still-seeping wound on his forehead. "Think of the original explosion as a wound. This wound of mine will heal, but only if Jennifer cleans it of all dirt and other foreign objects, and only if I make sure to leave it alone, and there may always be a scar. That's what's here—the original site of the wound between the worlds. And there's still 'foreign objects' here preventing this place from healing."

He swept his hands around. "Us," he said. "Me, Pete, Jenny, Struth—we don't belong here. Once we've gone back to our own timestreams, we tie up all the loose ends and the healing can begin."

"Sounds great to me," Peter said. "What are we waiting for?"

"There's still one problem," Eckels said. They all turned to the man. "Me," he told them. "There are two Eckels in this reality now. There are also two reasons you can't leave me here. First, I can't return to my own time without creating a nasty paradox, and you can't afford to leave me here with a working time machine, even one that will stop working in a few hours. You can't trust me, you can't send me back to my HomeTime, and you can't leave me here. I don't *belong* to this past. I'm not part of it. I'll step on a butterfly or kill some lizard, or some dinosaur will choke trying to eat me and the future will change again and again. So to do what you're talking about doing, you're going to have to kill me, right now. Is that what you're planning?"

Aaron had no answer to that. Eckels, for once in his life, was right. They couldn't leave him here, and he couldn't go home. Aaron knew none of them could kill Eckels. None of them would be able to simply murder him. And if they couldn't do that . . .

"Hay-ron," Struth bleated, calling Aaron's name with a breathy Mutata blat. Jennifer had been keeping up a running translation of everything that was said. Now she translated the Mutata's words:

"Tell Eckels that he is right," Struth said. "He does not belong in this past. There's no record of him—he is alien. But there *is* a record of him elsewhere. You humans have all forgotten it, but I haven't. He must go back to *my* world."

"What are you talking about, Struth?" Aaron asked. "That doesn't make any sense."

"None of this makes any sense. If I go back to my own world, I must stay away from my village, since an earlier SStragh is already there. That is true, and I understand it. There are other Mutata tribes I can go to, other places I can live. But Eckels must also go with me. Ask Jhenini. Jhenini and Peetah told me that when they first came to my world, this Eckels captured them and tied them up in his cave—yet when we found Eckels ourselves, he claimed to have never seen them before. I know who that other Eckels was, the one that Jhenini and Peetah thought was so much older."

Struth pointed at Eckels with a four-fingered hand.

"That Eckels was you," she said, "looped back through time just as we did with the rockfall that stopped the Gairk or the Far-Killer that you left for Travis. You talked about the Dreaming Storms being a wound in time—Jhenini said that she must stitch your wound to heal it. So we must also stitch this one—with our own selves."

A burst of laughter came unbidden from Aaron. "Struth, you're a genius," he said. "You've got the answer. She's right. Right now we're earlier in time in this world than our original arrival. In Green Town," he said, looking at Peter and Jennifer, "we haven't gone chasing that lousy triceratops yet. You and Peter haven't stumbled into Struth's time. Eckels is over in Struth's world, but he's wandering dazed and confused. Just like the rockfall and the gun, we've brought ourselves back into position to close all the loops, complete all the circles in time. We still have to hurry, though. Travis will show up here any moment, and I'll come tumbling through the portal myself. Peter, grab the pieces of temporal mechanism from the time machine. Everyone, let's go find a piece of the roadway to power up."

Aaron moved the time machine further down the path with the hatch open. He gave control of the craft to the computer, telling it to take it several miles away; as the vehicle passed the edge of the broken roadway, he jumped out. They watched the time machine move swiftly and quietly out of sight through the screening ferns and vines. "There—Travis and I never saw another time machine in this place, so that's taken care of. Now, follow me, and let's stay on the path that I made getting through here."

With a last glance back at the carcass of the Tyrannosaurus rex, Aaron led the group single file through the jungle until he saw the piece of roadway that had brought him here initially.

"Okay," he said. "Peter, you get underneath and pull out the piece of greenstone that's powering it, then I'll hand you another one for Dinosaur World."

"I'm getting good at this," Peter said, and crawled underneath the large fragment of white plastic. A moment later, sparks crawled the edges of the platform. "She's deactivated," Peter's muffled voice came. "Hand me the piece for Struth's world."

Aaron passed it to him. The limbs of the trees hundreds of feet above him were swaying in a quick wind, and the light under the green canopy had dimmed. "Time storm coming," Aaron called. "Struth, Eckels, are you two ready?"

"Wait a minute," Jennifer said. She went to Struth, who lowered her head to Jennifer. The young woman hugged the dinosaur's neck fiercely. "I'll miss you," she said. "You were a good friend."

"I still will be," Struth answered her. "That's all in the future, remember?"

Jennifer smiled at her sadly. "I guess so. Thank you, Struth. Without you . . ."

Struth reached out with one hand. Her scent was citrus and anise. She stroked Jennifer's cheek, caught up a teardrop that lingered there, and licked it away from her finger with her tongue. "Salty, like the ocean," she said. "I will never understand humans, no matter how long I live."

Jennifer smiled and hugged Struth again. The wind lashed her face with her hair, and she pulled away. "You'd better go." Aaron and Peter each came up to SStragh and said their goodbyes. They all shook hands with Eckels. "See you in a while," Peter told the man. "Listen, remember to tie those ropes a little looser this time, okay?"

"I'll remember," Eckels said.

Struth and Eckels approached the roadway. The sky was dark and the wind fierce, but there were no visions this time, no fleeting glimpses of other worlds. Thunder growled, but it seemed distant and there was no lightning.

"See," Jennifer said. "Things are beginning to heal already."

She gave Struth a last hug and stepped back. Eckels stepped up onto the roadway and vanished in a flurry of bright sparks. Then Struth leaped up. As she disappeared, she waved to the trio of humans. "I will never forget you," she said.

"Nor will we," Jennifer answered, but Struth was already gone. The time storm was already fading.

"Now it's our turn," Aaron said.

23

Home Again

Jennifer was crying, and there were tears in Peter's eyes as well. "Aaron!" Jennifer cried as he stepped through the portal. "We're *home!*"

Aaron grinned and leaped from the roadway. "Yes!" he exulted. He put his arm around Jennifer, and pulled Peter into the embrace. The three of them hugged fiercely, then Aaron stepped away with a sigh. "Okay," he told them. "There are still some things we need to check out—when I was here last, everything looked the same, but . . ."

Aaron stopped, remembering what Jennifer had told him—it seemed years ago.

"Your *Grandpa Carl . . . He's dead . . .*"

Aaron looked up the hill toward where his house was hidden behind the trees, and he was suddenly afraid. He didn't want to go that way, didn't know if he could deal with it if his Grandpa was dead, if his parents were gone forever, if Green Town was still dominated by the gray walls of the Compound. Jennifer evidently sensed his fear, for he felt her hand on his shoulder. "It'll be okay," she said. "I know it will."

"I hope you're right." He frowned. "Uh-oh . . . What's that sound?" A thousand hammers were thudding against the ground all at once, accom-panied by the chuffing of a steam engine, the clamor growing louder by the second.

"You obviously don't remember things as well as I do," Peter said. "I know what it means—it means we'd better get the heck away from here." He grabbed Jennifer's hand and nodded to Aaron. "Come on," he said. "We've got some heavy traffic coming."

They ran along the slope away from the path. Above them, saplings bent and branches snapped as a spiked head and body as large as a rhinocerous crushed the blackberry bushes at the top of the hill beneath massive feet. "The triceratops!" Aaron said. "Right! We were chasing it . . ." The huge dinosaur snorted, then the plated frill around its neck moved as it glanced back. Evidently it didn't like what it saw or sensed, for it quickly turned back, making the decision to try the steep slope. The dinosaur tried to gingerly walk down, but gravity quickly changed its plans. Bellowing in frustration, the triceratops had no choice—it came down the hill sliding and almost running, like a runaway tank. Halfway down, it hit the piece of roadway and disappeared.

"So *that's* what happened to it," Jennifer said. She started to head back toward the roadway, but Aaron held her back. "What's the matter?"

"Wait," Aaron said. He grinned at Peter. "There's something *you've* forgotten, too," he told the redhead. Aaron cupped his hands over his mouth. "Hey guys!" he called. "Aaron! Jen! Peter!"

"What are you doing?" Peter asked.

"Something else we need to accomplish before we're done," Aaron answered back, grinning. "Another one of Struth's 'stitches.'

"I get it—the Harper kids!" Jennifer exclaimed. "I remember now . . . We heard voices calling us, and we thought it was the Harper kids, lost in the woods."

Through the rustling of wind in the oaks and sycamores, they could hear faint voices answering—"Who's that? Where are you?"

"This way!" Jennifer called. "Down by the creek!" Jennifer looked at Aaron. "That's what you wanted, right?"

Aaron smiled back at her. "Right. And now I think we'd better make sure we're hidden."

"Why?" Peter asked.

"Because we're about to see someone I used to know."

The three moved behind a screen of trees and mulberry bushes. Not long after, a figure appeared at the top of the hill, staring down at the floating piece of roadway halfway down the slope. Aaron heard Jennifer gasp behind him. "That's . . ." she began.

"I know," Aaron told her. "Shhh . . ."

The figure, a dark-haired young man, turned and looked back the way he'd come. "Jen! Peter! Over here! Quick! I've found something." He listened for a moment, then jumped on top of a fallen log. From far away, they heard an answer: "Here we are!"

"Jen!" the youth shouted again, and at the same moment, his foot slipped. His arms pinwheeled as he tried to keep his balance, but he couldn't. He tumbled backward down the slope as he tried to stop his fall.

What he hit, like the triceratops, was the roadway. There was a blue flash, the faintest hint of the time storms that were to come, and he was gone.

"I was a lot clumsier back then," Aaron said.

"That was you!" Peter exclaimed. "That's how we lost you—you went somersaulting into Jaxon's world, while we found our own piece of roadway."

"Taking you to Dinosaur World," Aaron answered. "Right."

"Aaron! Hey, we're over this way!" they could hear Jennifer's—a younger Jennifer's—voice calling from somewhere in the woods. "Follow the sound," Aaron said. "As soon as you two—" He stopped and grinned. "Well, the people you used to be, anyway—go through the portal, we need to get that piece of temporal machinery and bring it back here. Then we'll close this one down, also. You remember where your part of the roadway was?"

"Sure do," Peter answered. "Come on—this way." Peter led them through the trees, following the sound of their earlier selves. They heard Peter's voice, calling Aaron's name over and over in increasing frustration. Finally, a long silence settled over the forest. Peter stopped; their breaths were the loudest sound they could hear.

"We're—they're—gone," he said. "They've jumped into Dinosaur World." He ran forward again; just around the edge of the hill, bridging the creek, they saw another piece of Eckels's roadway, floating there as if nothing had happened.

Aaron started to duck under it, but Jennifer stopped him. "Let me," she said. "I feel responsible for this one." Quickly, she swung underneath the floating white plastic and emerged a moment later with a twisted tube of glowing green metal. "Here we go," she said. "Now what?"

"The last step," Aaron said. "We go back to my part of the roadway . . ."

"Toss your part of the mechanism on the roadway," Aaron told Jennifer once they arrived back at the hillside. Jennifer heaved the lambent metal onto the pathway, where it promptly disappeared. "Okay," Aaron said. "Here's the last piece of business . . ."

With that, Aaron slipped under the roadway. Wriggling in the dirt, he found the piece of mechanism that powered it, and pulled it loose. Then, before the portal to Travis's world could close, Aaron rolled and tossed the final piece of temporal mechanism onto the roadway like Charles Barkley slamming home a dunk shot. He could feel the tingling all through his arm as the portal began to close.

"Aaron!" Peter yelled. "Get out of there! Now, buddy!"

Aaron kept rolling. Sparks were flaring from the roadway, fountaining from the middle of the plastic like a fireworks display and splashing in front of him as he got to his feet and stumbled away. The roadway itself was glowing blue-white, as searingly bright as an acetelyne torch. Then, with a thunderclap that nearly deafened them, it collapsed, sagging into itself as if it were melting, growing smaller and smaller and finally vanishing with a last flare of sparks that left glowing purple and red afterimages.

There were a few smoldering fires in the dry leaves where the roadway had once been. Beyond that, the woods were as they once had been.

"Wow . . ." Aaron breathed. "When time heals itself, it really packs a wallop."

"The rift is closed," Jennifer said. "We completed the loop and sealed it up."

"Yeah," Peter said. "And now we get to see if we're really in the right place." He looked up the hill, where Aaron's house was hidden behind the trees.

None of them needed any more of a reminder. The walk back to the house was silent, each of them lost in their own thoughts. Aaron could feel his stomach knotting as the rear of his home came into view through the leaves. It looked so achingly familiar, and yet he recalled how strange his grandfather had been when he and Mundo had last been here. He remembered Jennifer, weeping as she told him how she'd found Carl's body in Dinosaur World, ripped open by a Gairk spear.

"Be there, Gran'pa," he whispered to himself as they started up the long, grassy slope toward the house. "Please be there . . ."

The house appeared as he remembered from what seemed years ago. The windows were intact, the screen door on the back porch intact, but they could see no one there.

Then the door opened, and a figure limped out.

"Gran'pa!" Aaron shouted. He ran forward. "Gran'pa!"

"It's all true, then," Carl said, wonderingly. "The dinosaurs, other worlds, everything."

Aaron just nodded. His grandfather stretched out a finger and gently stroked the leathery, wrinkled surface of the dinosaur eggs sitting in their nest of grass in a cardboard box on the kitchen table. A *box of wonder*, Carl had called it. Now he was no longer so sure. "The dinosaurs all died millions of years ago. I know that. It's just . . ."

Carl stopped. He looked at Aaron, at this older, battered, and wounded version of his grandson, at the eyes which looked as though they'd seen far, far more than Carl could imagine. All three of them had that look, he realized: a maturity shaped by unguessed events. "Gran'pa," Aaron began, but Carl continued as if he hadn't heard him.

"I'd better get rid of these eggs," he told them. "They don't belong here, not really."

Carl groaned as he got up from the table. He pulled Aaron, then Jennifer and Peter, to him.

"But all of you do," he said. "You do."

DINOSAUR CONQUEST SKETCHBOOK

A Record of My Adventures
by Aaron Cofield

Pages 248 and 249: This world of dinosaurs, it seemed, was being assaulted by other times and histories.

Page 250: A velociraptor has it his way in a fast-food restaurant.

Page 251: The Mutata carefully built their nests among the time storms' devastation at the seashore.

Page 252: The Midgard Serpent remonstrates with Eckels (as described to me by Peter).

Page 253: Mundo and Jennifer find the Mutata nesting site scarred and littered with artifacts from a hundred alternate timelines.

Pages 254 and 255: Peter was put in the unenviable position of being chased up a tree by an Ankylosaur.

Pages 256 and 257: The one we left behind to face the Gairk . . .

Page 258: Slowly and laboriously dragging the time-travel craft to the Mutata Village.

Page 259: The Mutata sacrificial knife.

Pages 260 and 261: Eckels fleeing down the path, trying to escape the horror behind him.

Page 262: We come full circle. A box of dinosaur eggs began our adventure and also ended it.

Glossary of Mutata Terms

The Sounds of the Mutata

The sounds made by the Mutata (a race of sentient dinosaurs most similar to the duckbills of our prehistory) are produced through their long nasal horns. In the novels, they are omitted for the most part. However, the most common sounds are a nasal bleat, a snort, a full roar, and a trill.

Pronunciation Key

The Mutata language has been transcribed into an approximation of phonetic English. Most consonants are pronounced as they would be pronounced in that language. In most cases, "a" is pronounced as the "a" in cat; "e" as the "e" in met; "i" as the "i" in dim (though an ending "i" is pronounced as the "ee" in meet); "o" as the "o" in solo; "u" as the "oo" in moot; "ai" as "i" in ride; "ei" as the "ea" in heaven; "ah" as the "a" in tall. Some of the Mutata sounds cannot be adequately reproduced by the human larynx. In those cases, the closest English sound has been used, as in "jh", which for the Mutata is a glottal stop much like a very rapid "jeh-eh", the last syllable being a quick aspirant. In some cases, a literal translation of the Mutata word has been substituted, as in "Speaker" or "Giving." There are also subtle posture and scent aspects to the Mutata language which, unfortunately, must be lost in the written form and which humans can never imitate. Any human must always be partially mute and deaf to the Mutata language as spoken by the dinosaurs.

aii

An imperative: to be performed immediately.

Amath

The Mutata od of death, who comes to bear the soul of a dying Mutata back to the All-Ancestor.

Baosiot

Unintelligent predatory dinosaurs— the Allosaurus, possibly.

bhieye

"Thank you."

broaii

The Gairk war club, a massive wooden mallet tipped with several protruding blades of obsidian. The Gairk will usually carry two, one for the right hand, one for the left. Like the Mutata, the left hand is used when striking another sentient creature; the right is for "nonintelligent" lifeforms.

chodoe "Follow me." An imperative, used only by a superior Mutata to his or her social inferiors.

ciosie A demand for satisfaction. Ciosie means literally "The Decision of the All-Ancestor"—in other words, letting the right or wrong of an issue be decided by combat, with the All-Ancestor's influence supposedly determining the outcome.

daii soo Literally, "Pause [or wait] several breaths."

ehei To go outside a dwelling. Also, to wander.

Eikels Eckels.

Floraria Unintelligent predatory dinosaurs, possibly the Tyrannosaurus family.

gaedo An affirmative given by a younger to an elder. "Yes."

Gairk The racial name for a species of sentient, small Allosaurs.

geedo "Yes." As spoken by peers.

geiree "Come here" or "Approach me." An imperative form.

gheodo Literally, "I cannot do that," with the added emphasis that the refusal is based on a superior's orders.

Giving Translation of the Mutata phrase meaning "The time when the spirit is given to the All-Ancestor." The funeral rite for Mutata.

iado "Animal"—more specifically, an un-sentient creature, without language or anything more than animal intelligence. The type of being killed with the right hand rather than the left.

jhaka The village in which Mutata live, each under the rule of its own OColi.

Jhenini Jenny.

jhiehai Scavenger proto-birds—these are deliberately enticed to feed on the bodies of dead Mutata.

khiisoo A demand for obedience: "You must obey!"

LongDay Or OGhielas. The summer solstice. As with almost all human cultures, the Mutata and Gairk also mark the solstices for religious celebration and ceremony.

Mutata　　　The racial name for SStragh's species of sentient dinosaurs

niijeks　　　Mouselike rodents which feed on the stored grains within the Mutata encampments.

OColi　　　Literally, the Eldest. The ruler of a particular Mutata tribe is nearly always the oldest among them. Can be either male or female, though the males generally live the longest.

OColihi　　　The Ancient Path. The code of ethics and behavior which govern the Mutata. This code is handed down via a verbal tradition through the OTsio. The beginnings of the ritualized OColihi are lost in the long centuries of the Mutata past.

OColihi-ka　　　The Temple of the OColihi. A place of worship for the Mutata.

oei　　　A modifier. When used in conjunction with other words, it indicates "many" or "a large amount."

OTsio　　　Teacher. Each youngling Mutata, when the tribe has returned from the first Nesting Walk after their hatching, is assigned an OTsio to guide their development. The OTsio becomes a parent-analogue, though a Mutata of that age is considered independent.

otsioiue   The OTsio's student.

Raajek   Sstragh's OTsio, and a proponent of the OChiihi, or New Path—a mindset at variance with the old ways of Mutata behavior.

saitie   A flying insect. Each dawn, they chirp noisily as they rise from their nightly sleep in the leaves of the fern trees.

saorod   A species of pterosaur in Dinosaur World, with about a three-foot wingspan.

skyfire   Or "Holata." The sun.

Speaker   Translation of the Mutata title-phrase meaning "One who speaks the words of the Eldest."

SStragh   The Mutata who finds and captures Jennifer, Peter, and Eckels, and who befriends Jennifer.

Tiafer   The original name of the current OColi.

werada   A death caused by a Mutata—specifically, the left-handed type of killing, not the right-handed killing that would be done to an animal.

werata   Pain.

whiaso   A "right-handed" killing, or the killing of a simple, unintelligent creature.

yeie   A modifier, indicating a negative: "I will not" or "This is not so." Also used as a quick denial: "No!"

zhiotae   The Gairk "Reader of Omens" or shaman. Functions as an advisor to the Gairk OColi in spiritual matters. The Mutata have no analogue occupation.

We want to hear from readers!

Your opinion of the Dinosaur World series is important to us. We welcome all feedback about the series.

Write or email to the editors at the following address:

J. T. Colby & Company, Inc.
Purveyors of Time Travel Instruments and
Accessories™

Manhanset House
Dering Harbor, New York 11965-0342
bricktower@aol.com
bricktowerpress.com

RAY BRADBURY, one of the greatest writers of fantasy and horror fiction in the world today, has published some 500 short stories, novels, plays, and poems since his first story appeared in *Weird Tales* when he was twenty years old. Among his many famous works are *Fahrenheit 451*, *The Illustrated Man*, and *The Martian Chronicles*. He has also written the screenplays for *It Came From Outer Space*, *Something Wicked This Way Comes*, and *Moby Dick*. Mr. Bradbury was Idea Consultant for the United States Pavilion at the 1964 World's Fair, has written the basic scenario for the interior of Spaceship Earth at EP-COT, Disney World, and is doing consultant work on city engineering and rapid transit. When one of the Apollo Astronaut teams landed on the moon, they named Dandelion Crater there to honor Mr. Bradbury's novel, *Dandelion Wine*. Recently Mr. Bradbury flew in an airplane for the first time.

STEPHEN LEIGH is the author of several science fiction novels, including *Crystal Memory*, *The Bones of God*, and the best-selling *Alien Tongue*. He is also a contributing author to the Hugo-nominated *Wild Cards* shared-world series. Currently Mr. Leigh lives in Ohio.

www.ingramcontent.com/pod-product-compliance
Lightning Source LLC
Chambersburg PA
CBHW051638050726
47502CB00011B/1172